pineapples in paris

my sweet french life

pineapples in paris

my sweet french life

A TRANSATLANTIC LOVE STORY

VERNETIA COUTY SMITH

Book design by FlintlockCovers.com
Typeset in Athelas

IN LOVING MEMORY OF VIRGINIA,
WHO LIVES IN THE STARS,
MAY THIS STORY REACH YOU.

CONTENTS

ACKNOWLEDGMENTS

First and foremost, I can never adequately thank my devoted husband who walked every step of my journey with me. Without him my story could not have been imagined. "You are the spark that lights a fire of joy in my soul."

To Sam who pushed me to the limit and encouraged me to tell my story, interweaving the past and the present and digging into the heart of what I wanted to say in the most creative of ways.

A special thanks to Hannelore who proofread my story from beginning to end and gave a tenacious critique.

Caryle, your kind words "Congratulations on achieving a milestone achievement" meant a lot to me.

David, Bonnie, Marilyn, Hannah, Helen and Dan, thanks for your unwavering encouragement. Words cannot express my gratitude.

To my friend Kat who said, "Don't give in to the urge to rewrite endlessly. Cut the umbilical cord and share your beautiful story with the world."

My sincere thanks to the staff at *Château D'Agassac,* a Haut-Médoc wine estate, for providing priceless information on French wines and inviting François and me to visit their splendorous castle.

AUTHOR'S NOTE

I decided to write a story based on my life in Paris. The narrative I envisioned wasn't just a fairy tale romance. It was much more than that — PINEAPPLES IN PARIS: MY SWEET FRENCH LIFE is laden with love, grief, conflict, bold adventures and a sense of empowerment. Conversations are not verbatim. Names, places, individuals are products of my imagination and were inspired by real people including family. Many aspects of the Virginia character are based on recollections of my childhood. We were inseparable twins, enveloped in a shadow, real or imagined. We even dressed alike in vintage dresses, and her spunky attitude was an inspiration to me.

PROLOGUE
A SET OF TWIN RABBITS AND A SET OF TWIN GIRLS

I saw my twin sister, Virginia, everywhere — on every street, on every corner, in every store. Although she wasn't with me in a physical sense, we'd always shared an electrical connection, pulling us together even though we were miles apart. Two peas in a pod, we knew everything about each another, as if we shared the same brain — a swan song.

I had always wanted to share my life in Paris with Virginia. And sometimes I did. Like the day I was hanging out in the 17th arrondissement near Parc Monceau. Several feet in front of me I spotted a woman with two beautiful girls. As I watched one of the them whispering to the other with a plush rabbit clutched under her arm, I felt my twin sister's breath on my ear, her hand wrapped in mine — feeling a magnetic pull between me and the girls wishing I could meet them.

The girls were about five years old with long fat braids and milk chocolate skin. One of them had a round face, large eyes and elongated dimples. The other had an oblong face, small eyes and no dimples. They weren't identical but similar in many ways. They were dressed alike. Serendipitously, they were a replica of Virginia and Vernetia — our past lives.

As I surveyed the girls, I stood frozen in a web of remembrance from which I couldn't escape.

When Virginia and I were children, Mama came home from work one day with two twin rabbits as white as powder snow. We named them Snow Ball and Snow Flake. Our rabbits had a unique way of communicating through voice, eyes, touch, and smell. We knew they loved us because they licked us constantly. Our fuzzy bunny rabbits with bluish colored eyes and black twitching noses gave us love in the highest form of expression. They followed us around and jumped into our laps when we called them. Snow Flake was gravely depressed when Snow Ball died and shortly thereafter she joined her in heaven. It broke our hearts and we cried for days. They appeared in our sweet dreams showing an instinctual need for our affection.

Virginia and I were as close as two coats of paint. We even slept together. I slept at the foot of the bed; Virginia slept at the head and we had barely enough room for our quirky stuffed animals — our shy jelly cat with large black eyes, our cream colored kittens with pink paws, and our fat rooster with red protruding eyes, wattle hanging from his neck. Mama read bedside stories to her silly girls giggling like crazy at the tales she made up before we fell asleep.

Days before Virginia's passing I had a nightmare about a funeral not thinking in a million years it would be my twin. Maybe God was warning me before she left and I hadn't paid any attention. In hindsight, if I had seen a dream interpreter to analyze my night in terror perhaps I could have saved her. The images of Virginia in my head never went away. My world was turned upside down.

The family, especially me, held Virginia in high esteem and put her on a pedestal. She was like a string of rare pearls that needed special care to keep them elegant. We were scotched together, like threads connecting.

Born with an unlucky affliction — a hole in her heart – Virginia suffered a fatal heart attack at the age of twenty-two. When I received the call from the hospital that tragic evening, everything froze. My world had come to a dead halt. I felt alone in darkness even in broad daylight. When she died a part of me died too. While the taxi drove me to the hospital, I cried hysterically. I flew in and asked the receptionist:

"May I see her?"

Trying to absorb the shock of the response, I staggered unable to find the courage to deal with an unthinkable loss, the disbelief, the horror.

Then I collapsed.

Later that day at the viewing, I stood beside Virginia and kissed her face with tears rolling down. I let them linger, if only briefly, as it would be our last physical contact. I left the hospital torn apart dreading the funeral with a floodgate of questions about cardiac arrests, believing consciousness survives beyond one's death.

If only I could turn back the hands of time — I'd show Virginia my short street where I rented a *pied-à-terre* when I landed in Paris in the Marais near Place de Vosges and only spoke a handful of French. We'd take the elevator to the top of the Eiffel Tower and gaze at the most beautiful panoramic views of Paris. We'd visit the Musée du Louvre and admire the larger than life nude statues. We'd take an evening cruise on the Seine in a *Bateau-Mouche*. We'd sit in the exquisite Jardin du Luxembourg and later have a coffee at Les Deux Magots, once a literary haunt for the intellectual élite, or have a drink at Café de Flore where high-profile writers and philosophers once frequented. We'd take a stroll in the Latin Quarter and admire the bright lights in Paris at night with music playing in every nook and cranny. We'd rent bicycles with baskets to carry our French baguettes and wear a French béret and pretend we were Françaises.

Fast forward to the two girls I met at Park Monceau — Within a hazy instant, Virginia's face flashed in front of mine, her eyes piercing.

"*Go...Go ahead and talk to the girls.*"

I didn't have to move as one of them stood in front of me. "What are you looking at?" she asked. "Are you lost?"

Yes. I was lost in my memories, but I didn't tell her that. "No, I'm just enjoying this sunny day," I said and she smiled, her front two teeth missing. "What's your name?" I asked.

She shifted her head slightly studying me as if I were from another planet. But children are naturally curious. Maybe it was my Americanized French accent. Maybe she felt a puzzling connection.

"My name is Amelia," she said and then pointed. "My sister's name is Jasmine. We're twins." Jasmine raced up to us.

"Bonjour, Madame." She starred with a beaming smile.

"You're beautiful girls!" I said wanting to tell them I was a twin too.

"What's your name?" one of them asked.

"My name is Vernetia. And that's a beautiful stuffed animal you're holding."

"It's my bunny rabbit. Her name is Samantha. We call her Sam," said Amelia.

I asked the other twin if she had a stuffed animal.

"Big Bird from Sesame Street!" she said with a precocious giggle.

"I had a real bunny rabbit when I was your age," I said.

"Sam *is* real," said Jasmine, shaking her head with attitude.

"But I thought Sam was a stuffed animal."

"Sometimes she is and sometimes she isn't."

"What about Big Bird?" I asked Jasmine.

"Big Bird protects Sam with a long stick from the other animals. She also likes to dance."

I didn't want the twins' mother to become alarmed as I gawked at her girls, so when she approached me, I asked if she knew where Parc Monceau was even though I had been there many times.

"Yes, of course. We are going there now. If you want we can show you," she said and I nodded. "I hope my girls weren't bothering you. They're really quite a handful."

"No, not a bit, they're lovely," I said, watching every movement of the twins from the corner of my eyes.

Soon we had arrived at the park and sat on a bench and talked for a while. There were so many stories I wanted to share with the twins about Virginia and our beautiful white rabbits Snow Ball and Snow Flake but I didn't want to crush their joyful spirits. In the blink of an eye the girls and their mom had vanished. I choked up and then got up to leave, thinking, *if only I could turn time back, if only I could stop imagining my sister and me when we were young, if only I could let her go. But I couldn't. No, this dream was ours.*

Truth be told, the story about the twins in Parc Monceau may have been imagined. At the time it couldn't have been more real. Things like that happen to me often. Why, I've asked myself this question and the answer is simple. At the core of my soul and the purity of Virginia's, our spirits are intertwined, and happenstance can trigger what we know to be real even when we're not together. It may be called (ESP) Extrasensory Perception. I can't dismiss the thoughts when they arrive and neither do I want to because those memories ring true to my heart.

I have moved beyond the sad remembrance of Virginia's passing. Instead of bottling up my emotions as I did for many years, I think of beautiful memories and flashbacks whispered in my ear like the afternoon in Parc Monceau. I am sure Virginia had no idea what her loss would feel like and has forgiven me for using profanity after she left. She'd be so proud of the things I have accomplished and continue to do in her memory, especially after I arrived in Paris to see the Eiffel Tower. I'll always share my world of adventures with Virginia because we will always be connected. A profound quote which I ultimately understood, *"The essential things in life are seen not with the eyes, but with the heart,"* Le Petit Prince.

This is the story of my personal triumph finding love and laughter along the way.

PART ONE
FALLING INTO A
SWEET LIFE

"I do not think I should be acting foolishly. Even if I were to die for her; there is nothing so beautiful or so good in the world; And nothing that delights me more. I love my eyes which picked her out; From the moment I saw her, I left my heart with her as hostage. And there it has long resided, And never can it leave."

— LE CHÂTELAIN DE COUCY

1

NIGHTMARE AT THE PARK PLAZA HOTEL

One fateful night, I had an out-of-body experience — a wake-up call that left my soul shaken to the core. Insomnia brought on by tension, stress, and anxiety had made it impossible to sleep. Even when I managed to fall into the extremely shallow depths of slumber, it didn't last for long. I'd wake up screaming about missed timelines and deadlines, my job taking its toll on my entire existence. At the time I was working in Asset Management in Boston for Lucent Technology where I resolved grievances with stakeholders to achieve customer satisfaction and executed problem-solving methods to maximize inventory.

Why couldn't I solve my own problems? I wondered.

One thing I definitely knew, I couldn't go on like this.

Late one afternoon on my way to lunch, I was feeling down in the dumps when I crossed a charming man in the Prudential Tower and our eyes mysteriously met. He walked past me, turned and came back to introduce himself.

"My name is Lorenzo," he said. "I'd be really angry with myself if I didn't try to meet such a beautiful woman and ask her out on a date."

"My name is Vernetia," I said and smiled like a Cheshire cat.

He was stunning! His sex appeal was a combination of his dark brown penetrating eyes, thick eyelashes, black coiled curls, fairly large nose and dark skin, almost as if he had African heritage. His casual style was simple but sexy. He was dressed in a pair of fitted jeans with the sleeves rolled up on his sun-tanned arms, shirt slightly opened, exposing a sly look onto the hairs of his upper chest. I'd learn later that he was from Sicily, an island located in the Mediterranean Sea in Southern Italy.

I was dressed in a white long-sleeve blouse, a black skirt that fell below the knee, one-inch heels, hair straightened and pulled behind the ears. He could hardly have mistaken me for being beautiful. And hadn't he noticed the bags under my eyes from lack of sleep? If through the lens of Italian fetishism he was looking for an erotic Naomi Campbell "In the Closet" with Michael Jackson flaunting low down sensual dancing, I was surely not that sexy gal. Maybe I was flipping out from all the attention that I hadn't gotten in a long time.

My work obsessions had spilled over into late evenings and weekends and I had no social life. I had become a boring maniac and when I faced my reflection in the mirror I noticed how haggard I looked, although I'd acquired Mom's ageless genes — slim, long frizzy curls, dark eyes, low nasal bridge and thin lips that rarely smiled because of the gap in my front teeth. People of color have more melanin in their skin which has been scientifically proven to provide some protection against the sun and helps to prevent cracking, fine lines and keeps the skin looking younger. How sweet it is!

"Lorenzo must be desperate," I imagined. But, then again, maybe I was too. So I figured why the hell not and went out on a date with him.

Lorenzo and I had only been on three casual dates when he invited me to New York, also known as "the Big Apple". *Fast mover,*

I thought, but he seemed to be completely trustworthy, and very attractive, plus the fact that he was interested in taking me out as miserable as I felt inside, but had apparently disguised it on the outside, was a nice compliment.

"Give me a week," I said. "I have a lot on my plate."

Still, I desperately needed a break from the drudgery and the stress.

"I'll do all the planning," he insisted. "You don't need to worry about any of that." I worked most of the weekend going through stacks of papers and files trying to catch up. When I knew it was impossible, I panicked. I thought about trashing some of my customer disputes but realized it might come back to haunt me and make matters worse. It was imperative that I speak to my manager knowing that she only cared about her deadlines, and in order to meet them, she needed mine. I was on my own and became depressed.

I had previously worked for AT&T in New Jersey. When the company underwent a major reshuffling, many jobs — including mine — were abolished. Human Resource (HR) offices were located in different parts of the country to help employees find jobs. I was elated when I learned there was one in Boston that led me back home. During an informational interview, the manager was impressed with my sales results and created a position for me on the spot in his organization.

Fondly known as "Bean Town," Boston had become an electrifying city and finding a job was about as difficult as winning a lottery ticket. I hit the jackpot and was now in seventh heaven. My office was located in the swanky Prudential Tower in the heart of Back Bay — one of Boston's most iconic neighborhoods. The pink marbled walls, floors and elevators created a regal ambiance. I felt like a jolly tourist surrounded by fine dining and luxury stores.

In the afternoon there were concerts in the Prudential Tower gardens, which permeated the air with a mix of classical, jazz, rhythm and blues. I — like everyone else — was proud to have the Prudential Tower as my work address, second only to the John Hancock Tower Skyscraper, dominating the Back Bay skyline with a skywalk observatory on the 50th floor. As luck would have it, I found a cozy apartment a stone's throw away and could amble through the beautiful Marriott Hotel lobby directly to my office without having to go outside. I was ecstatic about being insulated from the fierce Boston winters.

Soon I realized that Lorenzo's obsessive work habits were a thousand times worse than mine. He owned a profitable construction business and never stopped. I thought he was gentle, but he was also tough, burning the midnight oil, raking in the bucks. Earlier on, I learned that when work becomes an obsession the best therapy is to take a vacation.

What the HELL should I do? I asked myself.

"Go to New York before you go insane," said the voice in my head.

Little did I know this trip would change everything, bringing on a night of shock, panic, and sheer terror.

The moment I left my apartment with my overnight bag I felt like a floating feather. When I arrived at the airport the plane was delayed, and I had more time to worry about the deadlines waiting for my return. I was supposed to meet Lorenzo at Logan airport and we would go to New York City together, but he phoned moments before the plane took off and asked if I would go alone and take a taxi from La Guardia Airport to the hotel. He said he received a business call that urgently needed his attention.

"We're booked at the Park Plaza Hotel in Manhattan!" he exclaimed. "They're expecting you."

"Wow," I said, although a bit disappointed, "How classy is that."

At the luxurious landmark hotel that was the Park Plaza, from our window we had a spectacular view of the enchanting horse and buggy rides in Central Park. I couldn't believe my good fortune after all my bad luck. It was a lovely daydream and late in the evening when the sun went down, it was a painting of a romantic night scene.

This will surely satisfy my sexual fantasies, I thought with a chuckle. Should I take a long soothing shower, spray my body all over with Sweet Temptation, and put on my sexy lingerie? Had my job pushed me to the point where I would act on my reveries or my overactive imagination? I hadn't even embraced Lorenzo nor had I done anything to seduce him, at least not yet. But I wanted to.

Around seven in the evening, the *Maitre d'Hotel* knocked on the door with a large bottle of champagne in a bucket of ice and a fancy dish with dark chocolates. I waited and waited but there was no Lorenzo. He called and left a message at the front desk apologizing profusely for being late. At 8 o'clock sharp, he knocked on the door and gave me a long stemmed yellow rose. After drinking several glasses of champagne, we stretched out across the bed, but there were no caresses or any form of intimacy.

"I'm burnt out Vernetia," he explained. "I need to get away."

"We've just arrived at the most glamorous, legendary hotel in Manhattan. Or is this a figment of my imagination?"

"No, but I want to go farther away," he insisted. "I have to leave here tonight."

"You must be joking!"

He got up and slammed his fist on the desk. "No. I'm not."

"Cut it out Lorenzo!" I yelled. "You sound like a damn fool!" He was frightening me, and I needed to show him I was no shrinking violet who could be jerked around on a whim.

"Don't you ever think about living on the edge?"

"You mean living dangerously."

"Why not," he muttered.

"Frankly, I'd rather play it safe."

"Come on. Life is an adventure. Let's live it up!"

"Our room is pretty nice for starters, don't you think?" I said trying to appease him.

His eyes swirled with madness, his face turned beet red then he yelled, "Let's run away tonight!"

This could not have been happening. But it was. This guy was insane. And this situation was so far removed from anything I'd ever experienced.

Sacred stiff, I wanted to make a run for it and get the hell away from him. But fear had me immobilized; and I decided it was best to go along with his little silly game, or I might have ended up chopped to bits and stuffed into a garbage can.

"Where do you want to go?" I asked, my shoulders shaking involuntarily.

"Italy!"

"Oh, really," I replied, trying to keep my cool. "And how do you plan to go to Italy tonight?"

"We'll take the Concorde."

"What?" I shouted, "The French supersonic airplane able to fly faster than the speed of sound? Surely, you're kidding!" My teeth almost fell out.

"No, I'm not kidding," he said, his arms crossed over his chest with defiance.

I had to get out of this. There was no way I was going anywhere with him. No, I didn't want to be near this madman. *Think, think, think.* "What about our passports?"

"I have mine. We can go back to Boston first and pick up yours."

"So you planned this without telling me?"

"I make decisions on the spot."

My jaw unhinged. "You can't be serious?"

"Of course, I am. I'm leaving for Italy tonight and that's that. I'd love to take you along."

What the hell is this 'Kook' smoking? Every nerve in my body was on fire, the hair on the back of my neck bristling.

"Thanks but no thanks. I have to get back to work," I said, taking a risk.

"I'll take care of the bill on the way out," he replied, glaring at me.

I knew something was about to happen. He flung the door open wide with fury in his eyes, slammed it in my face, holding his briefcase. Outside I could hear him yelling, "Goddamn!"

My heart raced while I sat on the side of the bed with my legs dangling. I didn't know what to think. I was terrorized but felt a sense of relief after he left. I thought I had come in contact with "Jack the Ripper." I hadn't seen any signs of erratic behavior except that night. I knew he was loaded with pockets of cash when he picked me up in his burgundy Porsche on our first date and invited me to a posh Italian restaurant in the North End of Boston. That evening, he was very sweet, even tempered and seemed to have his act intact.

Clearly, I'd been wrong.

I was left alone in the middle of the night in one of Manhattan's swankiest hotels, which clearly had no more importance to him than a fleabag inn, and it was too late to return to Boston. I pulled the sheets up to my neck scared to death. I hadn't eaten anything since lunch and stuffed myself with fancy chocolates to fill my empty stomach and calm my nerves.

What if he comes back?

I jumped out of bed, put the night lock on, and got under the sheets covering my face. The next thing I remembered, my head was spinning and I was floating in the air. The bed had been lifted from the frame, capsized and rotated to the ceiling. I'd lost control of my entire body, couldn't lift a finger, and was spooked by some kind of demonic anxiety. My mind, my imagination, went into overdrive. The key rattled violently in the door and a monster entered. He was tall and looked like a devil. He was wearing a black cape, red gloves, and his hair was long and straggly. His skin was pale and wrinkly like an old man. Evil spirits surrounded the room in the midst of white clouds. He reached up in my direction. "*Sono tornato per te*," I came back for you, he roared. When he spoke in Italian I knew it was Lorenzo and I was terrified that he was going to kill me. Suddenly, I shot straight up in bed screaming at the top of my lungs, sweating. How I ascended to the ceiling and eventually returned to my conscious state was a mystery I will never ever forget. It was the nightmare of all nightmares and it seemed so real.

Early the next morning, I was on the first flight to Boston sobbing my eyes out. A week later, I received a postcard from Italy: *You should have come, Vernetia. It's just what the doctor ordered.*

When I came to my senses, I believed Lorenzo was on the verge of having a nervous breakdown and needed to escape from his soul sucking job which was evident from his irrational behavior. After my rotation to the ceiling, I went straight to my doctor for tranquilizers to calm my nerves. Obviously, work pressures had begun to steer me out of control and I didn't want to make the same mistakes.

After my night in horror at the Park Plaza Hotel, I began my mental journey to chase my Paris dream and to live out the fantasies my twin sister and I wanted when we were young. Virginia wasn't with me any longer, but she still lived on in my heart urging me on.

Do it, Vernetia, came her whisper, sparking my soul. And I would do it. The looming question was how and when?

I'd always been somewhat of a miser and enjoyed reading investment books like *Rich Man, Poor Man; The Millionaire Fast Lane; and The Millionaire Next Door*, about the surprising secrets of America's wealthy, and my dream was to become one of them. I knew I would never climb the corporate ladder and become a

President or Vice President, playing office politics 24/7, and kissing ass for corporate giants to advance my career. It was not in my DNA. I did it my way.

With my company's 401-K retirement plan, matched with 80% of one's basic contribution, I found an investment specialist in New Jersey, Harry Stolick, who still manages my portfolio. Harry wasn't your usual investment advisor. He was a mix of an economist, a psychologist, and a stand-up comedian. When the market dropped and you just wanted to cry, it was great to have an advisor with a good degree of competency who could also make you laugh. Harry helped me grow my investments substantially over the years which gave me the luxury of having options in my life. Money wasn't everything but it sure helped.

The last time I had a rent increase, I decided to buy an apartment on Beacon Hill — one of the oldest and best places to live in Boston — a dream that I imagined each time I gazed at it from the Boston Gardens. With the Boston residence I could rent it out occasionally which gave me the freedom to go back and forth to France as I wished without cashing in on my investments.

Virginia did not get the chance to be with me on my life's journey filled with highs and lows, challenges and special moments, but her memories live on.

My life needed to be changed in a significant way and with sufficient savings, I quit my job. Then I signed up for foreign language lessons — because every now and then you have to say 'what the French' and follow your dreams.

2

SERGEANT'S DRILL IN BOSTON

ominique, our French professor, scurried into the classroom clutching a Larousse French grammar book and a folder stuffed with papers under her armpit. In her free hand, she carried a large cup of Starbuck's Dolce Latté with the potent scent of cinnamon infiltrating the classroom. Mornings without her caffeine fix caused noticeable mood swings. With it, she forged ahead captivating the class in eloquent French.

"Bonjour tout le monde!" Good morning everyone.

"Bonjour," the students responded gleefully.

"Sorry I'm late, Stéphanie is sick again." The "Sergeant's Drill" invoked the maximum level of proficiency — an uphill struggle for everyone. Speaking in a foreign language, while constantly being challenged, was laborious and intimidating. No matter how hard we tried, praises were rare.

A bit of an oddball, Harold — the youngest student in the class — rested his head on the desk in the back of the room waiting for Dominique's arrival. When she entered, he sat up spellbound. The way she spoke delighted him. He told me that he loved hearing his name pronounced in French as she glided over the "H," elevated the "air," and softened the last letter in "old." The class sensed it, too, and began calling him *Air-ol*. Once antisocial, he was bursting with pride and seemed to have a teacher's crush the way he smiled.

Despite her frequent tardiness, Dominique was adept at inciting her students to think in French. Humor is difficult to grasp in a foreign language but she had a craziness about her that made it translatable. She raised her long wicked eyelashes above her dreamy brown eyes and pirouetted in front of the classroom. Spirited and seductive, she wore spiked heels accentuating the height of her stubby legs and mastered her performance. She vacillated from fragility to indestructibility, exuding a powerful voice that emerged from a petite frame. I gawked at her *haute couture* fashion seen on the Catwalk and now — to my wonderment — in the classroom. And what a feast to the eyes! When the semester began every seat was taken. The "waitlist" was a waste of time. She transcended the language into an exhilarating experience and turned the students on.

"This is a French class," she raised her voice. "Please leave your English at the door."

The students were embarrassed when called on for fear of murdering the language. I had a plan and would not be intimidated by anyone or anything. I waited like a cat 'stalking a rat' hoping to impress Dominique when she called my name. I had memorized every line of my script. The *Larousse Dictionnaire* and *Bescherelle Grammaire* books were my bedside companions. I discovered that I only needed to master certain verb forms to speak French. The stems of most verbs have the same tenses. The convoluted irregular verbs were another story. Every day, I went to the language laboratory at Boston University and completed twenty dialogues of "Let's Go French." One day the director at the lab saw me nodding with my headphones on.

"Why not bring your bed in and spend the night? You're here all the time," she said.

"Perhaps I should." I snapped back, not in the mood for sarcasm. "I need to learn French quickly."

"How quickly," she asked.

"In three months."

"That's very ambitious! Why three months?" she asked.

"Because I'm moving to France," I responded. Saying it out loud made it seem more real.

"Oh," she replied, raising an inquisitive eyebrow. "Good luck!"

Soon, I stopped going to the language lab on a daily basis and heeded the director's advice — There is no substitute for time when learning a new language.

I fantasized about a city with over 2,000 years of history, which included hidden landmarks, the secret world of the Parisian Catacombs, the storming of the Bastille prison marking the beginning of the French Revolution, the stunning Notre Dame Cathedral, romantic night cruises on the Seine with illuminating lights and monuments. I'd envisioned walking in the footprints of legendary writers that celebrated the *City of Light* — Hemingway, Miller and Henry James. Their frequent haunts to Café de Flore, Les Deux Magots, Lipp and other meeting places seemed uncanny and intoxicating. All things French galvanized me — the art world, the culture and the cuisine. I had a long bucket list. I incessantly watched French films with subtitles, featuring Catherine Deneuve, Richard Berry, Jean Reno, Alain Delon and Gérard Depardieu. I wanted to devour the city of my wildest dreams — Paris dreams that began when I was a child.

After a long pause from the language lab, I was energized with 'feats of strength' to switch gears and found a new tactic for developing my language skills. I added a bit of French spice to my life, passing out French film programs at the Museum of Fine Arts in Boston. At the opening of the French festival, the audience was mostly French. All of my initiatives were to bring my voracious appetite to live in Paris, thanking the teachings of my parents and the dreams my twin sister and I had shared.

I reminisced about the past long gone. I remembered Mama would wake up at sunrise to spend time with her girls before going off to work. She looked so tired waking up at the crack of down to prepare our breakfast in her robe with a belt tied around her waist, her hair parted down the middle in a flipped bun behind her neck. Papa had left for his job at the morning's twilight. Mama, a domestic worker, performed a variety of household chores, as well as lavish cooking — crawfish, fried catfish, cajun Shrimp, glazed ham, collard greens with bacon, buttermilk biscuits, fried chicken, herb roasted turkey and gravy. The desserts of preference for the fancy dinner parties were hummingbird cake, peach cobbler, fresh lemon-lime and pecan pie with high peaks of fresh whipped cream and bourbon.

Every day Mama's boss drove her to and from work in the backseat of her fancy yellow Chevrolet that was so pretty it made you turn around and gawk. Why did Mama sit in the backseat of the car? Because that's the way it was when racial segregation was legitimized in the South. White bosses often treated their helpers abysmally. Mrs. Lila was no doubt a controlling boss but she had a tender spot for Mama. I believe she may have even loved her. It was Mrs. Lila who offered the bunny rabbits to Mama for our birthday, and at the end of each dinner party, she'd insist that Mama take leftovers in a pretty basket with flowered napkins so she wouldn't have to prepare an evening meal at home. On special occasions, she would offer Mama one of her fancy dresses and she'd get all prettied up for Papa when he got home and put on some red lipstick. When Mama wasn't feeling well she insisted that she stay at home. Those days reminded me of "Driving Miss Daisy" with Jessica Tandy and Morgan Freedman — except the driver was the white Boss Lady, and Mama, who sat in the back-seat of the car, was the driver's Black Helper.

We felt it in our bones when Mama would be coming home and we'd raced to the road. The minute Virginia and I spotted the fancy Chevrolet we'd jump up and down like crazy. As the car got closer, we'd wave to Mama and she'd wave back smiling at her babies, waiting impatiently for their loving embraces. Mrs. Lila would drive by the house turn around on the dirt road and drop Mama off directly in front of our door. When Mama got out of the car, she could barely move because we'd tugged on her dress tail until she lifted us up with big hugs and kisses. I could always tell when Mama had prepared a big dinner party because I would catch a sniff of the savoury odor in her clothes, especially from the roasted turkey with all the trimmings. Even today certain foods, especially turkey, trigger those beautiful moments.

We were neither a rich nor a poor family but we were property owners. Papa worked on our little farm in between building low-income homes. Our large abode with big windows and hand-me-down furnishings was surrounded by an orange grove on a massive plot of land in the countryside and so was Grandma's. Like any citrus fruit, it was all citrusy and sweet and boosted our energy. We carried the delightful smell in our clothes because we ate fruit constantly. Behind the house was a large tract of land where Papa reared two pigs, chickens, and a vegetable garden in beautiful rainbow colors — red, orange, yellow, green and violet. We'd feed the pigs various mixtures of leftovers from our dinners as well as sweet watermelons from the large field across the road. We even gave the pigs nicknames — Buzzy and Buddy — and loved hearing them grunting and squealing when we threw food in their pigpen. We listened to the hens cackling after laying their eggs and we held their baby chicks in the palm of our hands after they were hatched. We kept a watchful eye on the vicious rooster who surveyed the chicken coop for potential threats.

Food from our little farm was always plentiful. Papa also enjoyed fishing for bass and rainbow trout in nearby lakes that sparkle in the sunlight. Mama would bread them with hot spices baked or fried with all the sides — hushpuppies, lemon slices, tartar sauce and creamy cucumber salad. Grandma and our cousins came to our Friday night fish fries religiously.

Mrs. Lila, Mama's Boss Lady, and her husband Franklin vacationed in England every two years and would go to Paris for three or four days. They loved everything about Paris including the melody of the language, although they didn't speak a word of French. They ate at fine French restaurants, strolled down the Champs-Elysées, visited the famous *Musée du Louvre* and took boat rides aboard le bateau mouche on the Seine. She would bring Mama a vintage postcard of a beautiful Paris scene — Josephine Baker, who danced at *Le Théâtre des Champs-Elysées*, wearing a sexy skirt of palm leaves or her signature banana skirt; a portrait of a smiling young woman wearing a beret riding a bicycle carrying a baguette, the magnificent Cathédrale Notre-Dame, and the Tour Eiffel with extraordinary views of Paris. Mrs. Lila didn't socialize with Mama at work but when she returned from her European vacation she told her passionate stories about Paris. Mama sucked in every word. She even used her postcards as bookmarks in her bible and romance novels.

One very warm summer day sitting on the front porch in her rocker fanning and humming *La Vie en Rose* by Edith Piaf, Mama's boss called out, "Gertie it's time for a break. Bring us two tall glasses of Mint Tulip tea with plenty of ice." While she poured her heart out about the City of Light, she paused and asked, "Gertie, would you like to go to Paris one day?" Blown away and at a loss for words Mama nodded. Her boss stood up and said, "Good Heavens it's getting late. I've got to drive you home."

At the end of a Christmas dinner party, Mrs. Lila handed Mama a beautiful bag filled with gifts. "It's a little something for you and the girls! Open it when you get home."

Mama' eyes lit up with a broad smile stretched across her face and graciously thanked her. When she got home, she opened her gift first — "My Lord," she said glowing and holding a Blue, White and Red French scarf with Monuments on it: La Notre Dame Cathedral, L'Arc de Triumph, Le Bateau Mouche and La Tour Eiffel — all the places Mrs. Lila visited in Paris. It felt soft as butter. When Mama noticed it was made of pure silk, she grinned from ear to ear and put it around her shoulders twirling in delight like a burlesque showgirl.

"You look so pretty, Mama," we giggled. "Wear it tonight when Papa comes home."

Next Virginia and I ripped the paper off of our gifts and found two adorable French children's books, *Le Petit Prince and Un, Deux, Trois*. We were so happy we slept with them under our pillows that night. Before going to bed, we sat on Mama's lap while she pretended to translate the French to English. Eyes swirling, we laughed so hard because we knew Mama didn't understand what those strange words meant. We took pleasure in whatever she read but we mostly loved the stories Mama made up. Enveloped in darkness we fell asleep in her arms. We'd been very restless.

Mama was a seamstress at home and loved every minute. I can still hear the grind coming from the cast iron pedals under her feet on the old Singer machine passed down from her mother with the needles clacking up and down while sewing the rickrack on our dresses, bloomers and doll clothes. Virginia preferred soft colors for her dresses. I preferred bold sassy prints that matched my personality. We both had rickrack stitched around the waste with bows tied behind the back. Mama would sit behind the machine with her patterns all cut out and use her hands to guide the fabric. The stylish part was the squiggly zig-zag sewn on the collar and at the bottom of the flared skirt. She'd size us up in her sewing room where she kept threads, thimbles, needles, rick-rack on spools in a basket that her boss gave her on a regular basis. We'd sneak into the sewing room and Mama would remove one foot off the pedal to slow it down and yell over the crackling sound! "Girls come in and give mama a big kiss." Like Papa's foot pressed down on the gas pedal in his pick-up truck to speed it up, the more she pressed her foot down on the machine pedal the faster the needles would move. We always knew when it was time to leave Mama to her devices. After an arduous day at work, sewing at home freed her from stress. She'd always believed the proverb "a stitch in time saves nine" would give her more time with her girls.

Papa, a man of many talents, worked tirelessly to support his family. His principal job was carpentry and building low-income homes. One terribly sad day while engaged in rooftop framing he slipped and died a sudden death. Our dreams vanished in an instance. Shattered at age five, there were no words for the tragedy.

Virginia and I kept our sorrow in silence and pretended it never happened, but Papa often appeared in our sweet dreams. Then we'd come to the realization that those happy moments had vanished forever.

Before our eyes closed, one night Mama said, "Although Papa can't be with us girls, don't worry. Mama's gonna take you to Paris one day to see The Eiffel Tower."

And yet another devastating tragedy — An unforgettable night, Virginia and I were awakened by low voices. We got out of bed and found our bedroom door locked. We learned the next morning that Mama had a fatal heart attack. It seemed that Mama could not endure the pain from Papa's passing. Later that week, the funeral procession passed down the road in front of our home. We weren't allowed to attend Mama's burial. That afternoon we reminisced about the days when Mama came home after work and we'd jump into her arms and she'd give us big hugs and kisses. It gave us a bit of comfort in a time of sadness. Mama would have been touched but not surprised that Mrs. Lila attended the funeral. That day our happy lives had vanished yet again.

After Mama departed this life, there was a tug of war about who would become the guardians for the three children — Virginia and I and Carl. Aunt Ruby and Uncle Redmond felt it was their responsibility to raise us. Thelma, our oldest sister, and Charles, our oldest brother, would have been devastated. There was no way we would be separated from them. Symbolically they wore a 'badge of honor' with the hopes and dreams of our parents. After endless conversations, it was agreed that we would all move to Boston and live with our uncle and auntie who would share the responsibilities.

Before leaving Florida to travel North, we were filled with intense emotions, saddened to leave behind family members, friends and social connections — starting something new with conflicting feelings of fear and anxiety. Saying farewell to our *home sweet home* in the countryside that we'd known all our lives and our little farm with Buzzy and Buddy in the pigpen was unthinkable. The last day pulling out of the driveway waving goodbye to our loved ones was heart-wrenching. Our cousins moved into our home after we departed. There was no chance in hell it would become a forgotten past with so many precious memories and God only knew if we'd adjust to our new surroundings.

When we arrived in Boston we were greeted warmly by our aunt and uncle: *"We are thrilled to welcome you with open arms and hope your new abode becomes a little Paradise and that 'the world is your oyster.'"* Fond memories quickly emerged. A beautiful portrait of our deceased parents and grandmother hung on the wall in the living room. Thanksgiving day that we cherished with our parents was now being celebrated with Aunt Ruby and Uncle Redmond in Boston. It was a grand feast and joyous occasion, as well as Christmastime with a tree that reached the high ceilings, filled with dazzling lights and all sorts of unique decorations they had accumulated over the years. They were thrilled to have all of us living under the same roof with plenty of spare rooms. They had no children and spoiled us rotten. Uncle Redmond was a hotshot school principal. His friends called him Red. He was tall, slender and dressed to kill on special occasions, wearing double breasted suits, pointed black patent shoes and a chic flat cap. Aunt Ruby wore dresses with a silhouette drop waste that fell below the knee, a vintage box hat, tilted to one side of the forehead, revealing her angelic eyes when she sauntered around town. She was the epitome of black elegance from the Golden Age. They loved entertaining with style and grace and were admired dearly by their friends. It would take a bit of time to adjust to the city and we did.

Known for his political savvy, Uncle Redmond, a school principal, used his connections to hire Charles as a substitute teacher and later a head teacher. Eventually we moved into our own apartment. Charles and Thelma became strict disciplinarians like my aunt and uncle. It was their way of protecting us in the big city. Charles managed the external matters with the guidance of my uncle as if it were a formal business. Thelma managed the internal affairs. They shared things that couldn't be clearly separated. Should the children attend private or public school? Would co-education be more sustainable? How much money should they get for their weekly allowance? What genre of music was more suitable? We had very little input in decision-making. Deprived of the right to choose friends without their approval was also a part of their equation.

Having gone full circle Virginia and I found strength from each other — it held us together — two against the world. That catastrophic evening when she died completed a triple whammy that ripped us apart forever. After she left, my happy days and happy dreams suddenly dissipated. I'd wake up screaming with overwhelming sadness. *"Virginia, Virginia!"* I cried, but she was no longer by my side.

Traumatized, I hid my sorrow from family and friends for a very long time. Despite the void in my heart, I forced myself to take small steps and eventually found closure from that heart-wrenching tragedy. Life must go — Cheers to Virginia! She inspired the changes I was about to make.

Back in the classroom, I received kudos for my presentation on the usage of French courtesy; for example, "vous" and "tu" equals "you" in English but the meaning is different. The formal use of "vous" is used to address someone you don't know or have been given the authorization to do so. "Tu" is informal which means you already know the person. That said "vous" in some cases is used for the elite class even if you already know them. Use "tu" to address children. Always say "bonjour" when you meet someone you don't know or ask a question. I discussed the three verb groups in French: 1st group are verbs ending in –er (except aller). 3rd group are verbs ending in –re (with the exception of irregular verbs). 2nd group are verbs ending in –oir. Whew! What madness!

"Bravo," Dominique said with a smile. She pinched her fingers together. "But you made quite a lot of mistakes. You just need to practice speaking a bit more with native French speakers outside of class."

Which was *exactly* what I intended to do!

3

FRENCH RENDEZVOUS AT CAFÉ DE PARIS IN BOSTON

Pacing the floor in the middle of the night, I thought about writing an ad for conversation exchanges at the French Cultural Center, French Consulate, and English as a Second Language School in Boston wanting to move to France. The next morning, I toiled with my instincts: "For goodness sake! Go on and do it." And I did.

While I waited for responses, I went to Cape Elizabeth, Maine, and strolled around the ocean with my dear friend Margaret eager to get her spin on my crazy idea, leaving her husband at home with his business creations. We rolled up the cuffs of our jeans, locked arms, waded out into the ocean and talked for a while with the bone chilling water curling our toes. I looked at her, wide-eyed.

"I'm thinking about moving to Paris for a little bit," I said changing the conversation. For sure, she'd think I was nuts.

She tilted her head to the side. "You'd better invite me to visit. Why not go for it? You can always come back."

A cool breeze blew across the ocean while Margaret inspired me to pursue my dream. I absorbed the energy from the crashing waves frothing against the massive rocks, seagulls crying and gliding low overhead.

"I'd better get back to Dave," she said with a sigh. "You coming?"

"I'm going to hang out for a while," I responded. After she left, I sat on top of a bed of rocks and seaweeds tilting my head to the warm sun and found myself voyaging in and out of consciousness across the Atlantic until I reached the open doors of Paris. My eyes stayed fixed on the lighthouse across the blue and turquoise horizon until the sun went down.

When I returned at sunset, Dave was holding a rambunctious two and a half pound lobster (and two more to go) behind the claws plunging it into a huge pot with steam pouring out. Margaret was preparing an Italian salad that she perfected in Italy, grilling corn on the cob, and I could smell the scent of an apple pie with cinnamon, cloves and nutmeg fresh out of the oven. Our conversation around the dinner table about the City of Light lasted late into the night.

At one point, Dave stared at me holding a glass of red wine and begged: "There are many things to think about when moving to another country and things will come up that you hadn't thought about. So please stop worrying about matters you can't control. I've read that France is supposed to be one of the most expensive cities in the world. The key is financial independence, and since that doesn't seem to be a problem, you're golden, you lucky sun of a gun!"

"It's not luck, really, I've always been a tightwad and enjoyed saving rather than spending. Once that becomes your modus operandi that's where your head's at."

"Can we switch heads?"

"I have no friends there," I said worried.

"Not yet, but with your gregarious and outgoing personality, I can't see that being a problem."

"French is not the only language spoken in France," said Margaret, standing up. She left the room and returned a few moments later with a large album and talked about her life in Italy. "It was a fabulous five years. Yes, it was scary before I went but it was so fantastic I can't image not doing it. Of course every person I knew said, "Wow that's great but I wouldn't do it. I was so happy that I hadn't listened to any of them."

"Did you make friends easily?" I asked.

"I went to a synagogue a couple of times a week and made some very nice friends and also in my Italian cooking class."

"Good point," I said. "American churches are very friendly and have social hours right after the service."

I placed my elbows on the table, thinking. "Huh! Maybe I can make some friends before I go?"

"That's the spirit," said Dave.

While blasting music driving home from Maine, I sang and banged on the steering wheel. The driver in the car next to mine gazed as if I were insane. Inexplicably I felt as if I had been reborn but realized it was going to take a very long time to speak French correctly.

When I turned the key to enter my apartment in Boston, I could hear the phone ringing. I rushed to it leaving traces of sand from the ocean. I picked up but the call had already gone to the answering machine. An inarticulate message with a stunning accent came on.

"Allo, I call you. I'm French. My name is Isabelle. I want to know English. I am at Boston. I leave you my number." Ecstatic, I played it several times. Finally someone had responded to my ad. I called her back to set up a meeting place for conversations, thinking it would be the two of us but her husband Pierre would be joining us too.

The rendezvous was arranged at a mediocre coffee and sandwich shop but I chose it for the name *Café de Paris* and the fact that it was located in a very public place. It faced the Boston Public Garden — a picture postcard — where children fed pigeons and took swan boat cruises on the lagoon. I recognized the couple immediately at the entrance holding their bilingual dictionaries. She was a natural beauty with a stone face; he smiled delightfully.

Spring was on the horizon but it was still very cold. I tucked my hands into my pockets to avoid a freezing handshake from anxiety while we became acquainted. We chose a table by the expansive windows with an unobstructed view of the Boston gardens. The ordinary coffee shop seemed extraordinary that afternoon. Isabelle seemed restrained but clung feverishly to her broken English. Pierre was gregarious and eager for conversation. Comforted by being on my own turf, I took the lead trying to communicate in French. I didn't care if my empty words were inarticulate. Their English was also inconsequential. My puzzled trip to Paris was beginning to take shape and I was ecstatic about meeting them.

"Why did you come to Boston?" I asked.

"I will do research at Boston University," said Pierre.

"My Alma Mater is Boston University." I smiled.

"What's Alma Mata?" Pierre asked.

"The university where I graduated," I said.

"What will you do Isabelle?"

"I will study English while Pierre is working."

"We are very excited to be in America." Pierre gazed.

"Why do you want to learn French?" asked Isabelle.

"I am going to live in Paris for three months."

Her eyes widened with surprise, "Why Paris?"

"After college I went to the City of Light and fell in love."

"With a Frenchman," Pierre interrupted.

"No, with Paris," I answered. "I visited the City of Light a long time ago, and it's calling me to come back."

In my early twenties, a friend gave me a student's travel guide: *Let's Go Paris* before going on my first European vacation with two Irish friends, Charlotte and Beatrice. We visited six countries in three weeks. I missed the part that may have read "European women don't wear shorts even when it's hot." I ventured out on my own to make some new discoveries. My first problem was in Spain. I didn't speak a word of Spanish and no one spoke English. I was dressed in blue jeans and carried an English/Spanish dictionary — Useless! The boys snuck up behind me and pinched my butt. I had no one to communicate with and who could I trust? I managed to go to a bloody bullfight alone and couldn't wait to figure out how to get back to our pension (guest lodge) where I'd feel safe again with Charlotte and Beatrice.

But things got even more bizarre in Italy. Beatrice and I went out together in the late afternoon. "Have you noticed anything unusual Vernetia?" she asked.

"Noticed what?"

"Pay attention to your surroundings."

Several people were discretely taking pictures of me even behind trees as if I were a rock star. Shapely, slender, cropped hair with bangs, wearing a T shirt with Khaki shorts half way the thigh, casually dressed, nothing unusual according to American standards, and it was hot. "Why?" I wondered. It frightened me, leaving me with an uneasy feeling the rest of the trip. "Perhaps they think you're famous," Beatrice said with a grin. "Maybe you're right," I laughed. "Could it be you're wearing shorts?" It didn't end there — We went to Killarney, Ireland, a quaint town located in County Kerry, famous for its national park, Irish whiskey and knit sweaters. It is one of the most picturesque towns in the country's beautiful South West. I was wearing a long skirt walking down the street and cars slowed down when they passed by us. We could clearly see heads turning and staring like crazy at me until we were out of sight. I felt increasingly uncomfortable from the steady gazes. "I haven't seen one person of color," Beatrice said. "Maybe it's that?" Dublin was a great city but I'd never go back to the countryside of Killarney, picturesque or not.

When we arrived in Paris everything changed.

With every breath and every step I took Virginia was with me. We went here, there, everywhere. She was my shadow following me around and observing me secretly. Even if I'd wanted to step out of her silhouette, I couldn't, but neither did I want to. She was my shinning light that made everything glow even in the darkness. Even my friends could see that I was enamored with the City of Light.

"What are you thinking about?" asked Beatrice.

"Oh nothing," I lied. I couldn't explain that feeling inside of me. Only Virginia would understand. I knew that three days would not be long enough but I knew that one day we'd come back together and it would be just as I had left it, if not better.

I snapped back to the present, a reminiscent smile on my face.

"Do you know anyone in Paris?" Pierre asked as our conversation continued.

"No. What's it like?"

"We don't live in Paris. We live in Marseille, the oldest city in France. It's sunnier and runs along the Mediterranean Sea."

Soon I understood why Isabelle was astonished that I was bold enough to reside in a bustling city not knowing anyone or the language. She grew up in a small town on the outskirts of Switzerland where people smiled easily and were chatty with their neighbors. I was born in the countryside and had become a city girl in Boston and could not imagine living far from the heartbeat of Paris.

At the end of our first encounter, we planned regular meetings, developed a genuine friendship, and I was encouraged to pursue my Paris dream. Soon afterwards, I had a small network of conversation partners and my French was slightly improving. One endeavor led to another. Meeting them lit my fire and I was ready for the challenge. I was one step closer to my dream.

Reading the Boston Globe, was a temporary escape from reality but I avoided the business section, which reminded me of my financial losses. I came from modest roots, made an impressive climb in the stock market and my assets were riveting. "Don't put all your eggs in one basket," my financial expert strongly advised. Every day I walked around with my head in the clouds until the market spiraled downwards. Then I was spooked from the time I got up until the time I went to bed. The big Lucent stock crash was back in early 2000; the stock fluctuated for years and then had another big "leg down" between February and July 2006. Despite my misfortune, my motivation to live in Paris had not changed. I still owned a ton of worthless stock, my 401-K retirement plan, and a hefty savings bank, but money was not my overriding concern. My assets only brought superficial happiness. I longed for the real thing.

I decided to refurbish my apartment on Beacon Hill. I would withdraw funds from my savings account to pay for the renovations but it was difficult to find contractors. They were only interested in large projects. Home prices were soaring and purchasing property became the new investment craze around the same time as the market crash.

After three stressful months, I admired my beautiful new kitchen that should have taken no more than a month from start to finish. Aesthetically, it was worth all the headaches. My newly reclaimed space in soft warm colors became my "petit" retreat where I brewed coffee in the mornings and listened to French melodies. I even had a view of a tiny courtyard from my kitchen window with ivy climbing up a brick wall. A narrow dilapidated staircase five stories high in the rear of the building led to the rooftop terrace with a panoramic view of the Boston skyline. On Independence Day, my neighbors and I listened to the Boston Pops 1812 Overture and other popular American tunes, gazing at fireworks exploding in the air while sailboats and yachts anchored on the Charles River. The voluminous Fourth of July celebrations at the Hatch Shell were filled with jubilation. My cozy renovated flat in the city's oldest neighborhood in Boston was only a few minutes from all the action. It reminded me of Paris. I called it my *"pied-à-terre,"* a term I learned in my French class.

One day while scanning the Boston Globe an article caught my eye. A start-up company was about to launch an initiative allowing employees who recruited applicants with flawless credentials to bid on the CEO's classic automobile. I imagined the company was looking for talented, supercharged recruits ready to hit the carpet running. "What the heck, follow your heart, go make the call," I thought. Miraculously, the CEO answered.

"I read your article in the Sunday Globe," I said. "What a fascinating strategy to maximize employee participation, accountability and boost the company's image. I worked in corporate America."

"It's kind of you to call," he replied. Surely, I was intrigued by the article, but I had my own agenda. Familiar with corporate jargon and buzz words, I dropped a few appropriately during our conversation. They were archived in my brain.

"Sounds like a win-win for management and employees," I said.

"Indeed," he remarked and continued to praise his employees.

"If you need lodging for your recruits," I explained. "I have a charming furnished apartment on historic Beacon Hill that I rent to professionals."

"I'll take your name and number and pass it on to Human Resources." I clung to the phone not believing what I had just heard.

"Thanks for calling," he said.

"YES!" I shouted overjoyed after the call ended.

"If it feels right — do it. Don't over analyze. Have fear — lots of it. It keeps the heart pumping. Life is limited only by one's imagination."

I clung to this advice from a motivational speaker that I listened to at a conference. "Agonizing over ideas excessively can drive one insane. Indulge in one's reveries! Believe in yourself. Think wrongly if you will," the speaker encouraged. "Get off your rump *NOW* — and do something!"

Feeling exuberant after I contacted the CEO about renting my apartment, I walked around the Charles river and popped in on a friend. Not yet ready to share my life-changing endeavor, my conversation was strained. When I returned home, the flashing light on the phone restored my faith that there might be calls with infinite possibilities. For some strange reason, Thursday was my lucky day. I listened to my messages and deleted all but the last one.

"My name is Craig Rivers. Human Resources asked me to

contact you about renting your apartment. I'm temporarily living on the South Shore of Boston and would like a place on Beacon Hill. Please call me as soon as possible."

A few days later a statuesque vice president with copper tone skin, large sunken eyes, and pitch black hair knocked on my door. His long lashes fluttered and his dimples deepened when he smiled. Due to his extreme height he appeared to bend from the waist up when he entered the apartment. I felt tiny beside his muscular frame, personifying the perfect specimen, charismatic and drop-dead gorgeous. I lowered my head to keep from staring into his dreamy brown eyes while I showed him the apartment. I could easily imagine him known for his business savvy and management expertise. I kept fantasizing, romanticizing, bewitched by his charm. I wanted to make a few advances but that was hardly my style. I hadn't given a look to see if he was wearing a wedding band. Perhaps I didn't want to know lost in my admiration. Instead, I offered him a large cup of Earl Grey tea with steam pouring out and pretended I had no milk to cool it down. I was in no hurry for my imaginary man to leave while engrossed in conversation about Paris. After a while, he glanced at his watch and carried his empty cup to the kitchen as if he were family feeling the comforts of home.

"I love the apartment," he said, making a gesture to leave.

"Are you interested in renting it? It is available for three months."

"Yes, but I prefer to spend less."

A feeling of trust led to a burning desire to hand over the keys no matter what he offered, and I couldn't dismiss the fact that I found him attractive.

"It's a reasonable price in this neighborhood," I pleaded.

"Would you consider making a trade? What about airline tickets instead?"

Craig traveled long-haul flights regularly and accumulated

more mileage than he had time to use so leveraging a deal on the rent made perfect sense.

"Airline tickets?" I asked surprised.

"Yes, to Paris!" he reiterated. "Business class."

"Wow," I guessed, "Business class tickets most likely will exceed my asking price." What mattered was a complete stranger came to my home, encouraged me to follow my dream, and made an extremely interesting proposition. I nodded with approval but suppressed my feelings of elation.

"Thanks for your time," he said, reaching out his oversized hand. "It looks like we may have a deal."

After he left, I tried to focus on other things, but the meeting was all consuming. A week later, I listened to his message dumbfounded. We definitely had a deal.

"Pack your bags Vernetia," he said as if he were my lover or my best friend. "You have reservations for Paris. I had to put in a departure date, but you can change that. So there you go Ms. France! *Bon voyage*."

"Oh! My God," I shouted sitting in my rocking chair stupefied. Gripped by emotion, I could barely move. I stood by the window bewitched on a cool summer night, gazing at the stars in the pitch black, trying to comprehend a miracle that would take me to the City of Light.

"*All is within the realm of possibilities. Pay attention to your wildest dreams,*" appeared Virginia's voice, bursting into my head. "*Don't be imprisoned by those crazy ideas that may take you orbiting around the planet.*"

Piloting at an important moment in time, I wanted to shout it out to my friends but decided to wait. Unable to sleep, I walked the floor most of the night and called Pierre and Isabelle early the next morning.

"I have tickets to go to Paris!"

"*C'est une blague*," asked Pierre.

"No, it's not a joke!"

"*Vous partez quand,*" Isabelle asked and gasped for air in surprise from the news.

"I will leave as soon as I find a place to stay in Paris," I shouted.

"*C'est extraordinaire,*" she exclaimed. I had never heard her so excited.

"Goodbye Boston, Bonjour Paris!" I said with excitement. "May I see you and Pierre tomorrow?" I want to tell you everything."

"*Oui,*" they said in unison.

Isabelle and I fixed a rendezvous at the French Cultural Center on Marlboro Street and researched places to stay in Paris. The librarian recommended a traveler's guide titled "Paris Par Cher." We discussed the pros and cons of renting a less expensive apartment in Paris verses a small hotel.

Isabelle volunteered to make some calls after returning from the *Apple Big.*

"It's the Big Apple," I said, correcting her.

When she didn't get back to me right away, I became impatient and called myself. The first call to Paris was a no-brainer. The hotel clerk spoke charmingly in English. On my second attempt, the receptionist spoke so quickly I barely understood *bonjour* and *au revoir.* My expectations were flattened and I waited for Isabelle's return. Meanwhile, I worked on my "must do" list. Pressed for time, I was ready to do just about anything for accommodations. I glanced at the mail from the French Consulate to see if it contained lodging. It didn't. Blurred by all the chores that needed to be done, I turned the stereo on for a distraction. Jacques Brel, Edith Piaf and Charles Aznavour reignited the flames and things got magically done. Before I knew it, my suitcase was stuffed to the brim. Still my overriding concern was finding a place to sleep when I landed.

The next morning, I rushed to the library searching for apartments to rent on the Internet. My personal computer had gone kaput. I saw several home exchanges in Paris and fired off a short message to each one of them. I'd forgotten that I had rented my apartment and had nothing to exchange. Nevertheless, I received several responses and there were no vacancies remaining. I gave a quick look before leaving the library *et voilà* I had my answer.

"Thanks for your email," Olivier wrote. "Your apartment is much smaller than my home. However, I would gladly offer you free accommodations in my guest room, but I am leaving for Tuscany, Italy, on vacation. It would have been simply nice to 'work' my English. By the way, I love Boston! I have a friend who rents apartments in the *Marais*. I will give her a call on your behalf. I think she may have something." Ecstatic, I stared at the email until my time had expired on the Internet and then I flew home, hopeful.

4

FRENCH CONNECTION

I sabelle was the first to respond to my ad at the French Consulate's office in Boston for conversation exchanges. She would accompany her husband on a one-year sabbatical at BU (Boston University). Camille was the second respondent who came to Boston to perfect her English eager to find a job for an American law firm in Paris. A tough no-nonsense lawyer, Camille's attitude about work reminded me of the way I had attacked the corporate world — "*burning the candle at both ends.*" A younger clone of Sharon Stone, tall with blond cropped hair, she was not only beautiful but fierce. I encouraged her to slow down when she talked about the firm where she worked in Paris. Headstrong, she was capable of making "knock out" punches, and took my advice as frivolous. We discussed my dream about going to Paris to improve my French with native speakers.

"Great idea," she said. "Why limit your interest to French natives? French people are too darn complicated. We shield ourselves behind tall coded gates with closely guarded secrets. During the Second World War we trusted no one and hid our pride to save our lives. Enough said about us. You need to put an ad in *FUSAC* but first let's start speaking French together!"

"What's *FUSAC*?" I asked.

"A resource magazine in Paris created for Anglophones. That way, you are more likely to have conversations with many cultures eager to practice English in exchange for French. Most inhabitants learn English in school for years but rarely have an opportunity to use it."

"I can't do that."

"Do what?"

"Write a Paris ad," I said with frustration.

"Why not," she said giggling. "It's no different from the ad you placed at the French Consulate in Boston. Have you forgotten how we met?"

Once a week we visited the Museum of Fine Arts in Boston and critiqued American paintings. She was uncompromising when she corrected my French. I gave her the benefit of the doubt when she spoke in English. One late afternoon while having high noon tea in the museum's courtyard, she took out a pad and began scribbling. She lifted her head with piercing eyes.

"Don't waste time," she insisted. "Act quickly and decisively. You may need to re-run your ad a second time."

"An American woman seeks conversation partners fluent in French."

"Partners," I interrupted. "Can you change that to conversation exchanges?"

"What's the difference? Trust me Vernetia." She continued writing. "I will be staying in Paris several months and want to improve my French."

I asked if the ad could be written in English.

"Of course not, jump right in, don't dally around. If you get stuck, use your bilingual dictionary or send me an email." She gave me a devilish look.

"I'm not taking a computer."

"No problem! Go to a cyber café."

"What's that? I've never seen a cyber café in America."

"Many homes in France don't have internet access."

"Why not," I asked.

"Why should they?" she shouted. "That's such a pompous American attitude — We're the greatest, we have the latest, why can't the rest of the world be like us! We don't. Let's leave it at that!"

"Ouch," I recoiled and shut up. Our relationship had broken new ground. "You were just denigrating the French. Now you're fiercely defending them," I almost said but I needed her advice and admired her candidness.

"You'll find the French keyboard a tad different — the accented letters and a different layout for the letters, "AZERTY" — but you'll get the hang of it in no time."

Camille had a convincing argument but I hesitated thinking about the suppositions. Later I thought about the advantages of having contacts once I arrived in a new city and agreed reluctantly to do it.

Soon I received a small envelope from France. My hands were shaking when I opened one of the letters scribbled in indecipherable penmanship and my confidence sank as I struggled to read it. Camille had already returned to Paris so I went straight to the French Cultural Center on Marlborough Street — parallel to the elegant Commonwealth Avenue — to get help with the translation.

Commonwealth Avenue is a very wide thoroughfare filled with beautiful trees emitting sun and shade in a park-like setting, "punctuated with statutes and memorials and serving as a promenade for strolling, sitting and relaxing." It has some of Boston's finest townhouses with a blend of French architecture comparable to Boulevard Haussmann, one of the most elegant avenues in Paris. It is so quiet you never see anyone and I've always wondered,

"Who resides behind those stately doors?" Surely they are people with pockets full of cash. Minutes later, I arrived at the French Cultural Center on Marlborough Street and opened the tall, black gold-plated gate, took a deep breath, and went inside. Directly in front of me, the receptionist in her early thirties was speaking in French. I waited in an adjacent room where newspapers hung on rods, flipped through *Le Monde*, baffled by its contents, and waited nervously for the call to end.

"*Bonjour, puis-je vous aider?*"

"Yes, please. I have a few letters and postcards from France and I'd like your help with the translation." Intimidated, I made no effort to speak in French. I stuck firmly to my English.

"You need to see the librarian on the first floor," she said. I was already on the first floor but walked up the elegant spiraling staircase, as instructed. I learned later that the *rez-de-chaussée* is the ground floor and the next floor up is generally the first floor in Paris. At the landing, I found a middle-aged stern looking woman, hair twisted in a French bun, wearing thick-rimmed glasses, sitting behind a large stack of books. When I cleared my throat, she looked up with a half smile and offered to help. After the translation, she made a brief comment about a postcard I received with a magnificent scene of *Pont Neuf* on the river Seine. She wasted no time with superfluous conversation; I was babbling effusively unable to shut my big mouth. Walking down the elegant staircase to leave, I noticed that I had dropped one of the letters on the way up. I didn't want to return to the busy librarian, so I paused at the receptionist desk.

"Excusez-moi Madame," I asked in French. "Avez-vous le temps de traduire quelques lettres françaises?" Yes, of course, I will be happy to translate your French letters. She seemed to be surprised when I spoke in French this time. Moreover, she looked bored and thrilled to get a bit of gossip from the other side of the continent.

"Thierry sounds really interesting!" she said gloating over his message as if she were nostalgic for her country. "He has a vineyard in Bordeaux, the largest wine producing region in France."

"Is it unusual for Frenchmen to own vineyards?" I asked daunted by a topic I knew nothing about but wanted to keep the conversation going.

"*Ah, ben non.*" she responded authoritatively. "Of course not, if you are a Frenchmen with financial means."

"How far is Bordeaux from Paris?"

"About three hours on the TGV."

"Is it safe to go alone?"

"Of course, but he wants to meet you in Paris. Anyway, you need not worry," she added. "Frenchmen love to flirt but are rarely dangerous. I can assure you. I'm French." Unlike the librarian, the receptionist was 'all ears,' eager to learn more about my correspondents. Almost fifteen minutes had elapsed before she glanced at her watch.

"Good luck in France," she smiled standing up gesturing me to leave.

Metamorphosed — as if by witchcraft — I cut across the Boston Public Garden on my way home to Beacon Hill with my nose in the air, clutching my small envelope humming, "April in Paris."

When I got home, I'd received another small envelope but was too embarrassed to return to the French Cultural Center for the translation. "I can do this," I said sprawled out on my living room floor with my bilingual dictionary, my grammar book, nervous and excited.

François hadn't revealed too much personal information other than that he rarely had an opportunity to speak English and expressed an interest in conversation exchanges. He said he was a corporate lawyer, passionate about genealogy, tracing 2000 years of ancestral history. He was writing his second book. German was his second language in school. He also spoke some Spanish and Japanese.

Jacques was another interesting respondent who worked at *La Délégation Générale du Québec à Paris*. Both of these men tugged at my heart, seemed completely harmless, and were eager to engage in conversations across the Atlantic.

"*Umm*...What can I talk about with my sight unseen admirers — my job that I ended up hating and quit?" I began by revealing bits and pieces about renovating my kitchen. I was smitten by François' messages but I didn't know the reason why. I had read that France and America have always had a love-hate relationship.

The letters kept coming:

How are things in Boston? When are you coming to Paris? Tell me about you. Benoît wrote.

I am a French anthropologist-film maker and love American films. I travel quite a bit and am sure to spend more time in Paris. Can we meet up when you come? I await your answer. I send regards, Sélina.

I flipped to the next one,

Hi, how strange to write to someone I don't know. I would love to improve in understanding and speaking English. I work in Engineering Company of France and travel a lot, absent from Paris one week among four. I know it pretty well and enjoy it on my bicycle, motorbike or rollers. I would be pleased to work my English, offer you my knowledge of the French language and show you my beautiful city. I propose a rendezvous at my favorite café when you arrive and wake your Paris dream, Christophe.

Another,

When I came home to my Paris apartment tonight, I found the trash spilled over in the courtyard, and since no one else seemed ready to tidy it up, I did! On the edge of the spill was a copy of FUSAC. Looking to get some reward for my virtue, I flipped to the conversation section and 'voila' I found you. Hope to get news soon. Nicolas.

And another,

I am a French Cosmetician. I traveled a lot. It's my pleasure to meet new people. Don't worry about your French. I speak a little English. I'm waiting you, Agnès.

François and Jacques were the pick of the crop and seemed to be delighted to hear about the latest gossip of my new kitchen. To my surprise, another message came from Jacques this time via the US post office.

I would be pleased to receive a couple of photos of you in your new kitchen. If you send me your address I will send a photo of me in my garden!

My thoughts spiraled. What if he is a rapist, a madman? What if one day after meeting him I'm discovered under the soil in his garden? Suspicion accelerated in my mind. I was behaving like a lunatic but decided to send one. He thought I was concealing my identity because I hadn't disclosed my home address. François hadn't asked for a snapshot but, intrigued by his messages, I scanned a photo and sent him one too. He responded the next day.

Thanks for the photo of your beautiful kitchen. I like your choice of warm colors.

"What an insensitive jerk! He wasn't even courteous enough to compliment me, not that I was looking for love." I may not be a beauty queen but women enjoy a bit of flattery. My looks won't stop traffic, but I've been known to turn a few heads." I felt a tinge of rejection and lost my confidence. In another email he wrote: *It's the first step.*

"The first step to what — What the hell does that mean — a French romance?" Puzzled by his comment, my imagination ran wild which I loved as much as I fretted.

I went for a Sunday stroll on Newbury Street, Boston — the equivalent of Rodeo Drive in Beverly Hills where folks promenade like 'geese that lay golden eggs'— to window shop.

A large percentage of the *International Jeunesse Dorée* crowd with unlimited resources could afford the outrageously expensive stores. Window shopping on the multi-cultured street kept my Paris dream alive, and I was awestruck by so many foreign accents, especially French. My store was the famous Filene's Basement and I knew it inside out. Filene's basement was an actual Boston legend and even a tourist destination. It was known for its quirky and no frills discounted shopping experience, specializing in off-price designer and high fashion goods from the best stores, in the US and in Europe. Everyone shopped there, from tightwads like me, to the likes of Alan Dershowitz who might be seen examining the Ferragamo ties.

On Mondays and Wednesdays I clipped out newspaper coupons for "the Basement" as it was fondly called, along with the store rebate, and was entitled to a hefty savings of thirty percent on top of their already fabulous discount. One afternoon I found a lovely rose-colored evening gown and a matching shawl with white fringe. I looked at the label and, as luck would have it, discovered that it was made by a famous French designer. "Wow" I said, "If only I could afford it." My eyes scanned the tag and I discovered it was dirt-cheap. With my coupons, and the store's automatic mark-down system, I left the store with an exceptional discount of seventy percent for a designer gown. When I got home, I invited my best friend, Helena, for a glass of French wine and poured out the news about my Paris trip.

"I'm taking it with me."

"You are?" she asked, nose scrunched.

"Yes, of course. What do you think?"

"Do you want my honest opinion?"

"Please," I insisted.

"You look like a damn bridesmaid! And where can you wear it?" she asked. "At a gala," I said. "Are you sure?" She continued to nag me. "Hell yeah I can!" No matter what she said my mind was made up and I'd be a fool to leave my French designer gown behind. I returned to the basement the following day and purchased enough toiletries to fill a small suitcase. Laying my clothes out on the bed, a voice in my head unnerved me:

"What are you doing, for God's sake? If you think you're lonely now, wait until you arrive in Paris. Besides, you can't even speak French! You can still change your mind sweetheart!"

"No I can't," I hissed under my breath. "My heart is starving for Paris!" I fell across the bed thinking, "I've a few suitcases and a heart filled with dreams; I've my airline tickets in hand and damn it, I'm going." I tucked my letters away in my luggage and wondered if I would have the courage to contact my admirers once I arrived. After Helena left, I stormed off to the library to use the internet, hoping for news. And I had it.

"Chère Madame a friend asked me to contact you right away. I have a studio for rent in the Marais one of the liveliest neighborhoods in Paris, famous for hidden courtyards and cobblestone streets, impressionist painters like Monet and Renoir, and it's walking distance to stunning views of the river Seine. The trendy neighborhood is minutes away by foot to everything — restaurants, cafés, bakeries, florists, bookstores, clothing stores, two Métro stations and much more. Just around the corner, my husband and I drink frothy cups of coffee with delicious croissants at our favorite *Café Français* in the mornings. On the weekends, we buy fresh fruits, vegetables, fish and meat, at the open street market. I'm attaching a couple of photos of the apartment."

I forwarded the email to Camille and asked her opinion. She replied quickly.

Vernetia, I've spoken with Madame Guillot. She's very nice. The pied-à-terre sounds perfect, it's located in a vibrant historic neighbor-

hood and the price is right. I think you should take it immediately! It's very difficult to find an apartment in Paris. If I get a chance, I will stop by and take a look. A très bientôt, See you very soon in Paris!

Paris and my apartment were a done deal and I couldn't wait. My bags were packed, my ticket in hand, and I was ready to leave the following Friday, June 13th.

5

PARIS, ME VOILA! HERE I AM!

I managed to catch some Z's before arriving at Charles De Gaulle Airport stupid from fatigue. I breezed through customs and went straight to the taxi station to grab a cab. Standing beside two sharp-tongued men wearing turbans, I was nearly knocked to the ground when one of the drivers opened his door and the other slammed it preventing me from getting in. "This is my customer! Back off!"

"For crying out loud," I yelled and with very little strength I tugged at my suitcases and hailed another cab. When we sped away, the men were still in a battle of arguments. My driver apologized for the incident with an Arabic accent while he drove down the motorway to Paris.

"My name is Muhammad," he said and, too tired, I sighed out mine with a long slur.

"You're British," he said.

"No, American."

"Land of Prosperity, Zero Tolerance, Fifteen Minutes of Fame," he chuckled and spoke in flawless English. I suspected he was "kissing up" for a hefty tip from a worn out tourist feeling like crap with enough luggage to fill the trunk and back seat of his cab. Out of necessity, I sat up front blinded by the rising sun.

"Where are we going?" he asked. I handed him a card with the address.

"Good choice! The *Marais* is the oldest neighborhood in Paris."

"Alright," I whispered unable to lift my tired head. I nodded off and missed most of his boasting and babbling. He seemed to have a wealth of knowledge, but I was too exhausted for his *yackety-yak*. Under different circumstances, I would have been all ears. I was startled again when he continued his lecture aggressively as the traffic slowed down.

"Do you know that the Marais was once Marshland in the 12th century?"

"How would I know that, sir?" I asked.

"You wouldn't Madame? Sorry I didn't catch your name earlier."

"Madame Smith," I said with a sigh.

"Madame Smith," he said with a chuckle, as if he didn't believe me. "Your apartment is sitting on top of a swamp!"

"Sounds very attractive," I said. "Holy shit," I muttered.

"It's beautiful, in fact. Ages ago Paris was cultivated by a religious order under the reign of Philippe Auguste."

"What religious order was that?" My ears perked up. I vaguely remembered reading something about it.

"The Templars," he explained. "Several of the residences which were luxurious mansions resembling palaces known as — Hotel Particuliers — were constructed in the 16th and 18th century in the Marais for the French nobility before they left for Versailles. King Henry IV deserves much of the credit for transforming the neighborhood from the *Pits to the Ritz.*

"Can you tell me again who the Templars were?"

"Now we're talking!"

"No Sir, I was sleeping. Besides this is way over my head." I paused. "Sounds like you are passionate about history."

"Indeed, I am a French history buff, Madame Smith." A broad smile flickered across his face still not convinced of my name. "Louis XIV, King of France, wanted the court and the government to be under his control and had the Palais of Versailles rebuilt in the 17th Century in the Southwest of Paris to rule the nobility with a tight fist and absolute power. The decline of the Marais began after the nobility was forced to take residence in Versailles," he explained. "The Marais has long since become a very elegant and vibrant neighborhood with lots of restaurants, art galleries and museums. It has some of the most beautiful architecture in Paris, and I might add it is also very expensive. Don't expect to get bored!"

"Great! How much longer sir," I asked. I needed a shower and a bed.

"Less than five minutes," he laughed. "Is Smith really your family name?" "Of course," I said. My head began to bob and weave when he drove past the famous *Café Français,* turned onto a short street, and pulled up on the curb in front of a Prussian blue door. "*Nous sommes arrivés et bienvenue dans le quartier,*" he said flirting with me in beautiful French. We've arrived and welcome to the neighborhood! I sat up straight, short of breath, with knots in my stomach while he placed my luggage beside the taxi. I caught a glimpse of myself in the mirror and "Goodness gracious," I barely recognized myself.

"Do you have the code?" he asked.

"It's in my head."

Warned that I could not enter without it, I had it memorized. When he entered the code the door opened wide which insulated the interior from the street noise. My tired eyes gaped at a tiny courtyard with apartment doors, and a scattering of shrubs. At the top step of each door front, flowers were planted in small pots. I expected to see or hear some movement, but the quietness was ubiquitous. My landlords' private quarters were in the rear of the building. My studio was directly in front of the long walkway entrance. The driver carried my luggage to the door and paused for a tip.

"How long are you staying, Madame Smith?"

"Not sure," I said.

"Call me if you want the best tour of Paris." He handed me his business card, shook my hand and rang the doorbell. "Would you believe me if I told you my name is Mr. Jones? But, of course, it is not." I said "No, I would not."

The landlord greeted me with a perky smile and carried my suitcases inside. "Welcome to Paris!" she exclaimed and I could only nod a thank you. She could see that I was worn out and folded the sheets back. "I'll talk to you tomorrow after you've gotten some sleep."

I was dazed, staring around vaguely remembering the details in the photos, with a tiny kitchenette, circular shower, a large sofa bed which covered most of the floor's surface and a hideous painting of Paris on the wall. The phone blinked in red on the nightstand and a small chair was beside it.

"Holy cow," I mumbled and sat down not having the foggiest idea of how to retrieve my messages nor had I expected any. I kicked off my shoes, fell across the bed in my tiny pad and slept like a log. It felt strange being in a foreign country where things worked differently from my native land. I had already given my landlord the security deposit and the first month's rent, so I didn't need to deal with any immediate concerns except getting some money from the *distributeur automatique de billets* — the ATM cash machine.

Earl the next morning, my landlord stopped by to show me how to light the antique stove with an *allume gaz* — a gas lighter —

and how to retrieve messages on the vintage digital phone. I had one message!

Bienvenue à Paris! It's Camille. You must not be alone when you arrive. After you get some rest, call me Vernetia. I will come to your apartment, take you to lunch and give you a tour of the neighborhood.

A range of emotions washed over me — sadness, happiness, and fatigue. I opened the tiny refrigerator, found a bottle of Perrier, a French brand of bottled water, and drank it with my roasted peanuts I carried from the plane. In the cabinet, I found a box of sugar, herbal tea, and a small microwave was on the countertop. I sat on the side of the bed and sipped on a cup of warm *tisane*. I was feeling lonely just as my inner voice had warned me before leaving Boston. Jetlagged, I plunged my head into the fat pillow and within minutes I was sound asleep, dreaming about packing my suitcase in Boston getting ready to go to Paris.

The following afternoon, filled with exhilaration, I waited for Camille.

Bravo! You made it! Welcome!" She laughed.

Camille seemed to be as happy to see me as I was to see her when she entered the apartment grinning. She gave me a big hug and a French kiss on both cheeks, her smile wide.

"*Ce n'est pas mal ton studio, n'est ce pas?*" Your studio is not bad, huh?" she said.

"You're right, but I thought it would be larger."

"Then you should have found an apartment in the boring suburbs!"

"I just need time to adjust," I said.

"Don't worry, things will quickly change. Cheer up! You're in

Paris following your dream. Let's start the adventure by having a nice French lunch in your famous neighborhood."

Off we went to fantasy-land, my eyes popping, while we strolled in the Marais crammed with tiny restaurants and cafés. The neighborhood was different in every way from any place I had visited in America. My first observation was the magnificent Parisian Haussmann and Renaissance style architecture — bigger than life — and the charming narrow sidewalks spilled over with hordes of people. We paused at the Picasso museum, the Carnavalet museum and the house of Victor Hugo.

Camille chose a charming restaurant where we squeezed between tiny tables and followed the waiter who seated us by a window in an intimate dining room drenched with the aroma of charcoal grilled lamb and herbs. I salivated at the mouth while the waiter boasted about the specialties of the day. After our delicious lunch we continued our stroll in the famous *"Place des Vosges,"* once the residence of Alexandre Dumas, Victor Hugo, Honoré de Balzac, and paused to catch our breath in the enticing garden. Lovers were entangled in a passionate embrace in the garden, and pigeons were perched on top of the fountain taking it all in. We popped in and out of pricey stores under the arcades filled with trendy boutiques, galleries, vintage and antique shops. Before leaving we stopped for a drink at Brasserie Victor Hugo. I had flashbacks of Muhammad and wished I had paid more attention to his babbling. My afternoon with Camille was euphoric and suddenly I had an abundance of energy that exploded through me like a bolt of lightning. I had never felt that kind of excitement.

The first day I hit the streets of Paris alone, I had strong urges to piddle from nerves! Before leaving the apartment, I checked to see if I had everything I needed — the code to enter the courtyard, my antique key to open my Prussian blue door, my passport, bilingual dictionary, and "The Lonely Planet," a guide to the city of Paris. I also carried "What You Need to Know in Case of Emergency."

As I approached Métro Bastille, a ten minute walk from my studio, it started to rain. I ran back for my umbrella which was a good reason to see if my strange key would unlock my charming blue door. When I returned to the Métro, hurrying down a long flight of stairs, I noticed a crowd queuing up at the ticket window. It was obvious that I was among people who were different from me. We didn't speak the same language! While in line, I rehearsed what I would ask the agent when it was my turn. Nervous, I took in a deep breath and began speaking.

"*La direction Métro Charles de Gaulle, s'il vous plaît?*" I sounded so American even I couldn't bear hearing my awful accent. Having difficulty understanding my French, the agent scowled while lifting his head.

"What do you want to say, Madame?" he asked in broken English.

He raised his voice annoyed and rolled his shoulders as only a Frenchman can. As luck would have it, there weren't too many people queuing up. Ticked off trying to be understood, repeating myself over and over, I put my head against the ticket window and spoke in English with my teeth clenched.

"F... you," I said under my breath and then met his stoic face. "Sir, how do I get to *Avenue Charles de Gaulle*?"

He slid a miniature map of the Métro of Paris in a tray in the ticket window. It was so small I couldn't read it never mind figuring it out. A random woman, my guardian angel, came to my rescue when I stepped out of line. She pointed out the route on a larger map and assured me it was not difficult.

Days on end, I paced the streets aimlessly with French spreading rapidly in my brain. It seemed unnatural not hearing any English. In moments of self-assuredness, I talked to strangers, asked questions, and repeated phrases like a parrot. I quickly learned the importance of saying, "*Bonjour, excusez-moi de vous déranger,*" and I was eager to learn French customs. Insisting, repeatedly, that I say "Bonjour" when I approached someone (a custom foreign to Americans) was one thing, but asking for forgiveness at the same time seemed a bit too formal and ridiculous! Still, I remembered to do it.

I discovered first-hand what Camille had said in Boston: "The French are distrustful of people they don't know, especially in Paris. They are often formal and reserved. They need to be courted." After a while, I dazzled them with charm and won their acceptance. They were thrilled when I told them their city, and their language, was one of the most beautiful on the planet, as if it were a personal declaration. My physical therapist warned me that the French are very proud of their culture and their language and if you don't embrace it they won't think highly of you. Someone said I was not like most Americans. I didn't respond to that bogus compliment better left for another time after I'd improved my French and could stand my ground. I explained that living in Paris was a dream. "*Ah bon,*" said a smiling woman. "Wait until you see the rest of our beautiful country."

Fundamentally, the French believe in *Liberté*, *Egalité* and *Fraternité* and are strongly opinionated. Although the French love arguable debates and are pessimistic about most things, they admire American's optimism and our "over the top" Pollyannaish ways with unfailing cheerfulness. While there is no perfect place to live on the planet, one can adapt to some places more easily than others. I thought France was perfect for a long time, then I'd idolize America until I returned home and vice versa. *C'est la vie!* A metaphor, "The grass is always greener on the other side," and you find out later the grass "ain't" as green as it seemed.

Whether in a café intruding into someone's conversation or moving about aimlessly, I learned more French in a few weeks on the street than I had in my crash course in Boston. My only problem — remembering it! Sometimes complete strangers offered their assistance without my asking. On several occasions, I was escorted out of the Métro and was given directions on how to find a place. One day I was sitting on the train analyzing my map with my bilingual French/English dictionary resting on my lap and a woman tapped me on the shoulder.

"May I help you find your way," she asked in broken English and I nodded.

We got off the train together at *Métro Châtelet* and made the same connection for *Saint-Germain-des Prés.* "I want much to improve in English and you can improve in French. I give you my telephone number and invite you to a café."

Squeezed among hundreds of passengers, we talked about fifteen minutes. Madame LeClerc didn't need to exit at Métro Châtelet. She got off the train hoping to make an American connection. We exchanged numbers, parted with smiles, and disappeared into a dense cross section of humanity with the clacking sound of women strutting in high heels.

I had been thinking about François all day long and finally worked up the courage to call him. I was a wreck when his answering machine came on:

"*Allô, vous êtes bien chez François Duval. Je suis absent pour le moment. Laissez-moi un message et je vous rappellerai à mon retour."* Hello, you have reached the home of François Duval. I'm out at the moment. Please leave me a message and I'll call you when I return. For some strange reason and because I was highly strung I expected to hear his voice in English and hung up immediately. I called again at 9 p.m., excited and nervous when he picked up the phone.

"*Allô*," he repeated." *Allô, Allô.*"

I waited. The words wouldn't come. I found his French mesmerizing; his voice was deep and intimidating; I was frozen like a deer in headlights. He said "*Allô*" (hello) with an accent when he answered the phone.

"My name is Vernetia Smith," I said.

"Qui êtes-vous?" Who are you?

"Vernetia Smith from Boston," I repeated myself.

"Welcome to France Vernetia! When did you arrive?" He sounded surprised and pleased to receive my call with a charming British accent, weaving in and out of French.

"A couple of weeks ago," I said, remembering the moment I stepped off the plane but wanted him to think I was having the time of my life and lost track of every second.

"How do you like Paris?"

"*Paris est fantastique,*" I said, the only words in French that came to mind.

"Can you hold on for a second, please? I have another call." I was overjoyed with the pause. I needed a moment to catch my breath. My voice was cracking. My heart was pounding.

"Vernetia," he asked. "May I call you back?"

"Of course, take all the time you need," I said feeling a tinge of jealousy.

"What if he's talking to his girlfriend, his lover, or even worse his wife? Good Lord, am I flipping out here? What am I thinking? This guy could have an elephant nose and a camel's back. He didn't bother to send a photo and probably for good reason. Hell, I've done my part. The rest is up to him. I'll just have to be patient and see what happens."

Maneuvering the streets in Paris dating back to the Middle Ages was unimaginable. Old and new architecture were huddled together like a zigzag puzzle and occupied every inch of land. I took it all in exuberantly as if each day was my last. After a couple of weeks, I had gotten the swing of the Métro and the *RER*, the suburban fast train. I purchased a monthly Orange Card and ran around all day devouring the city and returned late in the evenings to an empty refrigerator. I consumed more snack food than I had in my entire life. I wasn't comfortable eating out alone in those daunting, cozy restaurants crammed with smooching lovers, speaking in foreign tongues.

One melancholy evening the phone rang. I thought it may have been Camille but it was François returning my call.

"Bonjour, François," I answered with my appalling accent. "Why is pronouncing French words utterly frustrating?" I pondered. After jabbering back and forth for almost fifteen minutes, he popped the long-awaited question.

"May I invite you for a drink one evening when you are free?" He sounded so dignified with proper French manners.

"Yes, I would love that very much." I answered graciously.

"A pleasure for me as well," he said." I'm going on a business trip in a couple of days. May I call you when I return?"

"*Oui*," I said, blowing out a happy sigh.

After the line clicked to a close, I snuggled in my sofa bed and slept like a baby for the first time since I had arrived in the City of Light and my *pied-à-terre* was beginning to feel like home. "Was that the first step?" I sighed. "I couldn't wait for the next step to meet him in person."

A few days later, Camille called and invited me to a cocktail party, which coincided with the day François was supposed to return home from his business trip. My feelings were mixed. I wanted to attend the party but preferred waiting at home for François' call.

"Please don't disappoint me," she insisted." It wasn't easy getting a guest invitation."

"Will anyone speak English?"

"Some, I'm sure, but I doubt they will." She raised her voice. "Vernetia, you're not in America!"

I agonized over what to wear on my first night out on the town. My clothes were too drab for Paris, plain and simple! I recalled Dominique's chic wardrobe in the classroom in Boston, and I needed to do something fast! To put my mind at ease, I popped into one of the neighborhood's chic boutiques where a salesman dressed to the nines, exhibited an over the top flair, chose my elegant outfit — a cocktail dress, high heels, and a handbag.

"*Vous avez l'air très chic. C'est parfait pour la soirée.*" You look very chic. It's perfect for the occasion. He spoke with brazen hand gestures and a runway swagger.

I smiled, thanked him, and left the boutique feeling very French in my changing world of fashion. Famished and full of confidence, I decided to have a late lunch alone on my way home. The waiter at Café Au Bascou approached me with a glass of Saint-Émilion wine.

"Bonjour, Madame," he said with a smile.

"Bonjour, Monsieur," I responded, impressed that he remembered me from lunch and the wine I drank with Camille. Each time he passed the table, he joked as if I were one of his regular customers.

"*Comment ça va Paris?*"

"*Paris est...super!*"

"*Alors,*" he continued. "*Our luncheon special today is snails cooked in a lemon garlic butter sauce.*"

"Do you recommend it?" I asked.

"*Oui, oui, bien sûr. C'est très bon,*" he replied puckering his mouth and pushing outward with the tips of his curved fingers on his lips indicating his approval while balancing a tray in the palm of the other hand.

"But it is not typically French?"

"*Si, Si, bien sûr!*" Yes of course, he insisted. "*Do you eat snails in Amérique?*"

"Not really," I said.

"*In France, we eat everything!*" he exclaimed.

The waiter asked how I met Camille who dined at the restaurant often. I couldn't have explained in French and neither would he have understood in English. After gulping down my delicious lunch, I left in haste leaving my evening attire beside the table. The waiter rushed to the door with the bag smiling. "*C'est un cadeau pour moi?*" It's a gift for me?

The next day I had to sprint to the ATM to withdraw some desperately needed cash. I was so elated I didn't care if I needed to get on a serious budget. My vacation was getting more exciting with every fleeting moment and I couldn't wait to meet my mysterious Frenchman with the sexy voice!

6

FIRST NIGHT OUT ON
THE TOWN

The lawyers' annual cocktail party was just a few blocks from the legendary Opéra Garnier in the ninth district in Paris. I had previously taken an unguided tour of the magnificent opera house and admired the red velvet seats, sumptuous Marc Chagall ceilings, and the ornate architecture of the mid-nineteenth century. I was somewhat familiar with the district but I had difficulty finding the street and arrived fifteen minutes late. Camille was engaged in conversation when I tapped her on the shoulder. She turned with a look of surprise and a cheerful disposition.

"*Vernetia, quel plaisir de te revoir!*" What a pleasure to see you again!

"*Je suis désolée d'être en retard,*" Sorry I'm late. I said in broken French. She wouldn't have tolerated my English.

"No problem," she replied. You're in France! We never arrive on time! And your French is already improving, *felicitations!*"

She then latched her arm into mine and introduced me to some of her colleagues. After dropping a few memorized phrases, the assumption was that I spoke French fluently until I tripped over my words and stuttered. Her confidants came to my rescue thrusting out a few words in broken English. After a few minutes, I glanced around nervously, then dashed to the powder room and outlined my lips with magenta, a tip from my dashing salesperson.

"Go girl," I said primping in front of the gold framed mirror. Fortunately, I was alone with my arrogant self. I left the powder room strutting with my shoulders held back and returned to the party with a new attitude in my sexy black French dress.

Across the room in the middle of a crowd a handsome man locked his eyes with mine. Stunned, neither of us wanted to be the first to look away. I hadn't noticed him coming in my direction, although I had hoped his stares indicated that he might. *What a cutie pie*, I thought and stopped myself from gawking.

Dazzling and alluring, he could easily make a gal's socks roll up and down, dressed elegantly in a dark pinstriped suit. His black hair paired perfectly with his outfit, and fell on one side of his face bringing my attention to his hazel eyes. His slim frame gave the impression that he was a tall man.

Some time had passed before my conversation ended with someone who didn't understand my French, nor did he speak English, and politely walked away. My heart fluttered when suddenly my admirer turned and gazed into my eyes.

"*Excusez-moi, s'il vous plaît. Madame*, where are you from?"

"America," I said with a smile.

"*Quelle ville*," he asked puzzled.

"Boston," I answered surprised by his question.

"Are you Vernetia Smith?"

"Yes, I am!" I wondered how this beautiful man could possibly have known my name. I hadn't met any Frenchmen in Paris.

"My name is François Duval."

"François Duval," I said with a high pitch squeal." Oh my God, are you really?"

"*Oui, oui, c'est moi*," Yes, it's me. His smile was a mile wide. After a few eye-popping stares landed on me, I quieted down.

"You sent me a beautiful photo of you in your new kitchen in Boston. *Vous en rappelez-vous?*" he whispered. Do you remember?

"Yes, of course, and now we're together in Paris! What an incredible coincidence!" No doubt he wanted to know how I got invited to the party but perhaps he was too polite to ask.

I smiled like a fool, let out a soft breath and thought, "He doesn't have an elephant's nose or a camel's back. He's gorgeous!" I was as high as a kite.

"I had planned to call you tomorrow *et voilà,* here you are. What a great surprise!" He moved in closer amused as if he wanted to embrace me.

"How serendipitous," I responded. "I am overjoyed to finally meet you."

"My sentiments as well," he said and then he asked me what I'd seen and done so far.

My Paris adventures captivated François attention. In a setting where people usually exchange superficial pleasantries, he hung onto every word while I gazed into his beautiful hazel eyes with a hint of gold. His slight dimples more profound on one side and his dazzling smile lit up his entire face. I was enthralled by his gracious and reserved demeanor. This was much more than either of us could have imagined. We were trapped at the party and would have preferred being somewhere else.

"Now that we've met, may I have the pleasure of inviting you to dinner next week?"

He must have read my mind.

"Yes, of course, I'd love that," I said joyfully.

We were, without a doubt, the happiest two people at the party that night. During our conversation, I imagined cuddling up to him on a plush sofa in the elegant lounge under dim lights. I had already experienced a heart-stopping moment when I caught sight of him, thinking he might be a crazy, hasty lover waiting to give me my first French kiss. I was smitten but didn't want to take any unnecessary risks. He invited me to a cozy bar and ordered two tall glasses of champagne.

Mesmerized, I drooled over his sexy French while he joked with the bartender. When his colleague joined us, he introduced me as his friend. François seemed impatient because he didn't speak English and he had no intention of excluding me from the conversation, at least not for long. At the point when they needed to talk business, I bowed out.

"It's been a long day," I said. "So if you'll excuse me, I'm going to say goodnight to Camille before leaving." I waved in her direction making it perfectly clear that I came with a woman and not a man. In French, Camille can be a feminine or masculine name with the same pronunciation. François seemed to be the serious type, not interested in competition or playing games, and neither was I with this beautiful man. He smiled and said goodbye with a twinkle in both eyes:

"I'll call you tomorrow evening if that's okay."

"Perfect," I said, feeling things were about to take a new direction. I wasn't sure how he felt about me, but I may have fallen in love at first sight.

On our first date, François invited me to *Le Gaspard de la Nuit*, one of the most luxurious restaurants in the Marais, nestled on the right bank of the Seine, spanning across the third and fourth districts of Paris. I woke up early for breakfast and lost my appetite. I was a nervous wreck as I usually am when I get all excited.

In the late afternoon, I began to pretty up for my date that evening. I wore a black satin skirt with white lilies sprinkled all over it with tiny pink petals shooting out of the flowers. It cinched my waist and flattered my thin hips. The skirt flared at the bottom to a v-line and fell mid-way on the legs. The outfit came with a black fitted top and cap sleeves that accentuated my breasts. I always got compliments when I wore it. I applied a dark rose-colored, matte finish lipstick on my lips, and strutted in my two-inch heels.

François was wearing a dark grey suit, pale blue shirt, necktie with stripes crosswise scattered with orange and aqua dots. When we met, he raised his eyebrows in a way showing amazement and his eyes, still dancing, gazed into mine. His smile was soft and mischievous, his cologne intoxicating.

When the waiter escorted us to our reserved table, I paused to admire the beautiful architecture. After being seated, I sashayed directly in front of François to the powder room and removed the pins from my hair. I returned to the table and made seductive gestures with my long tresses. Left-handed, I twirled a curly lock around my index finger flirting. François seemed to be amused by my antics and body language. We dined for three hours and had plenty of time to talk about all the places around Paris that he would eventually show me. He ordered the Saint-Jacques (large Alaska scallops seared) with a soft texture mildly sweet and a combination of mango, spices and grilled vegetables. I ordered veal with Armagnac served in a white sauce with garlic, parsley and vegetables. For dessert, I had *crème brûlée* (a rich custard base topped with caramelized sugar) and François had *moelleux au chocolat* (a rich delicious French chocolate cake made with dark chocolate). We drank a bottle of Saint Emilion wine. After dinner, we went for a stroll along Pont Alexander III, the most beautiful and romantic bridge in Paris.

When our breathtaking date came to a close, he dropped me off at the door of my apartment. It was a surreal evening and I thought I'd died and gone to heaven — even without a kiss to wish me good night.

I was on top of the world from all the attention that night and wished my American friends were there to witness the incredible event. I wonder what Virginia was thinking while François treated me like a princess.

During our teenage years, Virginia and I had similar taste in boyfriends. We were at a birthday party and I asked her what she thought of the boy I was chatting up with.

"You mean Sidney, the cutie pie that was covered with freckles on his face like spots on a Dalmatian dog?" I shook laughing.

"Yeah, he was really cute. I could have fallen for him too." The scary part was inviting Sidney home having him scrutinized and chewed over with a thousand questions by the family — Thelma, Charles, Aunt Ruby and Uncle Redmond. I loved Virginia's boyfriend that she met at the Methodist Church. He was tall, slender, Afro haircut, with killer dimples that made the girls heads spin. When Tommy joked she would egg him on like she did when we were four years old. I stood on top of the bed singing to the top of my lungs in my hairbrush microphone pretending to be a star while she sat on a stool at the foot of the bed laughing and clapping. Tommy and Virginia got the family's approval immediately. But then again Virginia could do no wrong. Sometimes the three of us would go to the movie together. Tommy would sit between the two of us and we'd share a big box of buttered popcorn and laugh our heads off over nothing. I asked if she had feelings for Tommy when they slow danced.

"Sure did," she said.

"Like what?" I asked.

"Like a little bolt of lightning running through my body."

It made me wonder just how close they'd gotten, but I knew she'd tell me when she was ready.

Thelma and Charles thought their rules would make us perfect girls. Oftentimes, we'd dismiss their harsh discipline and do exactly what we wanted to anyway. Their endeavors were done with the best of intentions, but it didn't always feel that way.

François surprise events kept coming. Two weeks later he invited me to a jazz concert, which included a saxophonist, harpist, drummer and a bass horn. He invited me to an outdoor musical performance with a female Swiss Cuban singer and composer, mixing rhythm and jazzy Afro-Cuban music together. Her voice was profound, sweet, and suave. After the concert ended, we had something light to eat at a bistro and, as always, he dropped me of at my door *sans baiser*, without a kiss.

François wasn't married and I had never suspected any disloyalty. I was smitten by a man completely different from the men I dated in America that I could read like a book. Always a gentleman, with old-fashion manners, who stepped aside to let me enter the door before him was his modus operandi. Any venture has an element of risk, but what was holding him back from exposing his feelings? We connected on so many levels. Could it be unrequited love? I longed for his display of affection in an unabashed way. Not knowing his intentions — if there were any — made him even more desirous. He'd become the delight of my life since the day we met and I couldn't imagine being without him. But what could be done to change the platonic trajectory to romanticism and understand his deepest truths?

When I arrived in France, I couldn't help but notice the difference in dating attitudes. We'd walk around in Paris and in the woods of Vincennes, and no one gave a dang that François, a white European Frenchman, locked arms with an Afro-American woman. Perhaps François was simply shy. When I was a teenager, I wanted to hold the reins and be in control. Upon reflection, I may have been camouflaging my need to be outgoing. Perhaps his lack of affection was not unique to him. Those mixed messages may have been coming from both of us — crazy in love but too timid to express romantic gestures towards each other. In my early teens I was very shy. I went to Church on Sundays and got all prettied up for the boys. They would stare me down when I passed by and I'd get so nervous my knees would knock in terror. I would have to be patient until we were in harmony like the pleasing sound of musical notes in an orchestra. But how long would that take? Men tend to be direct and upfront about their feelings but François was the complete opposite. I was often guessing what he was thinking. First I thought it may have been our cultural differences but that was not a logical reason. If I had met François in America I may have conjured up all sorts of racial biases but that was hardly the case in France. I was warmly welcomed by François' friends and, after I met them, his loving family. He explained how implicit biases can prevent people from meeting their soul mate. "I like you for the person that you are and not for the color of your skin." But what about love!

Several weeks had passed since the lawyers' cocktail party, and I hadn't heard from the workaholic, the nickname I had given Camille in America, where she studied English, got perfect grades, and was placed in advanced classes. Bursting at the seams, I wanted to see her reaction when I gave her the latest news about my Frenchman, particularly since she was instrumental in making it happen, not only by writing the ad for conversation partners, but also by inviting me to the lawyer's' cocktail party in Paris where, by serendipity, I met François. It was unbearable not having anyone to share my excitement. I wasn't ready to tell my American friends. The calls would cost a fortune and what would they tell me anyway. I can almost hear my best friend in Boston preaching:" For God's sake, don't be so trusting. For all you know, he could be a Paris strangler!"

Jennifer and I are as different as night and day. I am a peacemaker, sometimes emotionally fragile to a fault, yet I was fiercely competitive in the work place. She, decidedly old fashioned, speaks her mind at any cost and it's difficult to communicate with her about matters of the heart. Instead, I decided to call Isabelle and Pierre. They were still in America where Pierre's research position had begun. As fate would have it, I was searching for their number when the phone rang and Pierre blurted out, "Bonjour, Vernetia!"

Isabelle squealed, "We miss you!"

"How did you get my number?" I asked, confused.

"From your landlord," he said. "How are things going in Paris?"

"You won't believe it."

"Believe what?"

"I met a fantastic Frenchman."

"You see, we're not so bad," Pierre said with a chuckle.

"That's an understatement if I've heard one," I said, blurting out a laugh.

"You sound smitten. Are you in love?" asked Isabelle.

"I think so."

"On your first trip to Europe you fell in love with Paris and now you've falling in love with a Parisian, *Oh La La*."

"He's actually Lyonnais from the southeast of France," I said.

"That's amazing." Isabelle laughed easily.

"So what do you think?"

"You haven't told us very much."

"He invited me to a fabulous French restaurant — the first of several subsequent dates. He's not only good looking but he's a perfect gentleman. He said he would call this evening but it's already after ten. If I don't hear from him, I'm packing my bags."

"Relax," Pierre said. "You're overreacting. The night is still young in Paris. I'm sure he has a good reason."

"Maybe," I sighed. "I found an internet café close to my apartment. I'll send you an email tomorrow and give you the latest news."

"When we return to Marseille we plan to spend a couple of days in Paris. We would love to see you and meet..."

"François Duval is his name," I said with a smile.

"Congratulations from both of us and stop worrying," said Isabelle. "You're amazing!"

After hanging up, I took a long shower while humming a Bonnie Raitt favorite, *I can't make you love me if you don't want,* when the phone rang. I dashed to it buck naked, dripping water all over the carpet. I took a deep breath, grabbed the phone and held it from the opposite end. I was a nervous wreck.

"Vernetia, I hope it's not too late to call," said François.

"No, no, please. Your timing is perfect!" I almost laughed.

"The Métro is on strike today, and most of the lines aren't running," he explained. "If you're free tomorrow night," he said after apologizing profusely for calling late, "I would like to invite you to a classical concert."

"Of course, I'm all yours," I said, biting down on my bottom lip. "Where is the concert?"

"It's at the Swedish Cultural Center in the Hôtel de Marle in the Marais."

"Fantastique! I'm thrilled that you asked."

"May I fetch you at your apartment at 7:00? The concert starts at 7:30 and will end at 9:00 p.m. I'll make dinner reservations for 9:30 p.m. Your neighborhood has some excellent restaurants. Is there anything you can't eat?"

"Oh, I eat everything." I lied. I didn't bother to tell him how ill I was after eating spicy oysters in America. I spent the night in the hospital and couldn't eat solid foods for a week. Neither did I tell him that no one had ever asked to 'fetch' me but I loved hearing it just the same.

During our dinner conversation, I asked François if he were an omnivore or a pescatarian." "I've eaten more meat than not in my life so I guess that would make me an omnivore. Some of my favorite meats, and meat dishes were Châteaubriand cut from the tenderloin; the same as filet mignon — steak au poivre coated with coarsely cracked peppercorns and then cooked; coq au vin Burgundy, a popular speciality of the Burgundy region — a traditional dish made from a cockerel (a rooster) delicately braised and cooked in a red wine sauce — the breast of a duck or goose that has been fattened for *foie gras* and is France's favourite dish, especially for Christmas and New Year's celebrations; and beef bourguignon — a stew of meat slowly simmered in hearty red wine."

Just hearing about those mouth-watering dishes made me want to eat 'til I dropped, most of which I had never eaten. I nodded and he continued.

"For the last twenty years, I've only eaten fish and seafood knowing the unethical and maltreatment of animals for selfish reasons. Today we don't need meat nutritionally."

I'd soon learn that François found eating meat so offensive he could not bear the smell of it. I felt I was losing out on a long lived 'French experience' coupled with a tinge of jealousy, when I'd pass *la boucherie* where customers waited in a line that extended to the street, waiting to choose any number of beautiful cuts of meat.

Anyway, I rarely ate meat in Boston, surrounded by the harbor, known for its fishmongers and seafood that came straight out of the water.

After dinner I wrestled with the thought of inviting François for a late nightcap where I could survey his soft hazel eyes in the candlelight, hoping he would seduce me or vise versa. I even had an inkling of lying beside him in bed and he'd ignite a flame that would burn until dawn. God knows Ms. Proper Bostonian had fantasies of a naughty woman but I couldn't stop myself. After we parted and I had finally fallen asleep, I dreamt we were standing alongside an enchanting bridge over the Seine. He held me in his arms, kissed me deeply and fondled me underneath my winter coat. "I'll never let you go my *Chérie,*" he said. Then I woke up.

Still, the dice was rolling and I was enjoying the game.

Another unforgettable evening François fetched me at my apartment. In haste we took a taxi to a concert hall and sat in reserved seating in the front row. The house was packed. When the music of Saint-Saens reached a crescendo, I was aroused by the stellar performance and inadvertently plopped my hand firmly on his thigh, my heart beating. His head spun around and he gazed straight into my eyes. It was a dreamy-eyed shy glance lasting only a few seconds, and I believed it was a look of love. Uncertain, I quickly withdrew my hand. That was the first physical contact we had except *faire la bise,* a kiss on both cheeks to the wind each time we parted at my door. After the concert we had a romantic dinner at *Bistro Benoit* with brilliant red velvet plush chairs and a serene-blue-sky ceiling scattered with fluffy clouds. The *fillet de sole* with Nantua sauce from the Northeast region of

Lyon was out of this world, as well as the moist and savory scallops. We joked, laughed, held hands and made romantic gestures.

That fantastic evening was a pivotal moment in our relationship — Head over heels, and my feelings deepening, I had fallen hard for him.

7
LIVING THE FRENCH WAY

One Sunday afternoon while gazing at the crystal blue sky and puttering around in our tiny courtyard, I wondered why I hadn't seen any of my neighbors. It seemed a pity not to take advantage of the beautiful weather and finally meet some of them. I sat on the step of my studio filled with wonder and delight and began humming, *"I Love Paris."*

"Good afternoon, Vernetia," my landlady called out. "How's the apartment?"

"Great," I said. Tolerable would have been more honest.

"Have you gone to the open market?"

"No, not yet," I said.

"It's a great entrée to French culture."

"What do you mean?"

"You can tell a lot about one's culture by their eating habits. French people are passionate about gastronomy and eating is a big deal. It's our favorite pastime."

"Then I must check it out."

"We're going now if you'd like to join us."

"I'd love to," I said and I did. When we arrived at the market, there were hoards of people squeezed in narrow passageways all along the sidewalk. Covered stalls appeared to be the length of two city blocks and the traffic had slowed in both directions. After my landlords left, I stayed behind gawking at a variety of food, especially the meat, which I could not believe people actually ate: *viande de cheval* (horse meat), *ris de veau* (glands of veal), *boudin* (pork blood wrapped in the shape of sausages), and other animal parts that made me gag. I observed chickens plucked of their feathers, except for the heads with bows tied around their necks (*How chic!*), and whole piglets were lying on their stomachs with their ears standing up! There were myriad colors of farm grown vegetables, home baked breads, pastries, a cornucopia of sausages, gourmet olives, aromatic spices, fish mongers, and so delicious "stinky" aged cheeses — in abundance.

"Thank God for open stalls," I said holding my breath. Surveying the landscape and the enthusiasm from the crowds carefully selecting their produce was amazing. I noticed a bunch of pineapples, with tasty samples, and smiled to myself. Like me, like life, they were tough on the outside and sweet in the inside. Pineapples in Paris? Who would have thought? I decided to take one and then a glistening basket of plump, red strawberries caught my eye.

The merchant approached.

"Four, *uh*, kilos, please," I said.

She raised a brow and tapped on a calculator.

While the merchant handed me what turned out to be almost eight pounds of strawberries, I gasped and tried to explain that I had ordered too much. I lowered my head from embarrassment and walked away with a very heavy sack, surrounded by a variety of smells, including my sweet pineapple, luscious strawberries, and the melody of the French language.

When I told my landlady about the strawberries she was in stitches.

"Why didn't you order in pounds?" she said with a laugh.

"Because I thought I needed to order in kilos and guessed."

I offered a bowl of strawberries to my landlord and also to my next-door neighbor and sensed a bit of trepidation. She accepted, realizing I was simply trying to be neighborly. I returned to the market the following weekend skilled in calculations.

At the end of the open market stalls, I discovered a table with odds and ends that were super cheap — clothes, cosmetics, costume jewelry, etcetera. I fell in love with the open market, trashed my junk food and began eating like a native in my *pied-à-terre.*

When I arrived in Paris I noticed that the women were slim, chic and very sexy, which might explain their obsession for underwear. I went to a lingerie shop and saw underpants in every color and style imaginable. The mere sight of them made me think of flaunting a naughty 'G-string' in front of François. What might my old-fashioned girlfriend in Boston think of that? Without missing a beat she would say:

"You look like a prostitute in those raunchy things!"

I felt embarrassed fantasizing over the racy G-strings until I spotted a couple of middle aged Saudi Arabian women dressed in black from head to toe with only their faces uncovered. They purchased enough sexy lingerie to open up a boutique. The saleswoman asked if I needed help.

"You have too many choices!"

"Absolutely not, you need a set for each day of the week. I like to feel sexy even when I take my trash out," she said smiling. "French women are known for their panache which begins underneath their clothing and permeates throughout."

"I thought French women were reserved?"

"Perhaps on the outside, but we know how to have fun inside with our dash, splash and splendorous undergarments!"

The differences between French women and American women sometimes astounded me, especially the way they ate.

I met a couple of friends for drinks one late afternoon and suggested a side order of munchies. "I'm starving. Can we order some snacks?"

The woman who sat beside me was adamant. "We don't eat between meals." Hearing my stomach pang and growl, she said, "Here, take my tablet!" The waiter had placed a piece of dark chocolate the size of a 50 cent coin beside each of our coffee cups. Eventually, I gave in and began eating like French women, which explained why they looked like string beans and maintained their svelte figures eating small portions, and nothing between meals. Their obsessions also included a vast amount of perfume and dressing up in a classic black dress with an elegant scarf in bold colors tied around the neck.

As my confidence grew, I wondered what it would be like for a single woman to roam around in the *City of Light* at night. Before arriving in France, I read a frightening book about sex and drugs in Paris and was afraid to go out alone after dark. Nevertheless, I decided to go to the cinema to see my first French film.

"Does the film have English subtitles?" I asked the ticket agent.

"No Madame," she shouted. "You're in France."

Camille's comment leaped into my brain: "Why can't the rest of the world be like us?" An American movie with French subtitles was one thing, but a French film with English subtitles highlighted my international ignorance.

"Buy a DVD and choose your language," she mumbled underneath her breath.

Instead of festering over my stupidity, I stepped out of line and took a long leisurely walk around the tantalizing river Seine with thousands of roamers. I chatted with artists on *Pont Neuf*, browsed in and out of boutiques, stopped for a late night café and returned to my *pied-à-terre* after midnight. I curled up on my couch exhausted under a blanket, reminiscing about my childhood and family life in America.

Mama worked long hours and Grandma spoiled us terribly. We'd skip to her home across the orange grove and she'd have fresh squeezed orange popsicles on a stick waiting for us. I remember the day when Virginia and I arrived and I was wearing Mama's hot pink lipstick. She grabbed my shoulder raising her voice: "Here, take this damp towel and wipe it off!" She loved seeing her granddaughters in frilly dresses with pretty bows, but lipstick was forbidden. It was the first time she yelled at either of us. Standing beside me Virginia flinched and twirled her eyes. She was as stunned as I was. Our cousins lived a mile from us so Virginia and I spent most of our leisure time at Grandma's except when we were in school. Our homes were the only ones in sight for miles in the countryside. Grandma's home was like a picture post card, with hand-me-down antiques from her parents. The dining room was off limits unless there was a family meal. When we spent time with Grandma, she taught us so many things — how to bake cookies, how to dress and the importance of being polite young girls. Sometimes Grandma's rules conflicted with Mama's, but we didn't dare tell her that. We'd sit at our pretty pink vanity table with matching combs and brushes and play with our hair. Grandma would put fresh flowers from the garden on the vanity. When she gave us a spray of her perfume we'd giggle from the scent lingering around us. I asked Grandma if Virginia was her favorite granddaughter. "I love you both the same my cupcake." She squeezed me tight in her arms and pinch my cheeks.

I don't remember very much about Grandpa, except he was strikingly handsome, 6 feet 5 inches tall, jet-black skin, thick black eyebrows, large black sunken eyes and black hair on the curly side. He had an air of black aristocracy if there was such a thing back then. Grandma hung a beautiful portrait of Grandpa in the living room. His Indian heritage was alluring and unforgettable.

Grandma was a tall, slender woman with very long hair and very light skin sometimes referred to as high yellow. She wore her hair parted down the middle with one fat braid long enough to sit on. Every couple of years, she'd cut her braid, wrap it in paper tied with a pretty ribbon, and give it to us. She believed that long hair symbolized physical strength, a growth of the spirit and a connection to all things. It was her pride and joy embracing elegance. Virginia and I had a ton of thick frizzy hair. When it was washed it took the better part of the day. We would strip buck naked and jump into a large tub in the open air splashing water from the outdoor pump. The heat from the sunshine warmed the water and we'd play in it for hours. After Grandma washed our hair she'd take a sun drenched towel from the clothesline carrying the fragrance of lavender plants from the garden, and wrap it around us from head to toe. Then she would sit us down on a tiny stool between her legs in the sunshine combing out the tangles. "When was the last time your Mama combed your hair?" she asked, squeezing her lips to keep from swearing. She parted our hair down the middle and made twelve long braids on each of our heads. We dreaded having it done because it hurt 'so' bad when she got rid of the knots with a wide metal comb that took hours when all we wanted to do was go outside and play. When I yelled "*Ouch Gran'ma!*" she kept at it. "Be patient baby!" she yelled. "You're gonna look so pretty when Grandma's done."

Later that day, with my hair washed and still tingling, I sang into my hairbrush microphone as always pretending to be a star with Virginia watching. She kept me grounded even when I sang off-key. American Idol wasn't a thing back then, but if it were, surely, I'd take the stage and win. As I belted out "Hey baby, hey baby, let's rock and roll," Mama rushed into our room yelling, *"calm down girls for goodness sake!"*

Mama was a carbon copy of Grandma except for the color of her dark brown skin. She had slanted brown eyes, long coarse hair in texture, parted down the middle pulled back into a bun on the back of her neck with distinct features of a Native American. I learned that our great grandparents had Cherokee Indian ancestry. You could recognize some of the traits such as Mama's nose and high cheekbones. She didn't smile very much as if she were carrying the weight of the world on her shoulders. She always seemed to be thinking about something out of the ordinary.

Mama was wearing a full length "A" shaped summer dress when she came into our bedroom and placed her hands on her thin hips. "Vernetia, Virginia. Can't you find something better to do? You're making such a racket in here, I can't even think."

Virginia carried on chattering and flopped down on a tiny stool in front of me giggling and clapping. "You're gonna break your skinny legs," she roared. I made a face and continued bouncing on the bed.

"Come down for lunch girls," Mama yelled. "We're having fresh pineapple tuna-salad, French fries and cantaloupe with blueberries for dessert." She returned to our room, eyeing the mess on the floor. "Clean up your room before you come down if you want an ice cream cone later in the afternoon."

Our bedroom was always untidy. Mama had her hands full with her rambunctious twins. She would scold us about the clutter but that didn't always work, unless we were forbidden to go out and play, and then we'd find something naughty to do inside. The color of our room was soft pink. On the walls, Mama hung a poster of two adorable elephants, and another that read, "Dream Big" with stars hanging from it. There was a little fairy poster with blue butterflies and a stunning poster of the Eiffel tower colored in grey and pink.

I never broke my legs nor did I become a performer — but my childhood memories were more beautiful than the pitch-black night lit up by sparkling stars. And that poster of Paris perpetually fueled my dreams.

I had always thought I'd explore Paris with my twin sister. But that didn't happen so I was living out our dreams for both of us and somewhere up there among clusters of stars I knew she was smiling down upon me.

8

THE MYSTERY MAN

I reveled in François' attention to details. I called him my fastidious "minute" man. He'd record almost everything — past and present with dates and timelines in his bright red diary. Even if I wanted to be nosey I couldn't with his microscopic penmanship — vacations, family outings, date nights, and doing fun things.

My systematic planning was studying the map for places I couldn't wait to see like the *Louvre Museum, Notre Dame Cathedral, Sacré-Coeur, Jardin du Luxembourg, Saint Germain-des-Près,* and the *Eiffel Tower,* nicknamed the Iron lady.

I'd ramble around during the day and saw Paris at night under tantalizing lights through the eyes of my alluring Frenchman: cruises on the Seine, drinks at celebrated cafés, reputable jazz and classical concerts (sometimes free) at the Swedish, Portuguese and Japanese cultural centers, poetry readings at literary venues and dinners at choice restaurants. François is a loyalist and never broke a date, but I was completely baffled by his ambiguity. Why was it so difficult for him to express his emotions? I knew exactly how I felt but what was he feeling if anything? I had spent most of my vacation with François with little time remaining. Had I wasted it on him? There was one other pursuer who showed a bit of interest, but I graciously turned him down. I couldn't imagine being with another man. Lacking confidence, I called my French confidants in Boston with my new European calling card.

"I've been dating my mystery man almost two months and I don't understand him. He hasn't even kissed me yet, nor has he accepted my invitation for a nightcap. What's going on?"

"It's hard to tell," Isabelle replied. "Perhaps he's only interested in a platonic relationship."

"That's absurd," Pierre argued. "He wouldn't invest that much time and money in a casual relationship."

"Maybe he's married," Isabelle chimed in.

"Married?" I said with a huff. "Of course not, he's been divorced for several years. He has two boys and he doesn't speak to his "ex" unless it's about them."

Isabelle continued to badger me. "Have you met his family?"

"No I haven't," I rambled on defending him. I knew if he liked me as much as I liked him there should have been some physical display of affection by now, but that hadn't happened. Perhaps our relationship was doomed.

"Maybe he's shy which often stems from our education," Pierre said. "I am. At school we don't have the right to talk or have fun, we are taught to shut up, listen and learn."

"I would have never guessed that you're shy," I said, feeling more confident. "You've had a surreal vacation with François," said Isabelle. "Calm down for God's sake and enjoy the rest of your time in France."

She was right.

While living in Paris there were a couple of things I wanted to focus on like mastering the language and learning to cook — neither of which I had accomplished.

I was bewitched by the language and attempted to converse in French. I assumed if I enjoyed writing in English, which I did, I'd naturally adapt to writing in French and eventually it came to pass. François was tough as nails when he corrected my writing. "When using the *futur proche,* always use the *infinitif* after the verb. For example: *"Je vais acheter un ordinateur."* I am going to buy a computer, he explained. "French is not difficult. You must learn the rules. It's as simple as that." *Was he kidding or did he think I was an idiot!*

"And what about the hidden traps in writing French?" I asked.

A lover of linguistics, François was arrogant about the French language! I often felt that I was on my own like a 'baby thrown out with the bath water' to sink or swim. I'd get frustrated but ultimately he was right. Writing my book in English didn't help with my French. Code-switching two languages are difficult at best. Or was that just an excuse? He complimented me and said I mostly lacked confidence. Did his resilience come from his training at French school or having written so many words? He was now working on his 5th genealogical book.

Next on my bucket list was French cooking. While I had almost become *une gourmande* a lover of good food to an excess like François, I found French cooking very intimidating, especially when I watched the talented master chefs perform their artful tricks on television with expertly crafted dishes. *Gee. Golly. Gosh!* François bought me several French cookbooks and hinted about adding more to my list so it seemed he'd not given up on me entirely. He even offered me a class at *"Le Cordon Bleu"* a culinary school of the highest order and my excuse for not taking him up on his generous offer was that the class was unduly early in the morning. I explained that French cooking takes too much time, and I'd have to translate the French ingredients and utensils into English.

"It comes naturally, after a while," he said.

Truth be told, I'm not fond of cooking except making simple desserts like *une tarte aux* fruits or preparing *un goûter* with small bites of several dishes. I'd love to learn how to make a fancy French sauce like *béarnaise* but I'd never be able to master the exceptional techniques and decadent flavors. We both loved fresh fruits and vegetables and only ate seafood and fish, which was the basis for a lot of French cooking, so perhaps I still had a chance, *n'est-ce pas?*

Lastly, I fantasized about getting a French Driver's Permit when and if I become a French citizen but that would be razor-sharp and take a very long time. It was on my radar screen. For kicks, I even bought *"Le Code de la Route,"* rules about respecting signs and traffic codes. I had daydreams about buying a little French Peugeot where my friend Gabrielle works and I'd scoot all around town like a française. But why was I even thinking about all of this? Did I want to move to France permanently and live with François? The answer to this question gnawed at my brain; I did.

Still, where was this relationship going, if anywhere?

Sometime after arriving in Paris, my landlord invited me to her house party. Excited, I bought a box of expensive chocolates from *Maison du Chocolat* to take as a gift. I would have preferred bringing François *and* the chocolates, but I was embarrassed to ask because it was a sit-down dinner party.

When I arrived at the gala there were several people there already — a pianist, professor, journalist, artist, a wine connois-seur and more kept coming. I hadn't imagined how exciting things were behind my little *pied-à-terre.* The hosts greeted their guests at the entrance with a glass of French champagne and then escorted us to an entertainment room, with eclectic art dispersed on the walls giving the impression of a petite *galerie d'art.* A grand piano sat at an angle near the long dinner table and the guests hobnobbed before the gala began.

"How did you meet Madame and Monsieur Jourion?" an American woman asked.

"They are my landlords."

"You're so lucky. They love parties and have interesting friends."

"Apparently," I commented, eager to learn more.

"And what are you doing in Paris?" she asked.

"I'm following my dream. Perhaps I'll write a book about my Paris adventures."

"Paris is surely a city for dreamers and a writer's paradise," she said with a wink. "You'll become part of the Lost Generation." she smiled.

"The Lost Generation" was a young group of writers and artists from the United States who took up residence in Paris in the 1920s and 1930s." They included Gertrude Stein (who was credited with coining the term), Ernest Hemingway, T.S. Eliot, and F. Scott Fitzgerald. Members of the community frequented the Saint-Germain-des-Prés district at cafés like Les Deux Magots, Café de Flore and at La Closerie des Lilas, a favorite haunt of Ernest Hemingway. In his memoir "The Movable Feast," Hemingway talks about his high regard for Fitzgerald and the "Great Gatsby."

"What about you?" I asked.

"I'm a freelance writer."

"How exciting," I said with a smile, leaning forward completely curious. I wanted to pump this woman for information. "How did your writing career evolve?"

"Long story," she said. "Here's my business card, give me a call, and I will fill you in over a drink at one of my 'Lost Generation' favourite haunts.'"

Around midnight, after the meal had finished, the guests gathered around the piano and sang French and American songs, mostly out of tune, after drinking too much wine and champagne. I returned to my petit studio, a shouting distance away, saddened that François was not in attendance.

Time was flying by and I agonized, time and again, about not enrolling in a proper French school. *Do it before it's too late!* I thought. And that's what I did.

One morning, I woke up at the break of dawn and raced to Paris to register for French classes. In haste, I had forgotten to bring my passport. The lobby, packed with students in a mad rush, huddled around the receptionist.

"Merde," I mumbled under my breath, "Oh shit!" How could I have been so mindless? When it was my turn, I handed over my American driver's license thinking she was so busy she might not even notice.

"May I see your passport?"

Busted!

"Oops," I sighed, pretending to search my bag. "Sorry, I don't seem to have it."

"You should always have your passport or ID on you in case you're stopped by the police!"

"How dumb do you think I am," I wanted to say. "I'm afraid of losing it so I often carry a copy by choice. But I rushed over here and I forgot both the copy and the original."

Although the woman raised a defiant brow and shook her head, hope surged in my chest.

"May I register today and drop off my passport early tomorrow morning?"

"No. Absolutely not! Today is the last day for registration and you must have all your papers in order. You can register again next semester."

"I won't be here next semester," I pleaded, my bottom lip quivering. "I'll be back in America."

"*C'est dommage,*" That's too bad, she responded with a shrug. I whispered *bitch* and wittingly knocked the pen and pencils down onto her desk – then *poof!*

"*Qu'avez vous fait?*" What have you done? She roared rolling her eyes.

I gathered documents for internet courses knowing full well that once I returned to America, I would lose interest. Shuffling my feet, I headed toward the exit.

"Welcome to France," a student explained on the way out. "Rules are not made to be broken. Get used to the French bureaucracy."

I found the bureaucracy mindboggling but, with time, I'd come to understand it much better.

9
THE METRO'S GOT TALENT

I took a seat on the Métro with my back facing the driver wondering why the seats were so close the passengers' knees were touching. *This would not be possible in America.* Unable to cross my legs, I was uncomfortable sitting in such a cramped space. My eye was drawn to the woman facing me and what a joy it was scrutinizing her elegant outfit and her sky-high heels. As for me, I had advanced to two-inch heels and while there were moments of bittersweet pleasure, I couldn't endure more pain.

"*Excusez-moi, Madame,*" I said, leaning in to her holding a music composition book. I thought she might be American because the title was written in English, but I didn't want to appear impolite or presumptuous.

"*Vous-êtes française?*" Are you French?

"*Oui, oui,*" I am. I wondered why French people repeated "yes" sometimes three or four times – but my ears had grown accustomed to hearing it.

"Are you a musician?" I asked.

"*Non, non,* I am the choir director at Le Louvre and Le Musée d'Orsay.

"Does the chorus sing in English?"

"*Oui, oui, anglais et français*," she replied.

"I love the Musée du Louvre and the Musée d'Orsay," I said emphatically.

"Where are you from," she asked in English with a charming accent.

"Boston," I retorted.

"I love this town," she said with a smile, "although I've never visited it."

"It's a lovely city indeed."

"I've heard it's the most European of American cities."

Boston was and still is one of the oldest municipalities in America. It was founded in 1630 and played an active role during the American Revolution. Most famous was the Boston Tea Party raid that occurred in the Boston Harbor in 1773 when British ships, docked in the port, dumped shiploads of tea into the sea disapproving a tax on tea. It fueled tension that had already begun between Britain and America.

The passenger who was seated beside the woman with the composition book left the train and I sat next to her with a bit more room for my legs.

"I would love to sing in the Notre Dame Cathedral Choral," I confessed, changing the subject before she exited the train. "How amazing it would be floating in the clouds with St. Peter at the Pearly Gates and you'd have to pass him to enter into Heaven," I kidded.

"Or perhaps floating in a Castle in the Sky," she replied egging me on. I could tell she thought I was a dreamer gone mad.

"Is the chorus only for French people?"

"It's only for staff members."

"Thank you," I said, thinking I may have been too intrusive.

"Perhaps you should give Notre Dame a call."

"Do you have any contacts there?" I asked.

"Sorry I don't." she smiled and wished me good luck while she gathered her things to leave.

Anyway, I was going to give it a go —

One of the reasons I wanted to join the choir at Notre Dame was that I'd lived in a musical neighborhood in Boston surrounded by Berklee School of Music, where I took classical guitar lessons, Jordan Hall and Boston Symphony. Being that I was new in Paris, I thought it would be the perfect place to make acquaintances with church goers passionate about music and buffer my feelings of loneliness, with a sense of belonging.

When it was time for me to exit the Métro my attention fell on a strange man in his thirties sucking his thumb. However, he was not as weird as a young man I had seen the previous week in the Latin Quarter walking around in a diaper. This could only happen in Paris, I imagined. When I got home, I decided to make the call.

"Cathédrale Notre Dame, Bonjour!"

"Bonjour Monsieur, do you speak English?"

"Non, Madame, ne quittez pas." Please hold Madame.

"How may I help you?" A Frenchman asked with a heavy British accent.

"Is it possible to sing in the Notre Dame Cathedral Choir?"

"Do you speak and read French, Madame?"

"Not very well," I said.

"Ça alors, Oh my goodness, I don't think it's possible."

"We have an amateur choral that chants Gregorian prayers in song deeply moving from the twelfth to thirteenth centuries with our Sunday Masses. The choirs perform regularly with the organ and on occasion with a Baroque or Symphony orchestra. Sunday is the débutante's choral. You will need to speak to the *Directeur de la Musique*. He will decide if you can sit for an audition." That Sunday I did show up, reflecting on the magnificent gothic archi-tecture, the splendid rose colored windows, flying buttresses, and Victor Hugo's Hunchback of Notre Dame, Quasimodo, "and its ancient history dating back hundreds of years, making it one of the most important religious and political institutions in France."

My fantasy about singing at the renowned Notre Dame Cathedral choir did not materialize. Nevertheless, I was pleased that I was courageous enough to give it my best shot.

Christmas was right around the corner. A week before the holiday, François invited me to see the "Nutcracker," a popular Christmas ballet 'about a girl who befriends a nutcracker that comes to life on Christmas Eve and wages a battle against the evil Mouse King.' François knew that I enjoyed the ballet but he had never gone. After a delightful performance, he accepted my invitation for a nightcap.

"Wine or vodka," I asked.

"Vodka on the rocks," he replied.

I kept a bottle in the cabinet because he'd mentioned once that he enjoys it from time to time. As soon as he entered, I sensed there was something unsettling that he needed to shake off, and I tried my damnedest to figure out what was bugging him.

"Let me get right to the point, Vernetia. It's time to part ways. I've really enjoyed your company, but I'm not interested in a serious relationship, and I know that's what you want."

My body went rigid. WOW! I wasn't expecting this, Shit!

A whisper "inside my head" suddenly appeared, "You have a goddamn nerve to invite me to one of my favorite ballets to tell me this, you *buffoon*!"

It was my first time sipping vodka on the rocks and it sent me for a loop. My heart was racing, my head was spinning, and I was ready to blow my top. After a long ten minutes, which felt like an eternity, he put on his coat and gloves.

Be calm; don't let this clown get you down; take a deep breath.

Problem was I couldn't find my breath. The drama I just explained was "all in my head" and "not at all" in François' character. Let's be clear, sometimes you have to prepare yourself for the unthinkable. *Merci Dieu* thank God I only "imagined" it and it was not real. Perhaps it was the vodka.

He looked straight into my eyes — no dazzles, no emotions, nada!

"Vernetia," he asked. "Do you have holiday plans?"

I was almost knocked speechless. "Uh...Why do you ask?"

"I would like to invite you to spend Christmas with me and my family."

"Your family in Cannes," I asked with trepidation, "Really?"

"I don't want you to be alone in Paris."

I languished in obscurity not knowing what to say — *Alone, hell no. I don't need your pity. You're not the only pebble on the beach,* I thought tacitly.

"I would love to," I said choosing my words carefully. "But, unfortunately, I have already made Christmas plans."

I was dying to spend the holidays with François, but I couldn't accept his invitation after all the time we spent together and in light of his departing comment.

"Bon," he said, showing no sign of disappointment. "May I offer you a small Christmas gift?"

"Yes, of course," I said, surprised yet again. "How very kind of you," I smiled.

I wanted to squeeze him tight and kiss his lips when he handed me the bag with a small book inside by Alexandre Dumas entitled *les Aventures d'un Romancier"* the adventures of a novelist. At the time, I tucked it aside, having nothing to offer him in return except my fondest wishes for the holiday. We parted ways after swapping *les bises*. I sank into my bed, fighting with sleep until I passed out from emotional exhaustion.

A few days before Christmas, I was all alone in my little studio. Not a creature was stirring, not even a mouse. The streets were mostly deserted, but there were plenty of window shop decorations and echoing Christmas bells. In Boston, shops are packed during the holiday season. Here, I was spooked by the contrast. The liveliest scene in the city was the *Avenue des Champs-Elysées* where thousands of tourists promenaded the beautifully decorated avenue ecstatic to be in Paris.

On Christmas Eve, I met a delightful woman named Joy Smart from San Francisco at the American Cathedral in Paris. She was alone. I was sad and alone. We decided to go for an early dinner in the famous Latin Quarter filled with shops, bistros and restaurants on narrow cobblestone streets and alleyways. That evening the lively Latin Quarter, usually bustling with crowds, had come to a near halt.

Joy and I chose Chez Jenny — an Alsatian Brasserie. While we waited, we got acquainted. I asked if anyone had mentioned that she resembled Michelle Obama.

"Several people have," she said. "Michelle Obama is my role model and a trailblazer for all women." Joy was a tall, full-bodied woman with wide curvaceous hips, long legs and an oval shaped face. Sometimes she'd squeeze her lips tight when she smiled like Michelle and even spoke with the same voice.

"Would you like to be the first American female president?" A close resemblance to Michelle, the question popped into my head, flew out of my mouth and she starred into my eyes as if I were from another planet.

"Absolutely not," she smiled. "I am the president of an investment company that brings me to Paris and London a few times a year."

"So that's why you're here?"

"Yep," she said. I teased her about François Hollande's 'First Girlfriend' at the Elysée Palace, the official residence of the President of the French Republic. "Americans got a kick out of the 'First Girlfriend' at the Elysée Palace," she laughed. "I can't imagine a job with the weight of the world on one's shoulders. I'm extremely busy now and there's not an ounce of comparison. I'd be thrilled of course to see a woman of any race, color or creed rise to the occasion."

"Where's everyone?" I asked the waiter when he came to our table after fraternizing with a handful of customers.

"This must be your first Christmas in Paris," he said. "Mesdames, I'm going to give you a French lesson."

"Can we get us something to eat first? We're starving."

"Maurice?" he called out to the bartender. "Bring two glasses of wine from Alsace!"

Meanwhile, he helped us choose our menu. He recommended a typical Alsatian casserole dish for two — a steamy platter of smoked slab bacon, bratwurst, plump sausages, smoked pork loin in a long-simmered sauerkraut made with Alsace white wine, juniper, coriander, mustard seed, and whole white potatoes. I ordered a glass of Pinot Gris wine and Joy ordered a stein of golden beer. Stuffed after eating the main course, we shared a breaded cake with raisins and almonds for dessert. "*Alors*," he continued. "Many French families go to their provinces for holiday festivities. Tonight, for example, is the celebration of *Le Réveillon*."

"What is *Le Réveillon*?" I asked increasing my vocabulary, charmed by his beautiful French.

"It's a celebration for the Birth of Christ which varies from region to region. In Alsace, the province where I come from, a 'goose is honored' and served on a platter for the feast."

"Are you celebrating Christmas in Alsace?" Joy asked.

"No. I'm working late so I will celebrate Christmas tonight in

Paris with friends. We'll drink lots of good wine and champagne, feast on foie gras, oysters and our traditional *Bûche de Noël*."

"What's a Bûche de Noël?" I asked.

"It's a Christmas cake made with chestnuts, light cream and chocolate in the shape of a Yule log. There are many variations, but I prefer dark chocolate."

"Are there any special celebrations for children?" Joy asked thinking about her kids in California.

"Ah, the magic of Noël when I was a child still remains in my heart. Laurence and I would put our boots in front of the fireplace before our parents tucked us in bed in our proper pajamas. In the middle of the night, Papa Noël stuffed them with candies and fruits. The fairy tales, the legends, there were so many. My sister's favorite was the little homeless 'match girl' who sat on the cold pavement in the snow. She struck matches and imagined what it would be like to have a warm place like normal children. At the strike of the last match, she sat magically transfixed in Paradise feasting with the angels."

After our hefty meal we headed over to Notre Dame Cathedral where thousands of people were queuing up, shivering in the cold for the Christmas mass. There wasn't a snowball's chance in hell of going inside, so we waited for the broadcast on the outside of the magnificent French gothic cathedral, huddled together with foreigners from around the planet. And, for a moment, I felt like I belonged in Paris.

And then the music started.

While I was out, I tried not to think about François. When I got home, I was unable to control my emotions. I was comforted in some way knowing that in less than a week I would return to my sweet homeland, the *good ol' U.S. of A.* While packing my suitcases, tears rolled down my cheeks. I reminded myself that François was not the reason I came to Paris, but that was not enough to set my heart at ease and stop me from weeping. I pushed out of my mind that he was celebrating Christmas with his family on the Côte d'Azur. Grey clouds covered the Paris sky with a clap of thunder, a flash of lightening, and droplets of rain spattered against my window panes. The streets were as quiet as a quivering heart that would ultimately stop beating and a wave of profound loneliness took hold of me.

Moment by moment, I recounted so many special times together, like the night I inadvertently plopped my hand on his thigh at the concert wishing he had held on to it. Heaven knows there were so many wasted chances. After all this time, he hadn't once cuddled me in his arms or kissed me on the lips.

I reminisced about his passion for French history and his vast genealogical research. With his wealth of knowledge, I was never bored and could listen to his narratives endlessly. I couldn't stop myself from having second thoughts about refusing his Christmas invitation. If only I had accompanied him would things have turned out differently? Were we ever on the same page? Had I missed any warning signs believing my intuition was right on point? Were my expectations unrealistic? He pleased me in every way except his impassive heart and I couldn't find a good reason for his inactions. My Paris dream was turning into a nightmare. I lost my appetite, had no more energy, and all I wanted was to get on the damn plane and return to my family and friends who would have advised me against my frivolous pursuits if only I had confided in them. But no, I didn't want to hear the truth. Now, I would have to wallow in self-pity and suffer in silence.

It had only been a week since our last date, and I missed his dazzling hazel eyes, wide eyebrows, long lashes and thick black hair. I craved the way he cocked his head to one side, seemingly to contemplate our future together. I visualized his dimples, one more profound than the other, when he smiled like an innocent boy.

Desperate for a distraction, I rang my landlords' door. After the third buzz, I remembered they had already left for the coast in Normandy. I walked around in my intriguing neighborhood bored to death. After a short time, it rained so hard puddles filled my new French shoes and zipping cars splashed water against my pretty raincoat. Panic swelled within me, and I ran straight home as fast as my legs would carry me in the rainstorm. I needed to confront François and settle things in my mind definitively. I would come straight out and ask, "François what exactly are your feelings for me?"

No matter what he said, I'd rather know than keep on guessing and leave the country without closure. My heart couldn't bear it a minute longer. I picked up the phone then realized he hadn't given me his number in Cannes.

10

NEW YEAR'S EVE CELEBRATION

I pulled the curtains back and the sun-drenched sky spilled bright light all over my studio. The early morning rainstorm had stopped as quickly as it came. The sunshine lifted my mood and the tears in my sad eyes suddenly disappeared. I heard a knock at the door.

"Sorry to disturb you. It's Sabine, your neighbor."

"Not a disturbance at all. Please come in!"

"Sorry, I can't," she said as I opened the door. She held out a large shopping basket. "I have to run some errands."

"Would you like to stop by for a drink this evening?"

"I'd love to," I said with excitement. If only she knew how much.

"Around 6:30 then."

I could hardly wait to shoot the breeze and take my mind off François.

Before I set off for Sabine's, I put on layers of makeup to hide the dark lines under my eyes and I kept on my faded jeans and tee shirt. Just as I was about to leave, the phone rang.

"Hello," I answered in English. French irritated the HELL out of me.

"*C'est François,*" he said.

"François?" I said with great surprise. "Uh, I'm so happy to hear your voice."

"Really?" he said, sounding perplexed too.

"Yes, of course. I've been dying to get some news. How are you?"

"Other than having a mild cold, everything is okay."

I could tell from his hoarse voice that he wasn't feeling well.

"You're having lovely weather on the *Côte d'Azur*. I saw pictures of a bright yellow moon." I didn't know the temperature in Celsius.

"It's sunny, but not warm. Yesterday, I bathed my feet in the sea and the water was very cold. Is it still raining in Paris?"

"It poured all morning, but the weather is perfect now."

"Vernetia, I'm calling to ask if you would like to bring in the New Year with me."

I was shocked to get his call and I didn't waste a second beating around the bush. My time was flying by in Paris. Plus, I could finally find out if he had the same feelings for me.

"Yes, of course, that sounds fantastic! Nothing would please me more! When are you coming home?"

"I'll return on *La Saint-Sylvestre* — New Year's Eve."

"I miss you very much François," I said not caring if I sounded like his bonafide girlfriend.

"Bon," he responded. "I'll call you when I'm back in Paris."

Suddenly, I realized that I had completely misread François. But why was he so cautious and acted so strange? Perhaps he found me inscrutable and needed more time to figure me out, to sort things out. Perhaps it was his old-fashioned French manners. Perhaps he was shyer than I had imagined. Perhaps I'd never know the reason. But I knew then, although he didn't admit it, he missed me too. At last, I had a second chance after I declined his Christmas invitation. Thrilled to death, I giggled like an adolescent, changed into a proper pair of pants, a bright yellow blouse and visited my neighbor with a new attitude.

"Oh My God, this is amazing!" I shouted, and then I raced to Sabine's, my spirit lifted.

With excitement, I knocked on the door. Sabine opened it with a cheery smile, almost matching the one on my face.

"*Entrez, s'il vous plaît.* What a beautiful evening after the early morning rainstorm."

"Lovely weather indeed; it's incredible how quickly things can change," I said thinking about François' invitation as I entered her apartment.

"Would you prefer speaking in French or in English?" she asked.

Finding French very difficult, English was an easy choice. We sat on the couch and she set out some small snacks, like olives, tomatoes, and a savory onion tart, and then she poured me a glass of champagne. Our conversation quickly shifted from the weather to relationships, which interested me the most, and I told her about François. We also talked about her collection of American films and her dreams to visit Bryce Canyon in Utah, and gaze at the stunning views in variegated colors and hike in the spectacular Grand Canyon in Arizona.

"I'm afraid, to go alone," she admitted.

"I get it," I said. "But every now and then you have to say, 'What the French.' Look at me!"'

Her eyes crinkled into a smile. "You're right. Maybe I'll do it. I just need to find your courage."

Before leaving, she gave me what remained from the dessert, a scrumptious homemade strawberry tart, to take home. Standing in the threshold of the door she said, "François sounds very special! How lucky you are to have found love in Paris. You are a brave woman and I admire your adventurous spirit. Tell me, though, how can you maintain a relationship with François living on the opposite side of the continent?"

"I haven't thought that far ahead. When I decided to come to France, I was terrified but somehow, things have worked out extremely well."

"I think you should chase your dream, too, Sabine. I will help you in any way that I can," I said and we swapped *les bises*.

François had invited me to so many interesting places in Paris. My suitcase was packed for Boston, but I would be spending New Year's Eve with my Sweetheart in Paris. All revved up with a bundle of energy, I decided to do some damage at my favorite boutique again. This would be my last shopping spree and I would withdraw whatever cash was left at the ATM.

"Bonjour," said Nicolas, gesturing me to wait with a big smile while he finished with a customer. Meanwhile, I walked around admiring the extraordinary clothes for New Year's Eve, scandalous from the eyes of a proper Bostonian, outrageously expensive, and sexy as all 'get out' in the birthplace of *la maison de couture* — home of High Elegance and the famous Paris Fashion Week. I had spent a long pleasurable afternoon shopping at his chic boutique, and we quickly became friends.

Nicolas greeted me with a beautiful smile and a smooch on both cheeks. "*Ma belle*, you look absolutely ravishing! Are you in love?"

"*Oui, oui*," I said with a silly grin. "I think I am."

"How do you say in English? You look like a *chat* with a bowl of cream fresh! I adore les expressions American; why not a *chien*? "

"A dog with a bowl of cream," I asked. "Gosh no, give him a bone."

"No bones for my Chopin. He loves filet mignon, Haagen-Dazs ice cream and listening to Piano Concert No 1."

Supporting his chin with his pinky curved, he looked straight into my eyes.

"*Vous êtes aux anges, ma chère!*"

I laughed. "I'm in seventh heaven alright."

"*Il est français?*" he asked, wiggling his brows.

"*Bien sûr,* Yes, of course, he's French."

"*Extraordinaire!*" he said with a laugh. "It wouldn't be the same if you came to France and fell in love with an Italian, an Australian or *whatEVER!*" He placed both hands on his hips, leaning back with perfect posture. "How can I help you today *Ma Chérie*?"

"I need an outfit for New Year's Eve, something chic and memorable for my last date with François," I explained.

"*C'est triste,*" (that's sad) he said with a grimace. "You make it sound like a damn funeral! Good Lord, cheer up! Where is he taking you?"

"All I know is that I have to be ready at 7:30 p.m."

"If he wanted you to dress in a formal gown, he would have told you, *Chérie.* Anyway, it's better to play it safe and wear something in between. I want to infuse some Parisian elegance into your outfit. Be gutsy! Remember it's all about attitude, arrogance and how you cross your legs at the ankles that make you fiercely chic like Amelie Honore and Sandrine Marlier."

"Okay, you're the Fashionista!"

"I recommend something *classique* but sexy. Let me think for a minute." He brushed through the racks, pulling out dresses and placing them back. "*Celui-ci, Celui-là, Voila, C'est ça !*" (This one or that one? That's it!) He held the dress against my body. "*Allez,* go try it on *Chérie!*" He handed me a pair of black stiletto high heels to wear with the outfit.

"Jacques," he called out to his colleague, "*Venez, s'il vous plaît.*" Come, please!

"*Regardez, elle est belle, non?*" Look! Isn't she gorgeous?

"*Si, si! Tournez-vous, s'il vous plaît.*" Yes! Yes! Please, turn around!

"She looks like a runway model with the split in her skirt that almost reaches her buttocks." Jacques laughed, "How sexy!"

I interrupted while I eyed myself in the mirror. "Is the split too vulgar?"

"*Mais non!*" He raised an eye. "*C'est élegant, chic and seductive.*" I was convinced while I outlined my curvy hips in front of the mirror, caressing my plush velvet outfit and admiring how fantastic I looked.

"When are you leaving?" asked Nicolas.

"January second," I said.

Oh, la vache! "Damn," he exclaimed and fanned his face. "That's less than a week!" He handed me a large black bag, put one hand on my shoulder and whispered in my ear: "I threw in a small gift, something red and sexy. Wear it tonight for good luck!"

"Nicolas," I paused before leaving. "How will you spend New Year's Eve?"

"My partner and I will go to a couple of gay bars in the Marais and hang out with friends. Are the *bear cubs* cute in Boston?"

I smiled and winked. "Probably no more than they are in Paris."

Before François arrived, I spent the afternoon primping. I took a long shower with a silky scented gel, sprayed my body all over with 'Je t'aime' (I love you), and manicured my nails. After applying my makeup carefully I tried on my outfit several times. I lost my appetite but sipped on warm tea with sweet biscuits to keep my strength up and watched television for a distraction while I got all dolled up. Suddenly the clock was ticking away and I was worried if François would like my new outfit that I bought especially for him. When I put it on one last time, I stopped short of wearing Nicholas's gift and then I thought, *"Why the hell not?"*

At that very moment, I wiggled my way into my red velvet string ready for whatever might be on the horizon that night. The doorbell rang precisely at 7:30 p.m. I sprayed my neck, arms and hands again and again with "Je t'aime," refreshed my ruby red lips, and made a mad dash to the door excited to welcome François.

"*Bonsoir, Vernetia, comment ça va?*"

"I couldn't be better," I replied, succumbed by the scent of his French cologne. "And how are you?"

"Terrific," he said with a smile. And terrific he was.

Dressed to kill in a fine silk navy tailored suit, white shirt and red bow tie, he looked more gorgeous than ever. His gaze stayed on me for at least ten seconds and it was like sipping a fine glass of wine.

"Would you like a drink?" I asked.

"Non, Merci. We need to leave for the concert." He reached for my coat and paused. "You're very elegant tonight, Vernetia." He stared with a boyish shy smile, slight dimples and a twinkle in both eyes, utterly unaware of his reserved charm like the first night we met.

En route to the Saint Petersburg Russian Concert, the traffic was gridlocked. Vacationers had returned in droves to the *City of Light* for New Year's Eve, laughing, shouting and dancing in the streets. A large crowd queued up at the concert hall but François had already purchased our tickets so we went straight to the front of the line. The program was in Russian and French. He translated it to English to be sure that I understood every word. I don't ever remember feeling so pampered, so much in love. He held my hand and touched the side of my face, staring into my eyes, flirting. After the concert, we walked a short distance on *L'avenue des Champs Elysées* and stopped for a drink at a crammed bar.

Around 10:30 p.m. it was impossible to move with zillions of spectators and police flooding the avenue. It reminded me of Times Square in Manhattan where the Waterford Crystal Ball descended from a flagpole, attracting a mob filled with hopes and dreams for the 2000 millennium. That was my first New Year's Eve celebration in the Big Apple. This would be my first New Year's Eve celebration in the *City of Light* with my Frenchman.

"I'm taking you home," he said.

"Why?" I asked gobsmacked. "We haven't even eaten yet."

"It's New Year's Eve, you're returning to America in two days, and I've never invited you to my place." He grinned. "I'm cooking us dinner."

Back at François place, he switched on the lights in the foyer and my eyes scanned volumes of books bulging from bookcases. Stacks of *Science et Vie* magazines and newspapers were piled up in the corners. In the living room, an antique mirror hung over a marble fireplace and a small dramatic painting of the French Alps hung over the sofa. The dining room took on a cozier atmosphere with a load of books in a wall-to-wall bookshelf in every imaginable size and color. Sea blue curtains hung at the french door-sized windows. A beautiful red and blue Japanese tablecloth and a vase of peonies in a range of colors with big fluffy fragrant flowers, dressed the dinner table. Sea-blue trimming added a touch of color to the cream colored walls. A fireplace, identical to the one in the living room, was closed off for more books. It reminded me of a cozy library in the dining room. I was completely taken aback by the reality and the elegance. I observed that François is not very organized but is super clean. I was impressed with his fine taste — a buffet with delicate hand carving in exotic wood, an old antique bed from the region of Bresse in France, and other period pieces inherited from his grandparents.

When he went to the kitchen to prepare the meal, I poked my nose around, hoping to learn more about my private man who never boasted and said very little about himself. I craved more insight about his unique character. I noticed a beautiful Japanese calligraphy painting on the wall, a stunning Japanese kimono on a mannequin, American films and a variety of French artifacts. His vast collection seemed to be swayed by tender sentiments. François is a hopeless romantic, besotted with everything: old photos of the entire family dating back to his great grandparents, family letters, history books, Life magazine with the first astronaut walking on the moon. He could certainly have used a much larger apartment but that may have enhanced his insanity for hoarding things. On one hand, I found his preoccupation appealing. On the other, I found it unfathomable. I am the opposite, a fanatic about order and tidiness. I have to make a clean sweep periodically and chuck stuff I no longer need. My hatred for clutter came from abhorrent piles of conflict resolutions on my desk in corporate America.

I sighed, a photo album catching my attention. It was his wedding album and François caught me red-handed as if I were cheating on an exam. I spun around in a state of panic and put it back on the bookshelf. "She's lovely," I stammered at a loss for words.

He let out a *pffff* and returned to the kitchen. I thought I had ended the evening before it got started. Why had I meddled in the man's private business? Feeling guilty and embarrassed, I sat down on the sofa and didn't budge until he called me for dinner.

François' attention to details was extraordinary that night. The table was dressed exquisitely with china plates, crystal glasses, and sterling silver inherited from his grandparents. Then came the dinner fit for a King and a Queen — Extra large *Fines de Claire briny raw oysters* all salty and sweet served with lemon wedges; *gambas* the size of my hand; French Gold *caviar* with delicate texture and a fine nutty tang; *foie gras* with a rich buttery flavor that melted in your mouth served on toast with a sweet condiment; *escargot* with a savory taste of garlic and parsley butter; *crusty tradition and aux cereals baguettes;* an assortment of French cheeses and what a delight — *Bouton de Culotte*, a soft bloomy rind goat cheese from Haut-Beaujolias with the shape of a trouser button and pepper taste; *Bleu d'Auvergne,* a cheese made with ewe's milk and a pleasant perfumed taste; *Beaufort d'été* , located in the Savoie region, a firm, pale yellow cow's milk cheese with a smooth and creamy texture; a delicious bottle of red and white wine — *Château Margaux cru* — red wine from the region of Bordeaux with dried rose petals, sweet spices and dried red currant that fondle the palate; *Chablis grand cru* — white wine from *Bourgogne* with light bodied flavors of citrus; and plenty of bubbles — *La Veuve Clicquot,* nicknamed the "Widow." For dessert, we had pineapple sorbet and rich dark French chocolates straight from the chocolatier.

"Oh my God, this is truly amazing," I exclaimed surrounded by the most beautiful dishes I have ever seen. "How incredibly lucky I am to spend my first holiday celebration in France."

"I don't understand," he said with a puzzled expression, his eyes staring straight into mine. "You told me you were invited by a friend for Christmas."

"In fact, when I arrived at Jacques-Désiré's home, the family celebration had already ended. I ate leftovers alone at the table."

"*Ma pauvre,*" my poor little one, "I hope I can make up for that!" He sounded celebratory and perhaps relieved that I hadn't fallen for someone else.

"You've gone far beyond anything I could have ever dreamed of or imagined. Oh My Goodness — what an exquisite feast! I've never eaten caviar, foie gras or escargots."

He returned from the kitchen with another bottle of Veuve Cliquot and filled our champagne glasses. By then I was sloshed!

"*A ta santé, mon amour.*"

My heart fluttered. He'd just called me his love.

"Good health and happiness to you my sweetheart," I replied.

After eating the most exquisite delicious dishes ever with my man, I could hardly move. Later we scanned the channels and watched New Year's celebrations in different parts of the world. Close to midnight, François turned the TV off, put some romantic music on and asked me to dance. He held my face in his large warm hands and gently pecked my lips. I held onto the back of his neck with my hands locked, closed my eyes resting my head on his shoulder and drifted into a hypnotic state while we slow danced. My head was lowered when François gently lifted my chin, and at the stroke of midnight, our tongues intertwined into a long awaited French kiss — as delicious as the dinner!

"Happy New Year, my Vernetia," he said with a smile when we pulled away.

"Happy New Year, my François!" I smiled, breathless, my lips still tingling.

"Tell me," he asked. "Why didn't you accept my Christmas invitation?"

"Because I thought it was offered out of pity."

"*Ma Chérie*, how sad and untrue; it reminds me in some way of my first American vacation. People would ask me to stop by after one brief meeting. I wanted to ask, "Do you always invite people to your home that you don't know? I found it a bit superficial. Typically in France, we take time to get to know a person first.'"

"Two months," I intervened with a smile.

"The amount of time depends on the situation. Usually when we invite someone to our home, we mean it." He stroked my hand. "I can assure you that my invitation was not offered out of pity. I wanted you to spend the Christmas holiday with me and my family in Cannes in the worst way."

"If only I had known."

"Funny how we misinterpret things," he went on, confessing. "I felt rejected, heartbroken and thought you had fallen for someone else. If you had turned me down on New Year's Eve, I wouldn't have called again. Christmas was not the same without you. I am thrilled to have you back my *petit trésor*." He dimmed the lights, pumped up the volume and asked, "May I have this dance, *Ma Chèrie*?"

When he leaned over my curved body, the split in my long skirt almost exposed my red string. I raised my leg and kicked my high heel across the room, and tossed the other behind it. Swirling, twirling, drenched in sweat, we were having the time of our lives. While he seduced me, we were laughing, dancing and singing out loud.

"You're quite a dancer! Where did you learn such provocative moves?" I asked, breathless.

"I love dancing!" he said.

I had witnessed an exciting transformation. My reserved Frenchman suddenly took on the body movements of John Travolta. Tipsy and exhausted, I had difficulty standing.

"Would you like to lie down on the couch?"

"Actually, I would prefer the bed," I said with a sly smile.

When he cuddled me in his arms, I felt his heartbeat, his body heat and inhaled the scent of 'Euphoria" made from exotic fruits. He caressed my face, lifted my velvet top and gently ran his tongue over the curves of my breast. I drifted off while we were making love. He had placed my high heels beside the bed. Two misunderstood cultures had finally converged into a perfect alliance.

Around noon, I crawled out of bed and wearing his bathrobe, I went into the living room barefooted to the smell of freshly brewed coffee. I found François stretched out on the sofa listening to "Ne me quitte pas," (Do not leave me) by Jacques Brel, while reading a medieval history magazine.

"Good afternoon, my little 'Fluffy Puppy.'"

"What?" The tone of my voice demanded an immediate explanation. "Now I look like a dog, yes?"

"*Mais, non.* Fluffy was the family's poodle. She was as cute as a button and loved the rain. After getting soaked, she would waddle inside like a duck shaking water all over the carpet. It was impossible to scold her with those sad saucer eyes. You would have loved her. Unfortunately, she's dead."

I looked down aghast and embarrassed. My velvet ensemble lying on the floor was crushed like snowflakes. François must have imagined Fluffy reincarnated.

"I thought you liked my outfit?" I asked, nudging him on.

"Must have been all that dirty dancing," he said with an impish smile.

"I must have looked awful!"

"You were even cuter that way, *ma petite poulette.*"

"So now I am your little (poulette) chicken?" I rolled my eyes and he laughed. My attention was averted to the dining room table. I pointed.

"What's that?"

"A *Galette des Rois,*" he explained. "It's a round cake filled with almond paste served from January 6th to the end of the month in celebration of the Wise Men's arrival. A tiny fève is hidden inside and the one who finds the charm is crowned Queen or King. It's a bit early for the celebration, but I asked the baker to make it especially for my Vernetia."

"It's delicious," I said already on my second piece loaded with butter and almond paste. I ate it with a tall glass of champagne.

"Bon, we must continue until we find the charm," he insisted.

On the third slice, I bit into something tiny and as hard as a rock. I spit out a tiny Bugs Bunny.

"*Félicitations!*" He put a crown on the top of my head. "You found the *fève*. Now, you're officially my American Queen."

"A poodle, a chicken, a charm (fève), and now a queen," I said and then broke out into hysterical laughter holding Bugs Bunny in the flat of my hand. "Oh La La!"

I discovered so many remarkable things about François on New Year's Eve. He's very romantic and believes in everlasting love; he's honest, protective, has strength of character, and his heart can be easily broken; sometimes he's loquacious, but more often reserved, with a dry sense of humor. That night I felt as if I was at the summit of a mountain and all of my pinned up fears were forever silenced. When I reached the ground, he was patiently waiting, pleading with me to forgive him for anything he may have unknowingly done to upset me. He pulled me into his arms humming *Let Me Love You* while we danced the Spanish tango in the center of gravity. He danced his way forward, backward and sideways; I danced my way but our differences were inconsequential. We both knew in our hearts that we had reached the pinnacle in our relationship and were destined to be together. If only real life was as easy as living in *La La Land*, disconnected from reality, while we danced that night in search of our destiny?

Little did I know when I'd had my epiphany — my 'Oh My God' moment — that in a few meager hours I'd be on the plane, head pressed against the window pane gazing out at puffy white clouds continually moving, tears gushing down my cheeks, heart broken into a million pieces, not knowing if I'd see François again.

11

THE END OF MY FRENCH VACATION

I had less than 48 hours remaining with François and not a word was mentioned about my return to America. A week without François while he vacationed on the *Côte d'Azur* for Christmas left me sad and confused. I wondered what a permanent departure might feel like leaving behind so many precious and extraordinary memories. At times, I wished I had not come to Paris. Still, I had no regrets realizing I had not experienced love like this before. Late in the afternoon, we dined at my favorite restaurant in my neighborhood. I ordered a salad. François ordered enough food for two people.

"You're hungry," I said, thinking back to our extraordinary New Year's Eve feast the previous evening, leaving me with barely an appetite.

"Nerves setting in I suppose," he remarked, leaning on both elbows staring down. We didn't talk very much. The words wouldn't come. It felt as if we were mourning the death of a couple very much alive and crazy in love. He moved to my side of the table and wiped the tears from my eyes. After paying the check, we walked home, our steps as heavy as our sighs.

"May I stay with you tonight?" he asked.

"Perhaps it's better if you don't."

"Then, I will return at sunrise and wait at your door. I'm taking you to the airport and that's that!"

"*No. No. No,*" I cried. "That would be even worse."

"Nonsense!" he said, raising his voice. "Are you saying this is the last time I will see you?"

"Heaven's no, I hope not. I don't know what I'm saying." He held me in his arms for a long time and kissed me passionately at the door. Then he turned, head hung low, and walked away. I watched him until he was out of sight and felt his presence throughout the night. I woke up the next morning confused. Nothing felt right.

My flight to Logan Airport was catastrophic. Well into the flight, we were cruising along and suddenly felt a jolt, a rapid climb with violent turbulence among the clouds. Moans, groans and cursing shouted out, "Holy shit!" I sat facing two flight attendants clutching their seats with bulging eyes and frightening smiles. I was bawling my eyes out while the pilot announced it was the relativity of wind gusts that caused the plane to lift and fall. "I wasn't buying it!" My pent-up fear and my imagination ran wild: had the pilot fallen asleep in the cockpit? Were the wings going to collapse? I prayed, "Dear God please spare our lives." If only I had agreed to let François take me to the airport, things might have been different. At the very least, we would have had more time together. Will he forgive me if the plane crashes? I sorely regretted not being able to stay longer with him in France except for that damn visa. We braced ourselves when the plane went into a nose-dive and skidded on the runway perilously close to the edge of the landing. Right before the descent, the trapped air in my inner ear popped from the atmospheric pressure. "Holy crap, that sucks," I yelled. When we touched down, the lights came on! The passengers applauded! "We made it, Hallelujah!" An elderly woman walked off the plane beside me tapping her cane. "We've had a taste of Hell," she moaned. "What in God's name will Heaven feel like?"

Early the next morning in my Boston apartment, I bolted up in bed. Were all those good times in Paris just a dream? I pushed aside my goose feathered quilt, rubbed my tired eyes, and got up groggily. I was in the kitchen brewing coffee and found a note on the counter:

Hope you had a wonderful time in France. I'll call you when I return from my business trip and drop off the keys.

While inspecting the apartment, I spotted my ticket stubs near the door, and remembered my luggage had been put on another plane. The apartment was as calm as the night and four times larger than my *pied-à-terre* in Paris. While wallowing in the comforts of my apartment I thought, *what good is it if you're not happy here?*

I felt liberated in Paris with only my suitcases. The joy of living in the *City of Light* replaced my focus on material obsessions. I was already missing my little studio in a vibrant neighborhood not much larger than a big room. A bachelorette's pad can be more exciting than a grandiose apartment or better said, "One man's trash can be another one's treasure." I called my little studio DB *"Dream Big"* — the name written on a poster pinned to the wall in our bedroom with stars hanging from it when Virginia and I were kids. DB was a taste of the good life.

France is a country with emphasis on the *"joie de vivre,"* living one's life by happenstance, taking time to enjoy the aroma of brewed coffee in the mornings, romancing with flowers, and taking proper vacations. While I relaxed in a long bubble bath, I analyzed every detail of my life and wondered how I would manage without François. I understood what true love meant when we were together and although we were miles apart, I knew I'd found it.

Several hours had passed and I thought long and hard about our time together and how my perseverance transported me to an exhilarating adventure in France. I didn't know what I was doing on many occasions, but my mishaps and snafus along the way were sometimes exciting. I was no longer living in a country where the greed for money and an extravagant lifestyle replaced one's values. While there were exceptions, moderation was typically the norm. I recalled conversations around the coffee machine in corporate America about the importance of being a team player to get promoted. Money was the 'key to happiness.' But it wasn't.

In France people tend to have a greater appreciation for the small joys in life and family time around the dinner table with a fine glass of wine. Something as insignificant as a delicious French croissant to start your day can be unforgettable. A conversation about money outside of the home is taboo and being competitive is mostly about sports. Contrarily, I witnessed expressions of sexuality in ads at public places that were incomprehensible, but that's another story. Anyway, who was I to judge?

As I curled up on my long lavish couch, I thought about so many incredible experiences I'd had. How I wished I was back in Paris. I sighed. It was time to check my answering machine loaded with messages:

Ms. France you're finally back!
Welcome home, sweetie!
Hey, gutsy lady, I can't wait to get the low down on the French.
How the heck are you, babe?

Now that I was in Boston, I was dying to see my friends. They rarely crossed my mind in France, but I couldn't tell them that. It was unsettling readjusting to the American way of life after being in France. My neighbors had already left for work in the Financial District slogging out their guts for big bucks while I listened to luxuriating French melodies in my apartment. I was dying to tell François how much I missed him but it was 2:30 a.m. in Paris. I was already craving those French baguettes with golden crispy crusts and mouth-watering French cheeses with more than 350 varieties! Not a day passed by without devouring them. The artistic repertoire of decadent desserts in a *pâtisserie* was also an addiction. Reminiscing about French food, I got dressed and ran a few errands. I bought enough nourishment to stock my empty refrigerator and kitchen cabinets, which reminded me of the day I landed in Paris without a morsel to eat in my kitchenette.

I decided to take an early leisurely walk. Being home made me feel like a foreigner in my own country. Along the way, things that I hadn't paid any attention to before suddenly crystallized: obesity — which correlates with hypertension and strokes — eating on the run with a cup of coffee up to 20 ounces from Starbucks, the hectic pace and loud voices. Thank God, there was no hint of stifling cigarette smoke in cafés and restaurants like it was all over Paris. Most facets of American life were huge in comparison — apartments, restaurants, grocery stores, bathrooms and even rolls of toilet paper. Happily, the streets in Boston were much wider and cleaner — free of dog poop, *Merci Dieu*. One afternoon I stopped a stranger on the street in Paris and asked, "Where is the Imaging and Mammography Center?"

"*Je vais par là. Je peux vous guider si vous voulez.*" I'm going in that direction. I can show you if you want.

I nodded. Pressed for time I wasn't paying any attention to where I was walking — "*Merde!*" I shouted sliding on one heel.

"*C'est plus élégant de dire crotte de chien,*" she remarked. It is more elegant to say dog dirt. I didn't think any form of dog 'shit' was elegant. We hunched over laughing. "Keep your eyes to the sidewalk and watch your step," she said in choppy English.

The city I'd always loved had changed. Boston felt more like a vacation 'stopover' than my home. I headed back to my apartment. I was eating an unsavory Hershey bar I had picked up on my walk when the phone rang.

"*Comment ça va, mon petit chocolat en sucre?*" How's my little sweet chocolate?

"Not very happy," I laughed. "What time is it in France?"

"Very early," he said. "I've been having difficulty sleeping lately."

"Me too," I replied. "I feel out of synch in Boston."

"*Ma pauvre* (poor dear), you must not worry. I don't think it is Boston. Something is missing in France for me too and it's you! How was your trip?" he asked, changing the subject.

"My luggage is lost." I didn't mention my flight from hell.

"Vernetia, would you come back to France?"

"Holy Moses," I thought! "My vacation was far from being a foreign fling, but I hadn't expected an invitation and certainly not so soon." My excitement shot through the roof. I was thrilled to death and scared.

"I would love to come back," I blurted out. "Can you help me find a place to stay?"

"If you don't mind I would like you to stay with me this time."

Astonished, I was at a loss for words. "I need to get some sleep," he said "Let's talk later today."

Suddenly everything was shifting in the opposite direction —

slow to high speed, and it was the first time in my life that I had found true bliss. Bursting from excitement after François' invitation, I sought my British friend's advice. Katerina would have no problem counseling me on the dream of my life. She would even counsel the Pope if given a chance. "Welcome home," she shouted and I almost dropped the phone. "I've missed you so much, Vernetia!"

"I've missed you too," I replied but that was hardly the truth.

"How was Paris?"

"Fabulous. I need your advice."

"Of course. I'll need all the details so that I can advise you correctly." She was obviously making a pitch to get the lowdown.

"I'm thinking about returning to France!"

"You're not serious are you? You just got home."

"As serious as a heart attack," I laughed.

"So what's his name?"

"His name is François. He's really nice and very handsome."

"When does he want you to return?"

"Tomorrow is not soon enough. That's what he said word for word."

"Gosh! He's madly in love with you, isn't he?" She spoke with a charming British accent.

"Yes. I'm sure he is."

"And are you in love with him?"

"Star gazing, crazy in love."

"I'm so jealous, sweetie!"

"What should I do?"

"You've already done it. Your relationship is like a virgin and it needs nurturing. Think about all the women, including myself, that would love to be in your shoes."

"But what if it doesn't work out?"

"Come home!" She paused when I didn't reply. "Kidding here. You've found happiness with a handsome Frenchman who's madly in love with you and he wants you to live with him in Paris — of all places — and you're asking such a silly question? Are you out of your mind? Beautiful things happen when the heart is dazzled and life is also about taking chances. Remember the proverb: 'It's better to have loved and lost than not to have loved at all.' François sounds like a rare jewel. Finding true love is like harvesting flowers. Special seeds are planted in soil and in order for them to bud and flourish they need to be cared for. Some seeds produce rare flowers once in a lifetime. Some flowers attract butterflies, humming birds and other guests to your garden. Keep your dream alive and strumming. Rush to your man's side you crazy love bird!'"

"You've given me a lot to think about," I said with a sigh.

"Follow your heart and stop thinking so much."

Still, I remained apprehensive about packing it all in and rushing back into the arms of my Frenchman, even though it was unbearable being so far away from him. I've always had an independent streak, afraid of commitments, chasing rainbows and discovering new places; but it is another thing to go on a foreign vacation and move in with a man you hardly know that promises you everything.

The first snow flurries had begun to fall and the bitter cold was gripping Boston. I bundled up and went to *Café Vanille* on Charles Street close to my Beacon Hill apartment. I gazed at the mouthwatering French pastries while I waited in line. Vincent came out of the kitchen drying his hands on the bottom of his apron and his eyes lit up when he saw me.

"*Quelle surprise!* When did you get back?"

"A few days ago," I answered.

"*Comment cela a été à Paris?*" How was Paris? He continued, grinning from ear to ear, surprised to see me, and gave me a big hug.

"Paris was *extraordinaire!*"

"If you can wait ten minutes, I can take a fifteen minute break," he said and continued to dry his hands. I nodded and smiled.

Meanwhile, I sat at a table in the corner of the café and glanced at the Beacon Hill Times and waited. Before I went to Paris, Vincent encouraged me to stop by the café and practice my French. I went a few times, but he was always busy in the kitchen and it was difficult to understand his Haitian accent. Nevertheless, I tried on several occasions and he was always encouraging. After updating Vincent on my trip, I left with a few French pastries. Unfortunately, they didn't taste as good as the ones I'd devoured in Paris.

When I got home, I called François. He was disappointed that I wasn't coming right away. It took time to convince him that returning to France and moving in with him was one of the biggest decisions in my life, and naturally I was scared.

"If I were not working I'd be on the next plane," he said. "Perhaps I can come to Boston in April."

"That's perfect!" I said.

"Perfect? That's a very long time to 'not' see my love," he said. "*Et, je t'aime, Vernetia.*" And I love you Vernetia.

I sucked in a breath. He'd finally said it three times so I knew he was dead serious. I gripped the phone. "I love you, too."

Absence makes the heart grow fonder and I couldn't wait to be in the arms of François again.

PART TWO
LIVING IN A SWEET LIFE

"If you are lucky enough to have lived in Paris as a young man, then wherever you go for the rest of your life, it stays with you, for Paris is a movable feast."

— ERNEST HEMINGWAY

12

A DIFFERENT FRANÇOIS IN AMERICA

François seemed different when he landed in Boston — casual and more at ease. I hadn't ever seen him wearing sneakers and blue jeans. Formality and social nonconformity defined his dress code. It seemed as if I were greeting him at *Charles de Gaulle* airport instead of Logan. He held me close in his arms in those eye-catching jeans while the crowd rushed by.

"I missed you so much! Welcome to Boston!" I roared. "How was your flight?"

"Not bad. I sat beside a French couple and we talked about you and Bean Town."

"You're traveling very light," I said checking out his small suitcase.

"I always travel with a minimum of luggage. I want to go shopping at Filene's Basement. If necessary I can pick up another suitcase."

Arm in arm, we walked to the taxi stand and hopped in a cab, snuggling up in the back seat as we headed to my apartment.

"A Frenchman in Boston," the jolly driver chuckled." How sweet it is! I studied French in high school and I still remember a few words. It's music to my ears." He paused. "How's the weather in Paris?"

"Much warmer than in Boston but it was very cloudy before my departure," replied François.

Within twenty minutes flat, the driver stopped directly in front of my door.

"Go easy with the hanky-panky, love birds," he continued to joke. "What a toothsome sexy couple!" Suddenly he bellowed out the lyrics of Patti Labelle's Lady Marmalade, "Gitchi gitichi ya-ya here '*Voulez-vous coucher avec moi ce soir?*" Do you want to sleep with me tonight? He seemed delighted to have met us and we were in stitches from his sense of humor.

François was gloating when I gave him a tour of the apartment.

"You must be exhausted!"

"Thrilled and exhausted," he replied massaging my shoulders and neck.

"Would you like a glass of Perrier?"

"Perrier in Boston?" he sighed."That's perfect!"

"I'll prepare some California Cabernet Sauvignon wine and Vermont Aged Cheddar cheese. I hope you will not be too disappointed. Would you like to relax in a hot bath first?" I asked and he nodded.

François came out of the bathroom wearing a handsome navy and white silk robe with Japanese temples and shrines. He appeared to have Oriental features with thick eyelashes and black hair, epitomizing a younger image of Seiji Ozawa of the Boston Symphony. His hairy chest was exposed when I untied his robe and it fell off his shoulders. The next thing I knew we were both undressed and entangled on the floor.

"Ah, I feel like a million bucks," he sighed.

Should I tell him how sexy he looks?

I hesitated but the words flew out of my mouth. I rolled over on top of him inhaling his fragrance and we were laughing like crazy.

Beacon Hill is a charming neighborhood with "narrow cobblestone streets, federal style row houses and gaslit street-lamps," multicolor doors trimmed in elaborate brass and potted flowers in window boxes with narrow passageways and hidden gardens. Strolling up and down the Hill with vintage gas lamps at night is romantic and enchanting. After a light meal at Panificio Bistro five minutes from the apartment, we headed back home.

"*Ma Petite Princess*," he whispered while opening the door, "I am delighted to be with you."

"And I'm thrilled to have you in Boston *Cheri*," I said pointing to my WELCOME HOME sketch on the wall.

"I have a gift for you," he smiled searching his backpack. "We brought in the New Year with this in Paris. Do you remember it?"

"Of course, I will never forget," I said giving him a kiss. We sipped on *Veuve Clicquot, La Grande Dame* of champagne, capturing so many fond memories of Paris, including that passion-filled spine-tingly-body-quivering lovemaking late into the night.

But we had a lot to do. Our itinerary was jam-packed — restaurants, museums, boat cruises, the theatre. He spoiled me rotten in France, and I wanted to do my very best to reciprocate in Boston.

"Ma *Chérie*, he said vehemently. "You're very kind to have planned so many things to do, but I'm here to spend time with you. I couldn't be happier if we simply stroll around Charles River, enjoy a picnic in the park or dine at home relaxing."

There wouldn't be much relaxing. Derek, my nephew, called the next morning and invited us out on the town. He and his girlfriend, Lana, picked us up Friday evening in their little sports car with music blasting.

"Where are you taking us?" I asked as we hopped in the car.

"Surprises are fun. You'll just have to wait and see."

"What's that you're playing?" I said, cringing.

"Boston isn't Paris but we enjoy French Rap. We don't understand the lyrics but there's something about the beat and foreign accent that makes it exciting." he laughed. "It's so nice to finally meet you François."

"Likewise," said my sexy Frenchman.

I thought François would have preferred listening to something more soothing but he didn't seem to mind. As for me, anything that my darling nephew chose to play was acceptable for a short time. About an hour into the drive I asked again, "So where are we going?"

"Vernetia, surprises are the best," said Derek with a wink, "Don't you think so, François?"

"Yes, sure," he laughed.

"New York City here we come!" I shouted over the rap.

"Wrong," Lana answered.

While François rocked in the back seat, Derek and Lana laughed hysterically and fell in love with his antics. François has a great voice, but I was shocked to see his soulful gestures. I had never seen him acting goofy before.

"Love your accent," Derek yelled. "Maybe we should record something together." He teased him all along the drive to 'wherever.'

"You're such an adolescent," I said. François was completely relaxed and I was delighted to see him enjoying himself with my family.

Derek chuckled as he slid into the parking spot. "We've arrived!"

We all hopped out of the car.

"Where are we?" asked François.

"Look up! We're at the Foxwood Resort in Connecticut, the largest gambling casino in the world," he explained after opening François' door. "We're gonna have some fun tonight!"

"I'm going to get some coins," François said and darted over to the cashier. He returned with two large cups — one for me and one for him.

"Looks like we have a gambler in our company tonight," Lana said with a laugh.

By his expression, François was on cloud nine. The casino was jam-packed with folks sitting in front of slot machines yanking on levers playing their hearts out. The complimentary booze was plentiful for members, but that didn't apply to us. A quarter here, fifty cents there and nothing was happening; I emptied my cup and gave up. François kept up his rush of adrenaline and moved around like a flying squirrel.

"Isn't it better to play one machine at a time?" I asked.

"Why?" he responded. "It's all random." He kept on trucking.

"It's open all night, if you want to eat first," Derek reminded us. As soon as I walked away, I heard the thrill of a slot machine ringing, multi-color lights flashing and coins clanking and falling into a receptacle.

François yelled. "I hit the jackpot for a hundred bucks!"

"No way," Derek yelled back. "You hungry?"

We nodded and cut across the gigantic room with over seven thousand slot machines and headed towards the "All You Can Eat" buffet restaurant. François's eyes popped out like an inflated balloon when he saw large buffet pans with tons of food lined up — pastas, meats, fish, salads, desserts, drinks, etcetera. I had plenty on my plate but hadn't made all the rounds and waited at the table.

"Oh My God... Can you eat all that?" I asked François. "*Quel gourmand!*"

"When in America do as the Americans do. I read it in my Guide."

"Right on!" Derek laughed. "Eat your heart out, buddy!"

"That's how it's done in the *Good ol US of A*," said Lana, chiming in. "Vernetia, we're gonna dance until we burn off the calories so relax for God's sake."

After dinner, we rocked all night on the dance floor acting like fools and returned home at the crack of dawn exhausted, but happy.

Early the next morning, the phone woke us up. Groggily, I answered. "Mmmpf."

"Salaam, Chetori!"

He spoke with an Iranian accent and I knew immediately it was Kian.

I cleared my throat. "Merci, Khoban," Thank you, I'm fine — the only expression I remembered in Farsi.

"Can you and François come for dinner tomorrow night?"

I met Kian, a native Shiite Iranian, when I was looking for an apartment in Back Bay close to Boston University. He worked as a painter for a real estate agency. Very much underpaid without an education, he worked day and night in order to make a living. When he came to America he couldn't speak another language and gradually learned a bit of English. He greeted me at the agency covered with white paint from head to heels.

"I show 'U' bootiful 'partment' close at Siffanay Hall," he said trying to convince me.

"Oh no," I said tacitly. "Why am I wasting my time?"

When we entered the apartment five minutes from Symphony Hall, I was charmed out of my mind. It simply needed to be professionally painted. The neighborhood was vibrant and I could walk to Boston University where I attended college.

Years later, Kian bought a dilapidated building from the City of Boston for one dollar and refurbished it. Now he owns three buildings converted into several apartments and is richer than mud. To say that he worked 24/7 is not an exaggeration. Once his finances were in order, he returned to Iran for an arranged marriage.

"American women no good," he'd said. "I want to marry stupid girl, stay home, make babies and do as she told."

I thought he was kidding but he wasn't. A couple of years later, he brought his new bride to Boston. Totally dependent on him, just as he wanted, she spoke only in Farsi, their native language. Mondana, his beautiful young bride, was named after the mother of an Iranian King.

I turned to François. "You're gonna love Kian. He's, *umm*, most intriguing."

When François and I arrived at Kian's home for dinner, we gaped at the exquisite hand-woven Iranian rugs with geometric motifs in red (signifying power and strength), dark blue and green. The Persian carpets covered the sparkling hardwood floors in every room. We were astonished to see a carpet on the terrace where they grilled vegetables, beef, fish, and barbequed kabob. Mondana, full breasted, wore a loose fitting black dress with a hijab headscarf. Her eyes were at odds with her public persona. In deference to her guests, she held her head slightly down. Kian asked us to remove our shoes at the entrance, an Iranian custom. Their home was spotless!

Smiling shyly and lacking confidence, Mondana served us brewed black tea with a hint of cardamom, cinnamon and rose-water from an elegant porcelain pot. The tea had been brewing on the stove for hours. A Persian bowl with a motif of a 'prince on horseback' sat beside the teapot filled with pistachios served before the meal.

An Iranian custom, Mondana spread out a Sofreh tablecloth on the floor without cutlery.

We used our hands and bread to eat the delicious Iranian dishes. Rice, the center piece, was covered with saffron and slices of white grilled potatoes at the bottom. Chunks of salmon, sirloin steak and lamb marinated with garlic, onions, saffron and tomatoes were grilled on skewers. Everything except the flat stone bread was homemade including the yogurt. Sweet watermelon was the dessert.

We sat on the floor more than two hours eating with their children and listening to Iranian music. The conversation was serene but interesting. François and I were shocked by all the things Kian had accomplished.

"Vernetia was very kind to me," he said. "She treated the poor guy like everyone else. Over the years, she was like family, especially with my wife."

"She's like my big sister," Mondana smiled with her head slightly bowed. "We would like to invite both of you to Iran. Will you come?"

"We'd love to, wouldn't we François?"

"It would indeed be a pleasure, but we don't know when."

Before leaving, Kian took us down to the basement where there were at least a hundred Persian rugs in different pattern and sizes.

"Choose one for your wedding and take it back with you to Paris."

"That's very generous of you," I smiled. "But we have no plans to get married."

"You will," he said and then he winked. "I see it in your eyes. You belong together."

Like so many women, I'd wasted too many years craving affection in superficial relationships, akin to a compulsive eater, filling a void pretending to be happy. Things were different now with François. I had turned the page to a wonderful new life filled with happiness.

Except for the two fun packed nights out on the town, we hadn't done very much in Boston. François met some of my friends who adored him. A passion for genealogy, we visited the New England Historic Genealogical Society, a research center for genealogists and historians in Boston. We spent a couple of hours at the Boston Museum of Fine Arts, strolled around the Charles River and poked in and out of shops, cherishing each moment together from the time we got up to the time we went to bed. Boston hadn't changed. I had now that I was with the man I truly loved. Whether dressed in business suits in France or blue jeans in America, I knew he sincerely loved me too and that made all the difference.

I was going to do it. — I was moving to Paris!

While he slept in, I went over to list my apartment for rent. When I got back and announced the news, François was over the moon.

"So, you're really coming to France and moving in with me?" he asked, pulling me close.

"I am," I said, snuggling into his embrace.

"I'm very happy, Vernetia."

"Me too," I said.

A few days later a lovely couple came to the apartment with their son on his dad's back with a big round head, red curly locks, large marine blue eyes, playing hide and seek with me drooling all over my carpet. The couple handed over the signed lease.

The day François had to return to France, we were weepy as always with each separation. We were pleased, nevertheless, knowing that I had found a new tenant and soon we'd be together across the Atlantic where it all began in the *City of Light* with other love birds, young and old, in the park, on the train, in the drizzling rain, by the Seine — everywhere that makes "Paris an enchanting paradise!" François is truly a romantic and honest to the core. When I look into his eyes, I feel unconditional love that flows throughout my body, deep into my soul, and makes me feel whole. I didn't need to justify anything; I only needed to follow my heart and my dream.

13
RETURN TO GAI PARIS

I arrived at Charles de Gaulle Airport ragged from fatigue — sagging eyelids and flattened cheeks from lack of sleep. The melodic sound of the French language gave me a boost of energy and out of nowhere it seemed my face had lifted.

François reminded me that packing light would be a good reason to go shopping in *"Gai Paree."* He greeted me in the waiting room beaming, holding a long-stemmed red rose and wheeled my suitcases to the car.

"These are all yours?"

Perhaps he thought I had a hidden agenda. I carried enough clothes to stay forever. "Sorry for bringing so many things," I said. "Then you'll have no reason to leave after three months," he smiled and squeezed my hand. The moment he started the car, I was ecstatic about moving in with François and my fears had suddenly vanished. Soon, I was unpacked and settled in.

The next morning I was alone in the apartment adjusting to my new surroundings while François was at work. I found a love note waiting for me on the dining room table beside my tea cup and my breakfast — *"Bienvenu à Vincennes, Ma Chérie."* Welcome to Vincennes. "Call me when you're up and stirring."

While admiring my long stemmed roses left on the dinner table, I turned the television on. I didn't understand anything, nor could I read the books that covered a wall in the dining room. But I admired them, especially the Coat of Arms in beautiful colors used to identify the nobility in battles during the middle ages. My morning exploration reminded me of our New Year's Eve party when François caught me snooping around in his personal things, except this time he left me to roam as I pleased. After my second cup of tea, I called him at the office.

"I can't believe we're together again François."

"We're not. You're so far away from me *Ma Chérie,*" he complained.

"Less than an hour from door to door is much closer than Boston, sweetheart!"

Before turning in for the night, I slipped into a sheer white satin nightgown clinging to my curves and contrasting my chocolate skin. Lying beside me, François unfastened the tie and caressed my breasts in his warm hands. A patient French lover, he gave me sensual massages with sweet oil, pushed my curly locks to the side and fondled my face and neck. I raised my head and playfully kissed his lips. After sipping champagne under his gaze my body craved the lovefest. Hot and bothered, he removed his briefs, my nightgown and flung them on the floor. Lying on top of me breathing profoundly, his lips were soft and warm allowing my tongue to slip inside his mouth. He held me down while he pushed in gently, harder and harder until I was in Seventh heaven. Before drifting into a peaceful sleep, I was thinking, *Voila I'll have my man all to myself, 24/7 for the weekend.*

François was anxious for me to meet his two sons, JO (Jean-Olivier) and Xavier and said Father's Day would be the perfect occasion.

"What if we don't get on well together? What can I do to please them?" I asked.

"No worries," he said. "Just be yourself!"

Good idea in theory but still I was anxious. I decided to greet the boys over a home cooked American meal. Seldomly creative in the kitchen, I went straight to a French gourmet delicatessen in the neighborhood for some ideas. Feeling inadequate after seeing an extraordinary display of gourmet foods in the shop's window, I salivated at the mouth and returned home with lavishly prepared French dishes, thinking I should at least make the dessert! *And what could be more New England with a French touch than apple pie à la mode?*

I set to it, a whirling dervish in the kitchen. I had the recipe down to a science but had forgotten to add the vinegar that makes the dough rise. The pie fell flat in the center but stood upright and proper on the edges. *Put a hefty scoop of vanilla ice cream in the center, for goodness sake, and no one will even notice.*

I was struck by a tiny resemblance of JO to Brad Pitt when he appeared at the door, a handsome young man with light brown hair, blue eyes and a contagious laughter. Gregarious and polite he reached out to shake my hand. I could feel his warmth and eagerness to get acquainted. Not understanding his rapid French, I returned to the kitchen while he entertained his dad in the living room.

Why wouldn't the boys like me? I convinced myself.

Half an hour later, François youngest son Xavier arrived. Their personalities were starkly different. He was very restrained. I felt his dark brown eyes sizing me up the minute he arrived. I could almost tell what he was thinking: *Is she even good enough for my dad?* I was annoyed at myself for letting a young adolescent make me feel so edgy. Xavier and I played a game of cat and mouse while JO, a say what you feel kind of guy sugar coated with bullshit, gave me the lowdown on the French way of life in charming broken English and kept me laughing. I tried to engage Xavier, but he was unwilling. He needed to be sweetened up like pineapples — tough on the outside but sweet inside.

We sat down for the meal — a very awkward meal — me trying to keep up with inside jokes and the French.

When the boys got up to leave, I trailed them to the door. JO turned and kissed me on both cheeks: *"Bienvenue en France,"* he said Welcome to France. Xavier and I made eye contact for the first time.

"I liked your American pie," he smiled.

"Thank you!" I said. "I'll make a delicious Pineapple Upside Down Cake the next time you come for lunch."

He reached out and shook my hand. I suspected that I had passed the first test and would have other opportunities.

Organizing one's time in Paris is important because there are tons of things to do and I wanted to put French lessons back on my list. Ads for group and private French classes are numerous in the city. Teaching French is a popular means to make some easy cash under the table in a country faced with high unemployment. I've heard that it's easier to get a divorce than be fired by a French company, leaving little turnover in the workplace. There is usually a contractual trial period from three to six months.

Alliance Française is a renowned institution that disseminates languages around the world. I attended a few classes and enjoyed them tremendously but decided to quit after several weeks. I wanted a taste of everything. The weekly 'Pariscope' was my entertainment guide packed with numerous events: theatre, concerts, exhibits, etcetera.

One Sunday afternoon, I visited the *Musée Guimet*, which boasts masterpieces of diverse cultures and civilizations from the Asiatic continent. It has more than 60,000 works of art from seventeen countries. The sculptures, paintings and art objects are extraordinaire! Hypnotized in one of the galleries, I decided to sneak some photographs. A cold-faced security guard rushed over to me in the dimly lit room and pushed my hand down.

"You can't read?" he shouted in choppy English. "Pictures are forbidden!"

On my second visit, a staff member invited me to a Caribbean lunch prepared in the museum annex, *"Me like see you here,"* she said. After the meal, I was introduced to the book binding process, followed by a private viewing of an Afghanistan exhibit, bypassing a long line queuing up. I tried to communicate with my new friends with baffling thoughts of Asian art echoing in my brain, but, it was absurd!

Advancing on my bucket list, I watched the flashing lights at night filled with excitement at the Eiffel Tower in a jam-packed crowd. Built by Gustave Eiffel in 1889, the Eiffel Tower drew strong opposition against it from the 'Paris artistic and literary elite,' calling it 'unappreciated French taste.'" It was the tallest building in the world until the Chrysler Building was constructed forty years later. Maniacal tourists are drawn to it like bees to honey, making it the most iconic monument in the world.

The following week, François and I visited *Le Musée du Vin*, formerly a monastery built by mendicant monks. Near the arched cellars, waiters buzzed around serving lunch with a sampling of wines. While the noise from the crowd bounced against the masonry walls one could almost imagine the monks performing their daily chores. Dripping water falling on rocks gave the impression of living in another time zone.

Dating back to the middle ages, Le Musée du Vin was formerly a monastery surrounded by orchards and vines on the side of a hill bordered by the river Seine. King Louis XIII was known for enjoying a light red wine made by the monks on his way home after hunting in the Boulogne woods in Paris. Honoré de Balzac was supposed to have lived a few houses down the block. At the *Musée du Vin,* François and I were seated at a table with a large vase of stunning fresh flowers. For lunch, I chose *quail terrine* served with wine jam; François chose *frog legs* with *persillade.* Fancy desserts were wheeled around on a cart with a huge assortment of cheeses and complementary wines.

On the way out, François gave me a beautiful sea blue, white and gold scarf decorated with Bourgogne and Bordeaux wine bottles and coats of arms from Champagne. He purchased it in the gift shop while I had gone to the ladies parlor. What a man!

While Paris has over one hundred forty museums, one of the most celebrated is *Le Musée d'Orsay,* formerly a train station transformed into a palace of art specializing in some of the finest impressionist and post impressionist paintings in the world. One of my favorite paintings is Edouard Manet's *Le déjeuner sur l'herbe,* a nude woman picnicking on the grass with two men elegantly attired. Her clothes are lying beside the basket of fruit and a loaf of bread. In the background, a woman is bathing in a pond wearing a long sheer dress without under garments. When François invited me to go to his company's party at *Le Musée d'Orsay,* I jumped on the occasion.

For the special corporate event, the museum was closed off to the general public. On the first level of the gallery, there were private viewings, lectures and entertainment by a harpist, violinists and a dancing ballerina. At the entrance, the guests were given souvenirs and a young lady walked around on stilts wearing a tall hat and a dress covered with credit cards dramatizing the height of the company's success.

After the Chairman applauded his employees for having issued over twenty million MasterCards, we met in an exquisite room for a *dinatoire* buffet with massive chandeliers and gold plated framed mirrors while being serenaded by accordion players. More than three hundred guests from different banks in Europe were in attendance. At the reception *extraordinaire*, I spotted an enticing display of candied apples on a sterling silver platter, probably more for the 'French touch' than for eating.

"May I take one?" I asked.

"Of course," the waiter replied.

A man standing beside me raised an eyebrow when I took a bite and said, *"C'est bon, n'est-ce pas?"* It's good, huh?

It was. And, as I watched, François mingle, I thought, *and so is my sweet French life.*

One early Saturday morning, François and I took the RER C fast train to visit *Le Château de Versailles*. There were so many extraordinary museums and monuments that captivated me but when I visited *Le Château de Versailles* outside of Paris, I was blown away. In late summer, the weather can be stifling in and around the city. Air conditioning is often insufficient in buildings and almost non-existent on public transportation. When we arrived at Versailles the long lines had already extended from the gate to the entrance. It was so warm everyone in the queue seemed to be agitated.

François chose the line for the "Hall of Mirrors" with deluxe chandeliers designed by the best French and Italian artists of that era. The rooms were transformed into pure opulence, and the splendor of the nobility was unfathomable. King Louis XIII used a small palace on the grounds as his hunting lodge. It was later enlarged by his son Louis XIV who held court and maintained the government on the premise. The Palace was further embellished in the 18th century during the reigns of Louis XV and Louis XVI.

After visiting the world-renowned Hall of Mirrors, we strolled around the magnificent Gardens and visited *"le Grand Trianon* where the royal family escaped from formal manners and stuffy behavior of the court." *Le Petit Trianon* was built for Marie Antoinette where "she listened to music, staged and directed plays" for her guests. When the French Revolution ended, the *Royal Palace of Versailles* became the "favorite residence of Napoleon."

Flabbergasted and mentally exhausted from the convoluted French nobility, on the way home we stopped at an ice cream parlor with sweat dripping from our brows. Raspberry sorbet and sweet biscuits made with violet flowers was the perfect way to cool down. Blurred by my total lack of knowledge of King Louis' dynasty, I promised myself I'd take a French history class but not before attending some lectures at the Musée du Louvre.

The novelty and fatigue of traveling back and forth to America had run its course. François was left behind in France while I had the pleasure of getting together with friends in Boston who couldn't wait to hear the latest gossip. We had become a bona fide couple and each departure brought heavy hearts for both of us. Because of that damn visa, I couldn't spend more than three months in France to be with my love. Something had to change.

A week before one of my return trips to Boston, François and I visited the *Jardin du Luxembourg* — a magnificent garden *à la française* with epic sculptures in the open air. That day the sun was shining brightly and a soft breeze carried the scent of gardenias floating in the air. We wandered around the formal garden, admiring the statutes of the queens of France, and studied the delightful faces of children taking pony rides. We spotted two rarely available lounge chairs surrounding a large pool in the shape of an octagon with meticulously cut grass and hedges. *Don't even think about walking on the grass and please don't touch the flowers!* We continued our walk to the magnificent Medici Fountain (French: la Fountaine Médicis) with four statues. The Medici family dominated Florence and Tuscany during the Renaissance. *Marie de Médicis*, born in Florence, Italy, was the second wife of Henri IV and became Queen of France in the 16th century. Tired of life at the Louvre Palace, she decided to have the luxurious Palace of Luxembourg built the day after the King's assassination. "It was rumored that she feuded with the King's mistresses in language that shocked the courtiers of France." During the French Revolution, the Palace of Luxembourg was used as a prison. Today it is the seat of the French senate.

Snuggled near the trees gazing at the romantic Medici fountain, a perfect spot for lovers, François suddenly leapt to his feet.

"Vernetia!" he shouted. "Are you in love with me?"

"Yes, of course I am." I replied stunned by his outburst. "Why would you ask such an absurd question?"

"I'm fed up living this way."

I had never seen him so agitated and I was surely his target. His voice was vibrating, his stare penetrating.

"Living what way?"

"Living apart," he complained.

"Have you forgotten I'm American?"

"No," he stammered. "I'm not an idiot! When you return to Boston, apply for a *carte de séjour*."

"What's that?"

"It's your right to stay with me in France."

"Is it like a visa or Green Card?"

"Yes!"

"Are you serious?" I asked trying to absorb the depths of his stunning demand.

"Of course I'm serious!"

"Perhaps I should."

"Perhaps?" He shouted in a gruff voice. Nothing I said mattered.

"It was simply a rhetorical comment," I responded dismissively.

"Perhaps it's time to call it quits. I don't think you're ready for a serious relationship," he said with piercing eyes.

"And I don't think you understand!" I snapped back. "You're the perfect man for me!"

Suddenly, I had a lucid memory of a former relationship with a man who had no guts and couldn't make a commitment if his life depended on it. He was well traveled with pockets of cash and never offered me a penny, nor did I need his tight-fist assets. I was very independent. The best part, he was convinced, was his weekend visits. On Friday evenings he'd arrive at my apartment in the countryside as happy as a lark and left his nest on Sunday afternoon as fast as a peregrine falcon. The confirmed bachelor came with a bonus. Twice a year we'd wine and dine in the Big Apple and went to see a ballet at the Metropolitan Opera. Did those escapades make me happy? Of course not! I was often too angry to express myself. What on earth was I thinking? Had I listened to my heart and been honest with my feelings, I would have said farewell the first time I caught sight of him. Nope. I convinced myself that I didn't have time to find someone else. Fed up with his bullcrap, I decided to take control of the situation. I needed a man who truly loved me and knew what he wanted, a decisive man with certitude like François. I didn't need some coward full of empty promises without the balls to make a home run. I needed a winner. My soft heart hardened and I left.

Having met François, a loving, honest and protective man, helped me face my fears to 'get on with it' and stop beating around the bush. The obstacles I confronted in life made me realize just how much I wanted and valued the chance to confide in him. It was not until I was freed from the shackles of losing loved ones that I was able to trust and love again.

François and I made a pact that I would return to America twice a year after I received my Carte de Séjour (Residents Permit) which seemed reasonable since I was not working and he was.

François clasped onto my hands, his eyes pleading at the Medici Fountain — a hidden gem for lovers. "What's it going to be Vernetia? Are you in this relationship for the long haul?"

Of course I was. I loved him.

14

CARTE DE SÉJOUR

The bureaucracy in France is mind-boggling! There are mountains of laws and red tape that make the wheels of government move at a turtle's pace. After François' outburst at the Médici fountain, I wanted to do everything possible to make this relationship work.

A Carte de Séjour is mandatory if you want to live in France for more than three months. I needed permission to request a Residence Permit from the Police Headquarters in France. The process began in Boston with a police background check, verification of financial status — the most important in my opinion — valid passport, confirmation of French residence, and a statement of purpose for the trip.

While I waited for a decision at the French Consulate's office in Boston, I sat beside a Chinese-American woman in the back of the room sobbing clutching her handkerchief.

I leaned in being nosy. "Are you okay?"

"I've taught English to French students in France for a year now and I'm stranded."

"Stranded? What do you mean?"

"I feel like a hostage," she cried.

"Why a hostage," I asked.

"They won't approve my visa."

"Why not," I asked dying to find out. After all, I was there for the same purpose.

"I don't know why. Everything in France is a big Freaking deal, even the simplest things like opening a bank account, renting an apartment..."

"NUMBER 1," the clerk at the window called out.

"Excuse me," she said reaching for the document that fell from her lap.

"NUMBER 1," the clerk called again in French.

"*OUI, OUI*" she responded.

"Good luck," I said and handed her a card with my telephone number. "My boyfriend is French and he lives in France. Maybe he can help."

When it was my turn, I gave the agent all the documents I had received from the French Consulate in Boston. I was told that the *Carte de Séjour* would not be as difficult for an American with a French boyfriend and a visa-D stamp. I believed the visa-D stamp might have given me some sort of entitlement. In retrospect I should have asked, but I didn't. I was a nervous wreck while the agent made the analysis. Fortunately, my request was processed without a glitch.

When I returned to France, I went straight to *La Préfecture de Police* with copies of my documents from the Boston French Consulate. François insisted that I carry any additional papers that might be deemed important. When I arrived, I sat in a nervous state of anticipation for almost three hours in an odorous waiting room surrounded by a multitude of foreign accents. I clutched my ticket in my sweaty palm worrying if I had everything I needed. Applicants were dismissed for one reason or another — We need copies of this, that, or the other.

When my number was called I uttered, "Have you taken the time to read my damn file that was sent directly from the French Consulate in Boston that addresses all of your questions?" I didn't say it out loud but I wanted to.

At each follow-up meeting, I left with a different interpretation. One agent asked for copies of ABC; another asked for XYZ. Some were impolite, cold, unsympathetic and unyielding. They seemed to enjoy the theatrics of applicants jumping through loops and hoops as if it were a staged performance. My number seemed to be the bad luck of the draw each time I had an appointment. I became angry and sulked while waiting. I skillfully parried a question or two rather than show any sign of indignation, but nothing worked. I was doomed and had had it. It was time to take matters into my own hand before it was time to get on the damn plane headed over the Atlantic Ocean.

I called the American Embassy, wrote letters to the French Consulate and the Police Headquarters. After waiting several weeks and no response, François intervened. Time was of the essence. He sent a registered letter outlining my frustration at each visit and signed it jurist (lawyer). Thanks to his swift legal intervention, I received my temporary permit to live in France before the deadline had expired. We slapped high fives and celebrated with a bottle of champagne over the victory.

Not yet over, but closer to the finish line, I needed to pass a medical examination. No big deal. I was in good health. When I received a letter from the OMI (*Office des Migrations Internationales*), the last hurdle in the process, I was beside myself.

"*Il est impératif de respecter l'horaire indiqué sur la convocation....* (It is imperative that you 'respect' the time indicated on the summons. And if you need assistance, you may bring one person with you the day of the examination.) I had been hearing the word 'respect' used with inanimate objects like one's time schedule and found it strange.

Golden leaves were trickling from the trees when I arrived at the Immigration Office with an hour to kill. I was alone, nervous, and calmed myself by walking around the neighborhood observing very old, contemporary, high and low buildings, crammed together. Clearly, this was an unattractive district without architectural innovative solutions. Before entering the building, I waited in line with my comrades outside and positioned myself on the top step near the entrance. I had learned my lesson from being trampled on at *La Préfecture* (the Police Office).

When the door opened, I was among the first group to be shoved in like the force of a bull inside the lobby. Many of my comrades were from former French colonies and didn't need a translator. François said that I shouldn't worry because most French doctors speak some English. Nevertheless, I was comforted by a man in front of me.

"Are you American?" he asked.

"Yes, I am. And you?"

"Dutch," he said. "I'm here as a French translator for my friend from New Zealand and I'm happy to help you if necessary."

"I visited Amsterdam several years ago," I said.

"Did you like my city?"

"Indeed. I still have fond memories of bicycling and eyeballing windmills, multicolored tulips and boat cruises on the *Amstel*. My studio was on the top floor of a five-story building without an elevator. It was barely large enough to turn around but the view of the *Amstel* Canal from my window was breathtaking."

As luck would have it, the Dutchman's name was called first and mine trailed. A middle aged, sullen faced woman, wearing a white jacket and plastic gloves, sat stiff as a ramrod on a stool behind a large sink. Small plastic cups were neatly stacked on top of the counter. Sinks and hand dryers were lined against the wall. From all appearances, the room may have been used as a men's restroom at one point. Across from me, I eyeballed Erik, the Dutchman, drying his hands. The nurse mumbled something to me, which I didn't understand. Nervous, I knocked the cups down on her working space. Flushed with anger, she growled, *"Donnez-moi un spécimen et faites attention, s'il vous plaît!"* (Give me a specimen and pay attention, please!) I went inside a booth, filled the cup with urine and handed it to her.

"Put it on the counter!" she yelled as if she wanted to throw it in my face.

My guardian angel turned to me and smiled. "Don't worry, she's just annoyed!"

She dipped a strip into my cup, and noted the results on a form. I looked at her and she glared in disgust.

"Allez à la prochaine salle et attendez à l'extérieur!" Go the next room and wait outside, Erik explained. Later a male nurse called me into his room.

"Est-ce que vous connaissez votre taille et votre poids?"

"Sorry. I didn't understand your question." I no longer had the Dutchman nearby.

"Do you know your 'hate and wait'?" he asked in English with a big accent.

"About five feet six inches and a hundred and ten pounds," I said.

"Oh La La, in centimeters and kilos," he grumbled.

He took out a measuring tape.

"Stand with your back against the wall," he said. *"Voilà,* now stand on the scale." The French numbers rolled off his tongue like an auctioneer.

"Can you give me the measurements in English?" I asked taking a gamble. I didn't want to know, neither did I care, but I wanted to engage in some form of conversation to calm my nerves.

"*Non,*" he shouted. "Madame I speak French! Now take a seat outside."

I did, thankful to spot Erik again. He exited from the rear of the dressing room. I entered in the front, drew the curtain, disrobed from the waste up and put on a Johnny. I wasn't accustomed to a unisex dressing room. It made me uncomfortable. A pleasant, but tired looking Asian woman called me into a room.

"*Inhalez, expirez, s'il vous plaît,*" she said, Breathe in, breathe out, please. "*Encore, Encore,*" Again, Again! It was a test for tuberculosis, which I never had, but wondered if some foreign microbes had mysteriously invaded my lungs.

"You can get dressed now and wait outside," she said with a perfunctory nod.

Later she called me back with a long list of questions. She furrowed her brows while she breezed through them as if she had discovered something.

"How is your health?"

"Very good," I answered nervously.

"When was the last time you had a chest x-ray?"

"About ten years ago."

"What was the result?"

"Negative, I believe. I don't remember."

"Have you had any chest pains recently?"

"No, I haven't."

"Have you had any operations?"

"A bunionectomy," I said. I wasn't about to divulge any unfavorable information.

"When was that?"

"Five years ago."

"Are you taking any medication?"

"Vitamins," I said.

"You're very thin!" The tone of her voice was alarming.

"It's my normal weight, plus or minus a couple of pounds."

"Do you eat three meals a day?"

"Not always breakfast."

"Are you stressed?"

"Yes, I am."

"Stressed about what?" she asked concerned.

"The medical exam today," I said.

"No need to worry, everything is perfect!" Finally, she smiled and my nerves calmed down.

"Stop by the receptionist desk and take your paperwork with you on the way out." In Boston, patients rarely have access to their medical records so I wasn't sure if I understood correctly. "And don't forget to eat breakfast," she said, sounding like my mother. I trailed her to the adjacent room and she called the next applicant.

En route to the Métro, a man honked his horn trying to get my attention. "It's Erik from the medical exam!" He yelled. "Good luck and enjoy your stay in France."

"Thanks so much for your help," I said and we waved farewell.

On the way home, I recalled a delicate topic that I wanted to discuss with François long before my appointment at the *OMI*. Now was as good a time as ever.

"I can't accept money from you any longer," I said feeling like a pauper.

"Why do you think that way? We're living together. I can give you what you want."

"Please understand that I very much appreciate your generosity, but I want to be more independent."

"As you wish," he said.

"I do wish."

The next day, I went to a French bank expecting to open an account so that I could transfer funds from my bank in America.

"*Fermé tous les lundis,*" Closed every Monday. I returned on Tuesday morning, dressed in a business suit which I had not happily worn since I left corporate America.

"Bonjour," do you speak English?" I asked the bank teller.

"Just a lit-till," he said. Even with the one liner I knew I was in trouble.

"*Your Carte de Séjour, s'il vous plait?*"

"I don't have it yet," I pleaded.

"I can't open an account without it."

Having learned "NO" in France is etched in stone and bending the rules is seldom an option, I spent the entire week running around to different banks and got the same answer. The banks insisted I needed a *Carte de Séjour* before opening a bank account and the *Préfecture* insisted I needed a bank account before getting my *Carte de Séjour*. My head was spinning like a ball on a ping pong table. François left work early to resolve the discrepancy.

"French laws are archaic," he argued with the teller while I looked on. "I opened a bank account in America in fifteen minutes with just my French Passport, and I was only a tourist. The bank even gave me a king size red, white and blue umbrella and a beautiful picnic basket for their appreciation."

"But you're NOT in America, Monsieur!" He raised his voice in defiance.

Ouch! Monsieur, Francois is going to ring your neck. I sat beside him holding my breath.

"You're rude and impolite," François disputed, his eyes spitting fire. "Let me talk to your manager. Perhaps he knows something about Customer Service. You don't!"

Nothing happened that day.

A few weeks later, when my *Carte de Séjour* arrived in the mail, I was elated and called François at the office.

"I'm being deported!" I exclaimed.

"*Ah bon*?" He laughed as I filled him in on the good news.

"*Félicitations, Ma Chérie.* Now you can stay with me in France! It's even more official now that you have a French bank account!"

"I'm on my way to the bank now," I laughed gleefully.

15
BIRTHDAY PARTY ON THE CÔTE D'AZUR

Aside from work, François rarely went anywhere without inviting me to come along and I was beginning to feel like part of the family after meeting his two sons. After I regretfully declined his Christmas invitation, François was overjoyed that I'd finally get to meet his parents and his two sons would be joining us. To try and make up for my deplorable mistake, I would offer them souvenirs from Boston — a can of famous Boston baked beans cooked in molasses for his Mom and a Boston Red Socks Cap and Jersey for his Dad.

A birthday lunch was planned for his Dad's 80th birthday. Just thinking about it consumed much of my leisure time. I had already exchanged a few words on the phone with his mother that delighted both of us, but his father didn't speak any English. I was very excited and also very nervous about meeting them.

The day of the departure, we took the TGV, which held the world's speeding record at 320 miles per hour. The sleek train left Gare de Lyon in Paris at seven a.m. and we arrived at the train station near his parents' home at noon. I had barely slept the previous night and had dark lines under my eyes from being mentally and physically exhausted. The flying train was crammed with vacationers who usually take a minimum of four to six weeks' vacation around the same time.

Towards the middle of July, Paris begins to clear out, leaving the city for tourists, and in August most places are closed. It can be so hauntingly quiet that finding a baguette or a bottle of wine can be impossible. Many travelers go to resorts or the countryside often without urban amenities. Were they craving a long vacation or holding onto a family tradition, fleeing the city to help with home repairs or summer harvesting, or was it simply the French way of life? Whatever the reason, French people seemed to understand the importance of reviving the body and soul in a hurry-scurry society.

The TGV was within minutes of departure and JO (Jean-Olivier) was not yet in sight. In a world exploded by the annoyance of mobiles, Xavier was always gabbing. He called his brother frantically. "Where are you?" he asked.

"*Je suis là.*" (I'm here.) "Tell Papa I'm on the train."

"Ok, we're in car thirteen!"

Moments later, JO hurried towards us lopsided carrying a small suitcase and two laptop computers, one for him and one for Xavier, while the whistling train pulled out of the station. Surrounded by his sons and his sweetheart by his side, François leaned back tickled pink in route to his parents.

Part of the journey, I sat across from François and stretched out my tired legs under his seat. I dozed off from time to time preoccupied with how things might be when we arrived. I tucked Barbara Johnson's tiny book *The French Way of Life* in my suitcase and read it on the train. "While eating, the wrist should be touching the table edge," a custom that may have originated in the Middle Ages, suggesting perhaps that someone seated with their hands under the table might be hiding a weapon!

François hadn't seen his parents in several months and there would be lots of embracing and catching up, and I would be conscious of having declined their Christmas invitation for what appeared to be for no good reason. However, there would be plenty of time to ask for forgiveness. I imagined a loving family with refined manners. François' Sunday dinners for special occasions served on beautiful plates inherited from his grandmother was a reason to trust my instincts. There would be freshly cut jasmine flowers, his mom's favorite, carrying a sweet floral smell, fine china and crystal adding a touch of elegance to the table. François is a bit of a highbrow and I've heard him remark on several occasions that people in general are not very intelligent, preferring to socialize in a refined class. And what could Ms. America contribute to the conversation? I could barely speak French and debates on television at rocket speed were incomprehensible, plus everyone mostly talks at the same time. I'd hoped the family vacation would be entertaining with easy interaction and I would be able to communicate with my limited French.

When we arrived in Cannes, one of the most prestigious spots on *La Côte d'Azur*, the weather was splendid. A soft breeze and rising sun cast a glow over the city, and swept the delightful smell from the sea straight to my nostrils. François walked with his arms around me, knowing that I was nervous. I had only gotten a bird's eye view of a coastal scene in Cannes which I framed and hung in my Boston kitchen so I didn't know what to expect.

While we walked down La Croisette, the main boulevard that runs along the Mediterranean Sea with palm trees, flower gardens and parks, I gazed at the prestigious Intercontinental Carlton and Grand Hyatt Cannes Hôtel Martinez. I'd arrived in Cannes where the immensely popular International French Film Festival was celebrated every year on the Red Carpet. The Mediterranean azure blue sea with soft sandy beaches was minutes from François parents. They waited for us at the door, smiling.

"Bonjour, Maman!" François hugged and squeezed his Mom while their faces lit up with pleasure.

"Bonjour Chéri!" Renée's happy smile was stretched from ear to ear when she reached up to kiss her son's cheeks in her tiny hands. She was more petite and more elegant than I had imagined from her photos. When I got a whiff of her perfume scented with fruits and flowers, I recognized it. François had given me a bottle of Hermes 24 Faubourg for my birthday. François was a striking image of his dad except he was taller.

"Bonjour Papa," he said slapping his back, hugging and kissing him several times.

"*Bonjour, mon fils, cela fait longtemps,*" said René. It's been a long time my son.

I stood to the side while they got acquainted with long hugs and kisses. Then François introduced me while he held my hand.

"Maman and Papa, I would like to introduce you to Vernetia."

"Vernetia, I would like to introduce you to my parents."

"*Nous sommes très heureux de faire votre connaissance,*" We are very happy to meet you Vernetia. "*Bienvenue à Cannes,*" Welcome to Cannes!

"Merci beaucoup Madame et Monsieur Duval," I said making a nervous gesture similar to a Japanese curtsy. When the formal greetings ended, I was relieved.

"*Où sont mes petits-fils?*" Where are my grandsons? His father asked looking around.

"They stopped to reserve motorbikes," François explained.

The boys couldn't wait to hit the Croisette on their motorbikes, hair blowing in the wind, bodies washed in sweat from the unprecedented sun. En route, they would stop at the beach, check out the pretty girls, and take a dip in the sea.

While François carried our luggage to the bedroom, I waited in the living room gaping around. Lola, a large white fleecy bundle of joy, came in to greet me and purred her way onto my lap. I shared the feeling of her contentment and began to relax a bit. Sophie, standoffish, displayed a fair amount of politeness. She strutted by me, meowed and went straight to the kitchen for the catch of the day served on a beautiful dish and returned under the bed. I glanced into the dining room and it was mostly as I had imagined. The table was elegantly dressed with a Mediterranean Blue Provencal tablecloth with large lemons, crystal glasses and a stunning set of plates.

Shortly after our arrival, the rest of the family joined us. They were dying to meet Miss America. François' beautiful sister Celine, a psychotherapist, analyzed every word I said. I was pleased when she changed the conversation to Buddhism and American jazz. François' grand-niece, Véronique, painfully shy, communicated with her large brown eyes. I glanced at her sitting off to the side sketching children bathing in the sea. Her mother, Madeleine, a French cosmetician, couldn't wait to test her English on me. At the table, I was the point of convergence. The conversation began with easy talk but I had difficulty keeping up. I wanted to impress them so I devised my plan of action. After an aperitif on an empty stomach, my apprehension vanished. I leaped into the conversation like a roaring lion.

"*Est-ce que 'tu' aimes Américains,* Madame Duval?" Do you like Americans, Mrs. Duval?

I was taught in my French class that if you don't have a good vocabulary use words you know for table talk bantering. One should never address an unfamiliar person with 'tu' if you want to make a good impression and show that you have good manners. 'Vous' is imperative unless you are addressing a child or have been given the authorization to use 'tu' otherwise you may be considered uncouth and not very savvy! François' mother gave me a puzzled look, not because of my informal use of 'tu' clearly noticing that I spoke French at a debutant's level, but my question in general surprised her. François came to my rescue.

"Maman, Vernetia wants to know if you like America, not Americans."

"I like both, America and Americans."

"*Est-ce que vous aimez les films Americans,* Monsieur Duval," I continued my leap with his Dad using my limited vocabulary.

"*Je ne l'ai pas bien comprise, mon fils.*" Deflated! — Son, I didn't understand her French.

"She asked if you like American Films."

"*Oui, oui, j'aime les Western avec John Wayne.*"

"Vous speak français not bad with an accent *charmant,*" his mother said mixing French with a few English words, boastfully displaying her bilingual dictionary.

"*Merci beaucoup,*" I said, smiling from the inside, indulging in the pleasure of great company at the table with exceptional French gastronomy.

Our lunch consisted of an assortment of seafood — *jumbo gambas, freckled crayfish with their heads still attached called langoustines; oysters on the half-shell served with lemon wedges and a mignonette sauce with red wine vinegar and shallots, fresh garden salad with arugula lettuce, jalapeno peppers, teardrop tomatoes, carrots, radishes, zucchini with basil and a hint of mint herbs.* The scent of the sea from the seafood, all salty and sweet, wafted up to my nose, making my mouth run water. *Crusty golden brown baguettes* — a part of everyday life had a kind of sweet and yeasty smell. After the meal, Madame Duval served an assortment of cheeses on a platter: *Brillat Savarin* a soft-ripened triple cream cow's milk cheese with a bloomy rind — named after a famous chef, Jean Anthelme Brillat; *Tourmalet cheese from the Pyrénées* made from sheep's milk with a smooth texture; a little jewel from *Loir-et-Cher,* a goat cheese with raw milk — named after its native township, salted and ashed with charcoal which gives it a sweet taste. François offered his parents a bottle of *Château Moulin de Parc Graves, 1992* red wine and a bottle of *Chateau Tronquoy-Lalande Blanc* — white wine from Bordeaux.

As our hostess presented our last dish, whipped *mousse au*

chocolat with puffy clouds of Chantilly cream, my smile widened. For more than three hours, I was in heaven, completely engaged at the table with well-bred gentle folks. And, yes, I remembered to rest my hands on the table's edge, which meant I was not hiding a weapon!

The next evening we celebrated René's 80th birthday at his favorite restaurant *Miramar Plage* with elegant plates and delicious pastas, or traditional whole fish — dishes for all tastes in a chic atmosphere facing the Mediterranean Sea surrounded by palm trees with a few close friends and family. René was all smiles with tears in his eyes sitting in front of a *legendary Paris Opera cake with silky coffee butter cream and ganache au chocolat* and the crackling sound of sparkling candles as we saluted him with lots of delicious champagne.

Bright and early in the mornings, François, his mother and I went to the caterers after she got all dolled up. Although she was in her seventies, she dressed like a fashion plate. I hadn't ever seen her without makeup and the scent of beautiful perfume. A variety of French fragrances were lined up in her bathroom. It was a joy sniffing and trying to get an inkling of the beautiful intoxicating oils and aroma compounds.

Every other day at *Le Traiteur,* (delicatessen) François and his mom chose mouth-watering French dishes for lunch and dinner, outrageously expensive! She always asked, and François insisted, that I try a new French dish at the caterer. I couldn't believe my eyes and was struck by the importance placed on dining. Food was always at the forefront of our conversations. Rosline — the maid, or *la femme de ménage* — usually arrived after we left for the caterers wearing pointed high heels and long painted fingernails.

My stares were discreet when she stood behind the ironing board all dressed up for work.

After a few days of family gossip, and me bonding with his family, François and I romanced on the beach laughing about everything and nothing. Sometimes the force of the waves landed me under the water but he assured me that my long Afro braids were beautiful. But I was in Cannes and naturally concerned about my appearance. I chased him out of the sea and massaged him with tanning lotion, feeling a bit strange lying beside two topless bathers. The beach was crowded but we found enough room to stretch out our towels with our large straw hats shading our faces from the sun. François turned onto his side and held my hand.

"So how do you like my boys?" he asked.

"They're both great," I said and he smiled so big I thought his face would crack.

One evening, we went to a hip nightclub. I was *démodé* (unfashionably dressed) and gawked discretely at the sizzling chic haute couture snappy dressers. François, blinded by love, thought I looked stunning, but I wasn't.

Another day, we spotted a shopping cart in a boutique window covered with mink. It stopped me in my tracks. "Oh, let's purchase one and go shopping!" François joked. Not believing our eyes, we took a look inside. *Quelle decadence*, I thought. How pretentious! This was definitely a store for the rich and famous.

We made our way to *Le Suquet*, the oldest neighborhood in Cannes, located at the highest point of the hill at Mont-Chevalier. Still standing is the residue of a Medieval Château built to protect the harbor and the coast. The *Musée de la Castre* was partially replaced with acquisitions and exotic collections from Asia, Africa and South America. The magnificent view from the "*La Tour Carrée*," overlooking the bay of Cannes, (*La Croisette* and *les Isles de Lérins*, Lerins Islands) blew me away and so did the wind! François and I toured the museum and the famous gothic church, *Eglise Notre-Dame d'Espérance*, dating back to the 17th century. We kneeled in the last row of the church and I gave thanks to the Almighty and François for protecting me far away from my homeland. I pondered if we were the souls of destiny or divine intervention.

I trailed François through a cobblestone passageway saturated with boutiques, small cafés, and restaurants panting while climbing to the peak of the hill. The panoramic view of the Riviera was breathtaking. Residents surveyed the crowds on the harbor beaches at twilight from their balconies.

The following day, we dined with the boys at the summit after spending the afternoon window shopping. We stopped to eat at a charming restaurant, 'Number 13,' the same number as the car we sat in on the TGV in route to Cannes. We may not have given it a second thought until we realized it was also Friday the 13th.

"Maybe it's a lucky number," JO exclaimed. "Play it tonight, Papa."

From that moment on, No. 13 followed us incessantly.

François' parents lived in Lyon where he was born before moving to Cannes. They enjoyed Biarritz and were passionate travelers of the French Riviera where they spent a number of years in Saint Maxime, Saint Raphaël and Antibes, a charming city located between Nice and Cannes with beautiful sandy beaches, also known for jazz festivals and dolphin shows. I wanted to see the seemingly intelligent animals perform so François made reservations. We sat on the first row mesmerized by the agile champions twirling in the air. One of them glided in my direction flirting with his catch. Late that evening we headed to Nice and spent the next day strolling and walking down narrow streets gaping at 18th century architecture. The center of town was buzzing with tourists dining at local restaurants.

The last day of our excursion, we visited Monaco, a metropolis for the filthy rich, where massive yachts were moored in the harbor. My favorite spot was the exotic Jardin Albert I, constructed on the side of a steep rock with literally hundreds of species of plants, renowned for its gigantic cactuses. The panoramic view of the French and Italian Riviera was amazing. Narrow paths descended to an enormous cave with stalactite rocks. Our guide quizzed us while we paused to catch our breath. François answered all the questions while the rest of us looked on dumbfounded!

Another treasure was *Le Musée Océanographique*, showcasing turtles, jellyfish, crabs, oysters and sea urchins. The beautiful creatures swirled around the huge aquarium like dolphins. It reminded me of my scuba diving weekend in the Caribbean, long before I met François, where I swam with fish in a world of serenity.

The extravaganza and jet set glitterati, apparent from the car one drove to how one dressed, was too flashy for François's taste. I was in awe, especially with all the strange accents.

"Where are your brothers?"

"Brothers?" he asked.

"French people," I said not hearing any familiar accents.

"This is not the French way of life. Most of the tourists are Italian," he said with a shrug.

Before leaving we paused at a slot machine at *Place du Casino* in Monaco where I gambled with a hand full of coins and left with the equivalent of "thirteen" American dollars.

The day of our departure from Cannes, François' Dad, Monsieur Duval, gave me a delicious box of Calisson, his favorite candy. Tears formed in his round, dark eyes and I could see the identical face of François staring back at me when he kissed me on both cheeks. I was delighted and sad! He returned to his room and brought out a coin collection from his grandfather.

"Son, I want you to have these," he said.

François' Mom, Madame Duval, gave me a beautiful gold plated bracelet and a box of French chocolates to each of us. François's grand-niece, Véronique, gave me the sketch she worked on during the week rolled and tied with a pink ribbon.

"Madame and Monsieur Duval," I said tearfully. "It was the greatest pleasure meeting both of you. Thank you immensely for your generous hospitality."

"Our pleasure as well and we hope to see you again very soon," said Madame and Monsieur Duval.

I leaned down to hug the painfully shy artist.

"*Puis-je apporter le croquis en Amérique avec moi*?" May I take the sketch with me to America?

"*Mais non,*" she said, hiding behind François's back. Keep it in France! She turned and tugged on my hand giggling "*Je te taquine,*" she said. I'm teasing you.

While the driver placed our luggage in the trunk of his car, François hugged his parents.

"Au revoir Mom and Dad, I will call you tonight from Paris."

The driver sensed our dilemma, the sadness that overcame the family, and reluctantly started the engine. François' parents waited on the curb in tears waving until we vanished. JO and Xavier stayed on with their grandparents for the school vacation.

In route to the Train Station to take the TGV back to Paris, the weather was picture-perfect, the hue of the cornflower blue sky cloudless, sun beaming.

"I think we should stay a couple of days longer in Cannes." I said.

"You think so?"

"Your parents are so special. It would be a nice surprise for them!"

"At Gare de Lyon, the ticket agent said I could change the tickets if we wanted to stay longer in Cannes."

"I know. That's why I mentioned it."

We waited in line for about fifteen minutes at the train station in Cannes. François told the agent he wanted to change the return date.

"You can't," he yelled.

"Why not," François yelled back.

"Because I said you can't."

"I was told in Paris that I could, so change the date or give me a good reason why you can't."

"Once you purchase your tickets, they're final! Sir, move on. You're holding up the line."

"Let me talk to your boss!" François yelled.

"I am the Boss!"

François and the agent caused a bit of a ruckus yelling back and forth. If the glass window hadn't separated them he may have given the agent a blow in the nose. I grabbed his arm. "Let's go before we miss our train to Paris!"

He pulled back and yelled to the Agent. "I'm filing a complaint. This is not the end of it."

"François, I'm sorry. It's my fault for asking you to change the tickets!"

He put his arms around my shoulders. "It's not your fault. He's a low level idiot who wants to play boss!"

François and the agent had an unquenchable need to battle with words. Still, I wasn't sure if I liked this side of François's personality that I hadn't seen. Then again, I may have displayed my anger by giving him my middle finger and walked away.

16

BACK IN FRANCE TO STAND BY MY MAN

Once I'd taken the plunge to move in with François and started a new chapter in my life, I returned to Boston to settle my affairs. The most important thing was finding a reliable person to manage the apartment. My health insurance in America could not be transferred to France, so I'd have to apply for Overseas Health coverage. François assured me that with time he'd be able to add me to his complementary insurance. After I'd arranged all the essentials, I called my best friend Jennifer with the news:

"I'm moving to France," I said nervously.

"You're moving where? Have you lost your mind? This is your home, your country! Your family and your friends are in Boston."

"But François is NOT!" I said, pacing.

"Then ask him to come!"

"That's impossible. He's working — I'm not!"

"You're making a big mistake my friend and you're gonna regret it. What in God's name are you thinking? You can't run away from home and move in with a foreigner. Come on now. You're smarter than that. Men will tell you what you want to hear especially on vacation. Stop gambling with your life. That's crazy!"

My spine went rigid.

I should have known she would have responded this way. I clenched the phone and bit down on my bottom lip, livid. "I'll live my life as I choose." I said and then paused, wanting to say, "Where's your sense of adventure? That's why you're an old spinster." But before those words escaped my lips, I slammed the phone down. I'd always wanted to give her a piece of my mind and now was the time. I'd had it and called her back.

"Why did you hang up on me?" She shouted. I winched in pain when she yelled, and then I let her have it!

"Shut the hell up 'Ms. Know It All' and listen for a change! I can't choose my family but I can choose my friends. Your boyfriend was not a foreigner and your relationship ended. And you have the *nerve* to tell me what's best for me? If you weren't so damn controlling, he may have asked you to marry him. Stop being a dictator and start being more supportive. Otherwise don't call me again."

"Fine," she said and hung up on me. My body trembled with anger.

For a brief moment, I thought maybe she's right. Perhaps it is stupid to do something so drastic. But the more I thought about moving in with François the more it became an obsession and I wasn't about to let my selfish friend, who couldn't mind her business, talk me out of a relationship that made me happier than I had ever been.

A week later I received a call from François and he sounded very strange. Something was wrong and I knew it immediately. Was he having second thoughts about us?

"What's going on?" I asked, highly strung from worrying.

"My mother is in the hospital," he said, his voice cracking.

"Oh no," I said with a gulp. "What happened?"

"The doctor said she may have had a mild stroke."

"Will she be okay?" His voice shook.

"They have to run more tests. Vernetia I couldn't bear it if something happened to my mother."

"Try not to worry, my love. She'll probably be better in a few days. Have you told the boys?" I asked. "Not yet. Xavier will be here any minute." The only thing I could do was talk to him on the phone and that was hardly sufficient. I tried to keep busy but I was also frightened. At the end of the week, François called again with more shocking news.

"It's Papa," he cried.

"*Oh My God*," I shouted! "What?"

"Papa is at the hospital with Maman."

"Good grief, I can't believe it!"

"Neither me," he said. "Papa had a bronchitis attack and is on a respirator."

What a nightmare, I thought and took in a deep breath. "Have faith sweetheart and try to be patient. I will pray for both of them." He was terrified having both parents hospitalized at the same time and I was so far away unable to support him. Our happy lives in brilliant colors had suddenly turned dark in a matter of days.

"Can you come, Vernetia," François asked, his words catching. "I need you by my side."

"Yes. Of course I can. This affects me deeply. Meanwhile please try to be calm. Perhaps you should see a doctor. He can give you something for your nerves." I paused in thought. "How long would you like me to stay?"

"*Toujours et à jamais*," (always and forever), he said.

Come what may, I knew we belonged together more than ever! There were a few urgent things that I needed to do before my departure and wondered how I would manage. I thought about my wise and dependable nephew who could solve any problem. Derek and François had become buddies after our night out on the town at Foxwood and long chats on the phone. He'd surely be saddened by the news as well. After hanging up with François, I called him.

"François' parents are in the hospital," I said, my voice cracking.

"Parents, he asked, both of them? Holy Moses, what happened?"

I rehashed the dreadful saga that would change our lives forever across the Atlantic. I hadn't imagined being faced with such a calamity after being on top of the moon.

"Don't waste time agonizing over the small stuff," he said. "Go. Leave a list on the table and I will handle everything. Remember I have keys to the apartment."

Derek was the most precious person on the planet. His penetrating eyes, contagious smile, and loving personality were a joy from heaven. Without exaggeration, everyone he met loved him. I'd never seen him angry no matter what happened. He was optimistic, positive and always smiling. When anyone needed help, he was the first to arrive.

Soon I was on my way to France with a choice of seats on a fairly empty plane with overzealous flight attendants fraternizing with the passengers. On previous trips, I was wedged between passengers with barely enough room for my carry-on luggage and now I had the luxury of stretching out in the center aisle with lots of pillows and blankets. I'd finally fallen asleep and was awaken from the noise and the smell of Italian pasta with mozzarella cheese. The food on the plane was often tasteless but that day it was delicious mostly because I had barely eaten anything for days. I was starving, worried and happy to be going to France to stand by my man. Before landing, the flight attendants handed out tiny bottles of wine.

When I boarded the shuttle for the main terminal where I would meet François, I had nervous sweats and chills from the cool morning breeze. Despite his aching heart, François was waiting for me with a bunch of yellow Mimosas carrying a lovely fragrance.

"The Mimosas are beautiful!" I hugged him tight.

"They are Papa's favorite flowers," he said with a melancholy smile.

We arrived at his home where fresh bread, jam and brewed coffee waited for me on the table.

"You sound much better now," I said.

"Of course, you're here!" he smiled.

Despite our fears, we were getting stronger and closer by the minute. It was my first relationship where I was given unconditional love and was treated like a princess. He needed me now and I wanted to do everything in my power to take care of him.

"We'll leave first thing in the morning for Cannes," he said with tears welling in his eyes. "Thanks so much for coming, Vernetia."

François said his grandfather on his father's side died prematurely in surgery. When he passed, his grandmother took over the family business and ruled Duval & Company with an iron fist. Years later, she transferred the company to their only son René, François' dad. When René retired, he sold the company and moved the family to Cannes. The Duval's thirst for traveling could not be quenched. Passionate about the Mediterranean Sea, every few years they moved to a different city on *La Côte d'Azur* and eventually settled in Cannes.

I'd avoided the topic of his dad's fate at the airport as I didn't want to upset him in public. Worry sparked his eyes when I asked, "Is your dad getting any better?"

"It's too early to tell."

That evening, he called the hospital again. The doctor had removed the respirator, which gave him a glimmer of hope. François didn't sleep all night dreading to find him suffering the next day. Around 3:30 a.m. in the morning, his sister called from Cannes.

"Papa has just expired," Céline said, crying.

I held François's head on my aching heart feeling his pain. He was distraught from his father's death and I was overwhelmed with sadness. I tried to be strong and fought back the tears. Although I did not know René very well, I loved him very much and second-guessed what I had and had not done. I wished I had dropped everything and taken the first flight from Boston instead of waiting a couple of days.

When François was able to express his feelings, I listened quietly to his heartfelt memories of his dad through a floodgate of tears. Then I talked about my special day with his dad. The two of us were alone at his home in Cannes while François and his mom went to the caterers. We watched a French film together but he mostly watched me with his round black eyes. I didn't understand the film nor did he understand my French, but we bonded just the same.

"How is my French, René?" I asked.

"Pas mal, pas mal," not bad, not bad he said with a smile, gazing into my eyes so happy to have me there.

While grieving intensely, François paced the floor aimlessly. *"Mon Dieu, Il nous a quittés. "* My God, he's gone. I'll never see Papa again. Why did the doctor remove the damn respirator?" He fell into my arms and burst into tears, his shoulders trembling.

Renée had returned home from the hospital but was too weak to attend René's funeral. What are the chances of meeting and falling in love with someone with the same name, Renée and René, with the same pronunciation? I learned from François that their names meant "Born Again." In the *Province de la Marche* members of his family were lawyers, judges and prosecutors. During the life of *François René de Chateaubriand*, a famous writer and politician from Brittany, René was an aristocratic first name. The name later spread throughout France and was fashionable in the 1920s.

With trepidation I decided not to go to the funeral and kept Renée's company at the foot of the bed while she dozed from a mild sedative. After the death of Virginia everything about a funeral traumatized me — the display of flowers around the casket, mourners dressed in black, and the heart wrenching music that can put one in a trance. François finally returned.

"How did you say goodbye to your dad, François?" asked Renée, tears sparkling in her eyes.

"Before the coffin was lowered, I handed out multicolored roses and placed the mimosas which you chose for dad on top of the coffin. I wished you had been by my side to say farewell. There was so much I wanted to say but in those last dreadful moments I uttered, "I love you so much, Papa. Thank you immensely for everything you've done."

Renée gripped his hand.

It wasn't an ordinary day or an ordinary funeral. The forecast had predicted rain but it turned bright and sunny with a cool sea breeze. The sky was a pale blue. The mourners returned to the house dressed elegantly in black to comfort the family. Renée was treated as if she was royalty and the mourners showed a dignified respect for condolences. François sat up all night by his mother's side to help her cope with the sadness.

The next day at *Le Cimetière du Grand Jas,* the heavenly gravesite on the French Riviera, François encouraged me to go since it would be a quiet ceremony for the immediate family. I sat in the back seat of the car next to him struck by the beauty of the landscape as we made our way up the hill with a view of the sea behind us. Wringing my hands in distress, I gazed out of the window behind a veil of tears.

When we arrived, the grave keepers met us at the entrance. Each lane is named after a flower. René was buried on 'l'Allée des Jonquilles,' the Alley with Daffodils. We prayed at the final resting place for our beloved, known for its landscaped architecture with rich floral decorations, fruit trees and oranges hanging from the branches. The cemetery is one of the most beautiful gravesites in the South of France with the remains of tombs of poets, writers, artists and dignitaries, including Lord Henry Brougham (1778-1868), Grand Chancellor of England.

I did not have the good fortune of spending a long time with René, but I quickly discovered that François was a mirror image of his dad and, I assumed, his grandfather. The parting ceremony at "Le Cimetière du Grand Jas" was both emotional and peaceful at the same time. I was pleased that I attended and could not have imagined René's departure without saying farewell.

"I am the only son in the family and I hope that I can follow in Papa's footsteps and not disappoint him in anyway," François cried.

"You don't need to be a clone of your dad. You are a wonderful man and I am sure he's delighted to have left you in charge of things."

Back at the house, François and I combed through René's memorabilia. Flying was his dad's hobby when he needed time away from the business. He left a small collection of model planes for François, which he loved. Like his son, René kept everything. As we sorted through his personal things, we made a delightful discovery in his diary.

Vernetia est une femme spéciale. Vous formez un merveilleux couple.
Vernetia is a special woman. You make a very lovely couple.

His tender words of acceptance warmed my heart more than
he could have ever imagined. François smiled for the first time in a
long time.

"I think Papa was preparing to leave us," said François, gripping my hand.

When we returned to Paris things appeared to be normal on the
surface, but they really weren't. We had now gone full circle:
ecstasy, sickness and death. Our life had been turned upside down
and it was difficult to cope. I helped François through bouts of
depression, which lasted several weeks.

François' depression radiated to me and I thought about my
father who worked very hard before his death, managing the
family business. He'd come home late in the evenings flat out
exhausted. Sundays were Papa's favorite days with his twins. Our
special day of the year was Thanksgiving when Papa helped
Mama prepare the Thanksgiving feast. For starters, he'd land a
sweet kiss on Mama's cheek and pinched her on the buttocks.
"Yum, Honey Bun I can almost taste the bird and we haven't even
started eating yet!"

The preparation was intuitive for Mama after years of
preparing fancy dinner parties. Yet, nothing pleased her more
than having Papa beside her in the kitchen for this grand occasion.

Mama made the best stuffing ever with homemade cornbread,
sausage, giblets, butter, onions, celery, sweet red peppers and fresh
herbs. The side dishes were fresh cranberries, sweet baked yams
and roasted Brussels sprouts. She would surprise us with dishes
we hadn't tasted yet. Mama would even stuff the big bird's neck

cavity. The brown silky rich turkey gravy made from the drippings was finger-licking good, and the aroma coming from the oven was a mouth watering delight. Papa looked like a master chef carving the turkey and loved every minute. He removed the string and placed the big bird on a carving board, cutting off the legs and the thighs first. He split the wishbone and put it on our plates and winked. "One day I'm gonna take my girls to Paris, but first we'll go to Fat City in Louisiana and practice Cajun French." Papa already knew a few words in French: *mes filles, Chérie,* and *ville de Lumière à Paris.* "What do you think about that, Honey Bun?" Mama just smiled showing her pearly whites.

Sadly, Virginia and I never made it to Louisiana or Paris with or without our parents. I wished from the bottom of my heart it would have happened. *C'est la vie!* I longed to reminisce more about my family, but François needed me now.

One day on my way to French school, I sat across from a handsome elderly couple on the Métro. The man was dressed flamboyantly in an elegant navy suit, a white shirt and a classic red striped necktie. He had an air of shyness, confidence and success. A dainty woman attired in an imperial red tailored suit sat beside him holding onto his arm. He stared at her adoringly with a loving smile. They reminded me in some way of François's parents. I imagined a high browed stunning couple sitting in the backseat of a stretched limo behind tinted windows sipping on a glass of Dom Pérignon and eating fine French chocolates. They were being chauffeured to *La Place Vendôme* that housed some of Paris' most expensive boutiques. Well to do, with unguarded resources, he would offer her an extravagant gift — a cashmere sweater with sequins or a string of pearls from *Cartier.* She seemed to be the kind of elegant and stylish woman deserving such indulgences while being promenaded around the posh square arm in arm, after having lunch at the Ritz Carlton. When I got home, I told François. He found my story laughable.

"Papa was not a pretentious man and neither was my Maman. He was very modest and would never have been chauffeured in a limousine to *La Place Vendôme* or anywhere else."

René had now been deceased for several months and the harsh winter had come and gone. Spring had finally arrived. It was the golden hours lying in bed enchanted by birdsong melodies from the lower branches while our French shutters kept out the bright light from the bedroom windows. It was the perfect *April in Paris* with sweet morning breezes. I even found the light rain delightful. Slowly things were settling down and François was gaining momentum. He was back at work and I'd go to the local library and browse through *French Vogue, Science & Vie magazines, Astérix bande dessinée Française* (comic strip books). François had all of them. I'd spend time strolling around in Paris, visiting exhibits, and I'd rush home before François arrived.

"What are you doing at the moment, *Ma Chérie*?" he asked me on the phone.

"I'm waiting for you to come home, my love."

"Would you like to meet me for dinner?"

"Of course, where are you?"

"Stand by the window!"

There he was looking up. He waved and threw me a kiss. He'd snuck out of his office early to be with his Vernetia. I watched him walk briskly over the foot bridge in front of the building carrying his briefcase and a bouquet of spring flowers. I rushed to the door perfumed in *Guerlain Champs Elysées*, and flung the door wide open.

"Peekaboo," I said.

"Coucou," he replied. "*Ahhhh...*You're here my one and only and you smell so nice."

"How are you feeling?" I asked.

"Things are finally getting better," he said grinning.

At dinner there was no mention of the past. We were on our way now — off to a new day and a new chapter in our lives.

17
THE SHOCK OF A LIFETIME

"Vernetia, can you reserve a time slot on your calendar for June 14th?"

"Yes, of course, what's up?"

"I'd like you to meet some old friends."

"Marie-Laure and Philippe," I asked. He often spoke of them.

For several weeks François had been overwhelmed with deadlines at work, dental appointments after work, and looked completely worn out when he came home late in the evenings. In America, one usually makes dentist appointments during office hours and I found it disconcerting. Nevertheless, meeting up with Marie-Laure and Philippe was a great idea and a nice break for both of us.

The week I was supposed to meet up with François' friends, I caught my first case of French flu while having high noon tea with our neighbors.

"Are you okay?" I asked the sweet young girl who snuggled up beside me on the couch coughing and sneezing.

"I was sick Monday, Tuesday, Wednesday and Thursday. She counted the days on her fingers. "*Maintenant, c'est bien fini.*" Now it's completely finished. She let out a hack and wiped her nose.

"I think not," I said to myself. "I'm going to sit in the armchair."

"*Bah non*," she said with a cry, "*Je ne suis pas contagieuse!*" Oh No, I'm not contagious.

A few days later I had a fever, sore throat, intestinal cramps and stayed in bed all day, my head pounding.

"You should see a doctor," François insisted.

"I should be fine in a few days," I said. Since I wasn't getting any better I took his advice. The doctor enjoyed speaking to me in broken English but I could barely respond with a throbbing headache. I left with a bag full of medicine and overdosed on Doliprane, the equivalent of Tylenol, and trashed the rest.

I asked François if we could reschedule our appointment.

"We still have a full week," he said. "Let's wait and see how you're feeling in a few days."

Miraculously, the day of our rendezvous, I was in great shape! Before leaving for work, François left a love note on the dining room table with Mickey — my adorable puppet that he gave me on his first visit to Boston — addressing me with one of my many nicknames:

"*Mickette, you looked so peaceful this morning. It was difficult to leave you. Please don't do too much, big kisses all day through.*"

Each time I dozed off, the phone rang. I didn't have the heart to ask François to stop calling so that I could get some Z's before our meeting in the evening.

"How's my *petit ange* feeling?" he asked, sounding perky.

Groggily I said, "The same as your little angel felt when you called an hour ago."

Finally, I fell into a deep sleep but was now awakened by the neighbor's two German Shepherds. The dogs were barking and howling like a gust of wind in the courtyard behind our bedroom window. As soon as Javert stopped, Julian began. It was not until they were vocalizing that their master intervened. I called François.

"You up?" he said surprised to get my call.

"The crazy dogs woke me up."

"Feeling okay?"

"I feel great! I may even attend my French class this afternoon."

"Have you forgotten about our appointment this evening?"

"Of course not, it's only an hour and a half."

"Please stay home and rest."

"How shall I dress tonight?"

"Dress smart," he said his expression for dressing up. "I will fetch you at 6:30."

"I can meet you in Paris."

"No. It's not necessary," he insisted. Surprisingly, after being awakened by the dogs from a deep sleep my mood was elevated. I stretched out on the coach and relaxed with a large cup of *Mariage Frères* green tea made with sweet spices, red fruits, vanilla, and I thought about how to "dress smart" for the evening. I opened my old closet and there it was straight in front of me, the last beautiful outfit Virginia was wearing before her departure — an elegant sleeveless satin blouse surrounded by ruffles in pale yellow, a pair of misty green colored silk pants and two inch heels in light green. My ensemble for the evening would be a happy reminder — a cream colored satin blouse with layered ruffles that extended around the shoulders, silk brown pants, shoes matching. I'd carry Virginia's clutch bag from the closet covered with sparkling gold fabric, and an eye catching gold chain that could be converted to a shoulder bag. Cherished memories of Virginia had me smiling while I dressed for the special occasion.

My straightened black hair with chestnut hues reached my shoulders with loose curls at the end. I gushed with joy in front of the mirror knowing Virginia would have given me a 'thumbs up' before leaving.

Precisely at 6:30 p.m. François turned the key in the door and entered. He stared me up and down. "You look beautiful *Ma Chérie.*"

"I'm excited about meeting your friends tonight."

"And I've got to get ready," he said. He kissed me on the nose. "I'll see you in a few minutes."

He brushed his teeth, changed into a beautiful suit and put on my favorite cologne. Then he grabbed a bag off the hook and slung it over his shoulder.

"You're taking your backpack?" I asked.

"Yep. Throw in a pair of ballet shoes. The weather is perfect for a night stroll." I was not comfortable stylizing in sky-high heels and he knew it. The few times I did my feet ached for days. We took the Métro and hurried down *Rue Marboeuf* near *Avenue des Champs-Elysées* with fancy restaurants and exuberant strollers. The blue sky and evening breeze gave me a renewed surge of energy.

"Are we going to be on time?"

"Of course," he said. "Don't worry. See that restaurant over there?"

"Which one," I asked.

"The marvel across the street," he pointed. "I'd love to take you there one day."

"It's gorgeous from the outside." I said.

La Fermette Marbeuf was a gourmet restaurant near Les Champs-Élysées Avenue in the 8th arrondissement of Paris. The Belle Époque (Golden Age) Art Nouveau "1900 room" at La Fermette Marbeuf had been an official Historical Monument since 1983. The Golden Age was a period of European history synony-mous with peace, and economic prosperity with many scientific and cultural innovations. The arts flourished in Paris and elsewhere.

"Let's take a quick peep inside," he said glancing at his watch. "We have a few minutes."

And so we did.

"WOW," I shouted. "It's breathtaking! It's drop-dead gorgeous!" After gazing around I went to the powder room to freshen up before meeting up with Francois' friends in the lobby of the restaurant down the street. When I came out, François walked towards me and reached for my hand.

"Your table is ready Monsieur Duval," said the *Maître d' Hôtel and he* escorted us into the formal dining room and seated us in a reserved private corner.

"I'm confused François!" I exclaimed as I took my seat and gaped at the magnificent baroque décor with stained glass and mosaic tiles. What a tantalizing work of art! "We're dining here tonight?" I was in a state of shock. "What about your friends?"

"Chérie," he said with a wink. "It's just the two of us tonight."

Surprises were not rare for François, but I was knocked for a loop as I fixed my gaze on the most handsome man in the posh dining room dressed in an elegant pin striped suit.

"Where'd you get that beautiful tie?" I said, leaning forward flirting.

"It's a gift from my Boston lady. I wear it on very special occasions. You don't remember it?"

"You two look ecstatic," our devoted waiter smiled. "Is a bottle of champagne in order?" After a long consultation, François chose one of the best bottles in the house. I sensed a bit of anxiety when he began blinking his eyes, rolling his shoulders and adjusting his tie. A fancy restaurant like this could make anyone edgy, I guessed.

"How are you feeling?" he asked.

"I couldn't feel more special Sweetheart. This restaurant really has class."

"You had me worried that I would have to cancel tonight."

After several glasses of delicious champagne, I began to feel topsy-turvy and giggled a lot.

"*Ma Chérie*," he spoke nervously. "I have known you more than two years now and I love you very much."

In retrospect, what followed should have been obvious but the alcohol had gotten me tanked and clouded my reasoning.

"And now," he proclaimed, "I would like to be committed."

"I thought we were committed!" I said with a laugh.

"Yes, we are but when two people truly love each other a permanent bond is the next bold and logical step."

Truth be told, I had always feared losing my independence and any mention of it deadened my brain.

He looked deeply into my eyes; his face was flushed.

"*Je te fais ma déclaration d'amour.*" I am making my declaration of love.

"Declaration," I asked myself not wanting to appear dense, "What the HELL is that?" In America, men go straight to the point and not beat around the bush with formalities: "Let's tie the knot baby!" "Wanna get married honey cup?" "Could it be that?" My jaws locked. My words froze. I'd never heard that expression before. *You're drunk! Go ahead and ask him what it means; who cares if you sound like a dunce.* "You are making what?"

"My declaration of love," he repeated. I'm asking for your hand, Vernetia."

"My hand," I stammered.

"Yes. May I have your hand in marriage?"

Shocked, I hesitated. Worried, he waited. After a few seconds of contemplation and intense exhilaration, I leaned in, bubbling over with joy.

My voice roared. "Yes, of course, my darling!"

"Really?" he asked as if he feared rejection.

"*Really, Yes, Yes, Yes, Really!*" The words rolled off my tongue.

He ran his fingers through his thick black hair, cocked his boyish face to one side and pushed his shoulders back. I hadn't seen him so relaxed in months. His face was aglow; his dimples reappeared.

"It will be wonderful having you for my wife. I want to spoil you and take care of you for the rest of our lives. I want you to be a part of my family, and I want to be a part of yours. The best part is we won't be separated again."

The waiter sensed it was the right time to intervene and placed the wine lists and menus in front of us. Tears rolled down my cheeks.

"Are you crying, *Chérie*?" asked François.

"Tears of joy," I assured him with a *sniff*.

After dinner and before the digestives, he took out a large bag from his backpack and placed it in front of me — the ballerina shoes for a night stroll was just a pretense!

"I don't know how it's done in America, but in France when we ask a very special lady for her hand, we offer her a gift." His smile broadened and my heart raced when I opened the large bag. Inside it I found a smaller one. I took it out carefully and admired it for several moments.

"*Allez, allez*," he said excited and impatient. "*Go on. Open it Ma Chérie.*"

My hand was unsteady while I took the red velvet box out of the decorative bag. François had been planning the surprise celebration for months and hadn't breathed a word to anyone, not even his mother. The stress that I sensed for weeks was not from his job or dental appointments; it was the stress of having to choose the perfect ring, the perfect restaurant and the uncertainty of not knowing if I would accept his marriage proposal and move permanently to France.

"I'm a very happy man tonight," he said, his voice cracking. My hand was shaking when he reached for it and put a stunning sapphire gem, surrounding by thirty sparkling diamond chips on my finger that he had taken from the little red box. My eyes nearly popped out of my head and my mouth flew open with excitement!

"*Oh my God,*" I giggled out loud. "François it's gorgeous; it's sublime!"

"I love you, my American Queen," he whispered and kissed me on the lips.

"I love you too, my French King."

Early the next morning, the florist delivered thirteen long-stemmed voluptuous red roses as soft as velvet. The card read: *Toujours je t'aimerai; toujours à jamais.* I will love you always and forever. He scooped me up into his arms and closed the door. "Love is an endless ocean, with no beginning or end..." A quote he had written in the card.

"François, when did you decide to ask for my hand?"

"The first time you left me and returned to Boston," he said.

I laughed. "What took you so long?"

"I know you are an independent woman and I didn't want to pressure you in any way; and when Papa died, it was difficult for me to make important decisions. There is one thing that breaks my heart."

"What's that?" I asked.

"Papa won't be around for the wedding."

"Would he have approved?"

"Absolutely, he would have been elated!"

When François asked for my hand in marriage, I was thrilled beyond words and I could not wait to share the news with my future *Belle-Mère* (beautiful mother) which defined Renée to a Tee. There was not an ounce of doubt in my mind that once we shared the news about our engagement she would be as excited to have me as her daughter-in-law as I was excited to have her for my mother-in-law. I knew it because we had already become the best of friends and she treated me no differently from François whom she cherished from the bottom of her heart.

Renée, Madame la Reine (Madame Queen) — I sometimes called her didn't like cooking very much after seeing her mom work tirelessly in the kitchen and never complained. Frankly, I didn't like cooking either so we had that in common. During our visits when *la cuisinière* (the cook) came to prepare the meals Renée would ask her to give me some cooking lessons. She would take me along to the open market to buy fresh ingredients for the meals. When we left, that gave Renée and François some private time together. François was a tad jealous and felt he was left out of our playful antics — but what joy we shared together.

When Renée realized the cooking lessons were overwhelming, she would give me a wink. *"Venez ma petite Chérie."* Come, my little darling. It's time for our French/English conversations. Then we'd go and sit on the terrace where our *goûter* (snacks) were waiting — a delicious assortment of dark and milk chocolates from the *chocolatier,* a glass of *Cabernet Sauvignon* (sweet wine), *Assimil* (a French bilingual French book), and we'd come apart at the seams cracking up laughing.

Renée was always loving and supportive. She understood our cultural differences and graciously invited me into her family and the French way of life. There was a "tug of love" between the three of us, but I was fortunate to be in the center of so much affection. As we expected, my future mother-in-law was thrilled with the news.

PART THREE
LOVING THE SWEET LIFE

"We are given a block of marble when we begin a lifetime, and the tools to shape it into sculpture...We can drag it behind untouched, we can pound it into gravel, we can shape it into glory."

— RICHARD BACH

18
RENÉE'S AMERICAN VACATION

For a very long time, I had been thinking about inviting François' Mom to America. She'd always made me feel as if I were part of the family and showered me with kindness. This would be a nice way to thank her for her extraordinary generosity. I asked François if he thought she might accompany us to Boston.

"Knowing *Maman*, I think she would go in a heartbeat. Her birthday is coming up.

Let's ask her."

In haste, I called. Her answer had me jumping up and down with excitement:

"When I was a teen girl, the boys American came to France in 1944 as part of the liberation force to save us from the German occupation. I had a pen pal *sympathique*. I felt love in Frank's eyes *bleu*. He invited me to *Amérique* to visit his *famille* but *mes parents* said *bien sûr que non* (of course not). A French girl had to be a fiancée before accepting such an invitation. It's my dream American. I'm very happy to go. What can I do?"

"You will need a passport," I said. "We'll take care of the rest."

We began to organize Renée's first visit to the land she

dreamed of so many years ago. Excited to share my American life with her, I arrived in Boston a week before François and his Mom to welcome them to my home. Madame Duval's first American vacation had to be extra special because she was a warm-hearted generous person and she treated me like family. When I landed, I sought my nephew's advice, thinking that my secret plan might be too outlandish.

"Should I have François and his Mom picked up in a limousine?"

"Heck yes! A Stretch I hope!" He let out a deep breath. "That'll be really cool."

"You're sure?" I needed to be convinced.

"Absolutely, auntie, please do it!"

"But I've never seen a stretch limo in France. It's an American luxury. The French prefer something more subdued, like the Mercedes Benz."

"When in America, do as Americans do. François read it in his guide, remember?"

"Call now Vernetia and stop wasting time."

And I did, only to learn from an obnoxious reservationist that it was graduation week and a stretch limo could easily run around five hundred dollars. I wanted to slam the phone down on Mr. Rude but hung up nicely. Although my wish was unsuccessful it made me even more determined. I combed the yellow pages and spotted an advertisement with a tall, cool looking dude wearing a chauffeur's cap, black suit, white shirt and necktie. He was leaning against the limo, arms folded, with an attitude.

"International Limousine Service, how may I help you today?" Within minutes, I was given a more reasonable price. Lesson learned: Never give up! Keep on trying!

After giving him the flight details, he said, "If you'd like, I can arrange a mini tour from the airport."

"How much will that cost?" I asked.

"It's free for you, Madame. We'll drive through the North End, Financial District and end up on historic Beacon Hill."

"Sounds great, but Madame Duval doesn't speak English."

"In that case we'll just have to send 'Madame' a French speaking chauffeur!" He chuckled trying to impress me.

"May I order a bottle of champagne?"

"It's included but don't expect French champagne, Ma'am."

"Perfect," I said, "Absolutely perfect."

A week later, I waited nervously at Logan Airport reading the flight arrival screen. The plane arrived on time, but it took them almost an hour to go through customs. When my guests walked out into the lobby, arms locked, Renée looked flabbergasted. I rushed over to greet them with big hugs and kisses and gave her a beautiful bouquet of spring flowers.

"*Merci, Ma petite Chérie!*" She said. I loved hearing my endearing name that she had given me in France. She tried to speak a few words in English but was too darn exhausted.

"*Je suis très contente de vous revoir.*" I am very happy to see you again. She clasped onto my hand.

When we got outside, I spotted a white stretched limo even longer than the one advertised. "Could it be ours?" I guessed. François and Renée were stunned when they saw the chauffeur posed against the limo holding a card with their names, and I was flabbergasted.

Surprisingly — though no one can ever be certain in New England — the meteorologist had predicted beautiful weather and it wavered by no more than two degrees. It was a picture perfect sunny day with a light harbor breeze. I took a few photos of them standing beside the limo with the chauffeur before leaving the airport. When we got inside François popped the bottle of champagne.

"*A votre santé et bonheur. Bienvenue à Boston*" I said. To your health and happiness. Welcome to Boston.

We tipped our champagne flutes. "*Cheers! Cheers! Cheers!*"

"How do you like our limo, *Maman*?" François asked.

"*J'ai l'impression d'être au Paradis,*" I feel like I'm in heaven. She sat between both of us squeezing our hands.

Maneuvering the narrow streets on Beacon Hill in a stretch limousine can be challenging. Performance requires precision moving back and forth. We held up traffic for nearly fifteen minutes while pedestrians gawked to see if we were celebrities. When we arrived at the door of the apartment, the chauffeur carried our luggage to the second floor graciously, unperturbed by the cars waiting to pass.

"Kindness matters," I said and gave him a generous tip, thrilled with our limo excursion.

For the next few days, we visited Boston's most important historical sites, which included the top of the Custom House Tower with a panoramic view of the Boston harbor, off limits to non-residents. The concierge, pleased to have an opportunity to practice his French, happily escorted us in.

We attended a wonderful classical concert at Boston Symphony and Jordan Hall. Renée especially enjoyed the intimacy of Jordan Hall, renowned for chamber music, yet large enough to accommodate a full orchestra. A passion for violin, she started playing at age seven. We attended a Tchaikovsky Violin Concerto at Jordan Hall and miraculously sat beside the Conductor's mother and exchanged contact information. After the awe-inspiring concert, she invited us back stage to meet her son who was fluent in French. When we returned to France, I received an unexpected email.

"It was a joy being at Jordan Hall with new friends who shared my appreciation for the evening. It doubled the pleasure! My oldest son whom you met is a Conductor and my youngest son is a pianist. He teaches at the New England Conservatory. Warm regards to François and his delightful mother. Perhaps we can meet at another concert. Let us know when you are in Boston again."

While Renée was in Boston she had a surprise visit from my nephew and his Japanese wife. Raymond was in Boston for a couple of days and was very anxious to meet her. A multinational businessman his schedule was hectic but he managed to find time. First we went to the most scenic part of the Charles River, a 10 minute walk from the apartment, gazing at the sail boats taking loads of pictures in perfect weather with a soft New England breeze. François said to Raymond, *Nihongo ga sukoshi dekimus.* (I can speak some Japanese). Meanwhile I spoke French with Renée like a Spanish Cow. It was like a comedy show on the bridge laughing like crazy. Then we headed over to *La Voile* for lunch, a popular french restaurant in Back Bay. The head waiter spoke French and a Japanese waiter spoke with Raymond. The staff was engaging and the French food was delicious. "Karai," Raymond cried. "The seafood curry dish is SO spicy it makes my eyes run water, but it's awesome!" Before leaving, Raymond and his wife Aiko gave Renée the bise and took a flight back to Japan.

Madame Duval loved Boston but the biggest surprise was yet to come!

New York City — like Paris — is one of the most visited cities in the world that gives immediate gratification. We told Renée we were going to Connecticut to visit friends. When referring to NY, we said the Big Apple, which means *Grosse Pomme* in French. When she heard that expression she didn't make the connection knowing only a smidgen of English. I spilled the beans a couple of times but weaseled my way out of it.

Enthralled by the American landscape and the Brooklyn

Bridge, Renée was in fantasyland. When we arrived at Penn Central Station Lavel, our New York pal, had planned an exceptional weekend. We strolled through Macy's annual flower show, lunched at a very old pub, and relaxed at our Marriott Hotel. That evening, he surprised us with a dinner cruise on the Hudson River and invited some of his family. At the onset of our departure from the South Street Sea Port on calm and gentle waters, we sat at tables with white tablecloths and long stemmed spring flowers. Cruising along, the boat rocked downstream. When François and I learned that the theme for the evening was *"April in Paris,"* we were on "cloud nine." The waiter came to our table, stood directly in front of Renée, and made an announcement.

Bienvenue (welcome) to New York City, Madame Duval.

We were lead into a Happy Birthday song while we saluted her with a flute of champagne. Everyone sang *April in Paris* and *I Love New York.*

Shocked, Renée turned beet red. After dinner, François and his mom waltzed around the dance floor and some of the passengers joined in. Soon the red sun dropped and disappeared behind the Manhattan skyscrapers. We circled Ellis and Governors Islands, cruised by the Brooklyn and Williamsburg Bridges, turned at the Manhattan Bridge and paused in silence in front of the majestic *Statue of Liberty.* While the lyrics of *America the Beautiful* by Ray Charles soared across the Island, the passengers joined in.

Hypnotized, I had tears in my eyes. Ms. Liberty held her torch high above the horizon and I gazed at her spellbound falling in love all over again with America. It was easy to imagine how the most magnificent statue ever constructed took twenty-one years for the French sculptor to conceive. Thanks to the genius of Frédéric-Auguste Bartholdi and the generosity of France, it resides on American soil.

The following day, Lavel gave us a whirlwind, hodge-podge tour, in his car giving us a taste of it all. Mad about NY, he took it all in strides. At some point of our convoluted tour on both the East and West side of Manhattan, we drove by Madison Square Garden, the Empire State Building, Rockefeller Center, Opera House and Carnegie Hall in no particular order, which brought back sweet memories along the way. Eventually, we purchased souvenirs from Greenwich Village.

On Easter Sunday we wanted to attend a Mass at Saint Patrick's Cathedral on Park Avenue, famous for its stained glass windows and organ, but the line was half way around the block, so we wandered down 5th Avenue, the most prestigious street in Manhattan closed off for the famous Easter parade. Dogs, cats, ferrets, gays, and straights were decked-out for the special occasion. Cross-dressers posed for the cameras wearing outlandish outfits; some had painted eggs propped on top of their Easter bonnets.

Late in the evening we drove northward across the Franklin D. Roosevelt Drive among robust magnificent skyscrapers and connecting bridges. Driving along 125th Street, we passed the renowned Apollo theatre in Harlem admiring the architecture where jazz and gospel music were founded. Renée was completely worn out and nodded off. In route to our hotel she was awakened from a symphony of horns and yellow cabs zigzagging in and out of traffic. On 42nd Street, the 'Buzz and Glow' from Giant Neon Signs gave the city that 'never sleeps' a feeling of explosion, engulfed with theatres, restaurants and the hustle and bustle of pedestrians. François sat beside me in the back seat singing the lyrics of *On Broadway*. His mom sat straight up in the front seat gazing out at the dazzling multicolored lights, her lifetime dream fulfilled.

Although spooked by the memory of 911, we wanted to visit the site of the fallen Twin Towers. "May God be with you," I sighed weakened by the sight of the Open Pit surrounded by construction. A tall fence held the visitors at bay but there was space between the boards to peek inside. It was a feeling of déjà vu all over again at Ground Zero when I watched the saga in disbelief on TV, the Internet, and listened to the radio at the same time in Boston. François watched TV across the Atlantic terrified of what might happen. I remembered the reportage of 'stabbings in the cockpit,' the 'falling towers engulfed with fire and flying debris,' the 'carnage from planes crashing into stone buildings.' Hundreds of observers were coming and going in an attempt to bring closure to an unprecedented atrocity. I read that "Our heroes were gone but not without a battle; our symbolic towers were destroyed but will always be remembered."

At the end of the two weeks' vacation, I took François and Renée to Logan Airport saddened to see them leave. I stayed behind in Boston to meet old friends and I interviewed a new tenant to rent the apartment before leaving shortly for France. Renée's broad smile radiated happiness when she thanked her *petite amour* a million times for inviting her to America and for celebrating *April in Paris* in the Big Apple, and then she gave me a beautiful gift of JOY — a French perfume by Jean-Patou scented with Jasmine and rose buds that she brought with her from France. She hugged me tight and gave me *les bises* three or four times on the cheeks teary eyed. François stepped to the side.

"You're the best," he said, locking onto my eyes. "I'll call you when we arrive and I'll see you in a couple of weeks. *Je t'aime. Gros bisous* (I love you, big kisses)."

I stayed at the airport until the plane left the ground.

19
MARRIAGE CEREMONY IN FRANCE

International marriages are not always easy with lots of flying parts but we hadn't expected a bureaucratic nightmare. Our Civil Ceremony was going to be performed in France and our Church wedding later on in Boston. Before leaving for America, François asked if I had read the French marriage requirements. Turned off by the size of the document, I left it on the coffee table for weeks on end thinking, *How complicated can it be for God's sake?*

There is a three-day waiting period in the state of Massachusetts to get married. You will need a birth certificate, passport or state ID, social security number, and a payment of fees ($50). In Texas, a person can get married without a birth certificate.

In France, the separation of Church and State laws require that marriages be performed by the French Civil Authority in the town where one of the parties reside. The law also mandates that the names be posted on the outside wall at City Hall no less than ten days prior to the religious ceremony or thirty days prior to the forty days required before the marriage is to be consummated. For good reason, I supposed. Imagine learning that the bride's fiancé or the groom's fiancée was already married or had committed a crime. I'd blow the whistle if I discovered such a dreadful thing. Other requirements include a form requiring two witnesses with their names at birth, spouse and profession, address, valid passport, and birth certificate. If one or both parties were previously married, and François had been, an affidavit of marital status and a judgment of divorce were required. It was a never-ending paper trail.

"Don't forget to bring back your birth certificate," François said.

"I don't have a birth certificate."

"You're joking?"

"No, I'm not."

"How could that be? You exist?"

"Yes, without a birth certificate."

François was dumbfounded.

In France, your birth certificate follows you from cradle to grave. Essential is the *Livret de Famille,* an attractive plush booklet about the size of a business envelope in warm colors (beige and red, eventually, in my case) with the French logo: *"Liberté, Egalité, Fraternité."* One's *Livret de Famille,* a meticulously organized family record for registering marriages, births and deaths, are the most important documents one has in his or her possession, as I would soon discover. When I returned from America, François and I went straight to City Hall with my documents expecting there might be a problem.

"Votre copie d'acte de naissance, s'il vous plaît."

"She doesn't have a birth certificate," François chimed in. "It was destroyed in a fire."

The receptionist gave him a distrustful eye.

"My fiancée and her twin sister were assisted at childbirth by a *sage femme* (mid-wife) and the certificates of birth were not filed at City Hall. Later there was a fire in the home and the records were destroyed."

"*Oh La La*," she said, mystified. "Then you will need a signed copy of our customized certificate proving one's identity and place of birth in America.

As instructed I took the customized copy straight to the American Embassy in Paris to have it embossed.

"I don't know why City Hall sent you to the American Embassy. You'll need to contact the state where you were born and ask for an Apostille to authenticate your birth with a seal," said the agent.

Ready to try anything, I gave the agent about sixty Euros and made a sworn statement in the presence of an officer and left with an American Embassy Seal on the document from City Hall.

It is possible to apply for a Delayed Certificate of Birth in America, which requires original documents, witnesses in some cases, or filing through a circuit court. It would take a long time and would be costly. Now that I was spending most of my time in France, we didn't want to wait forever to get married. I can't remember a time when my birth certificate was mandatory in America. A passport or driver's license — both of which I had — was sufficient.

I was born in a small town with relaxed laws, a place where nothing really mattered except a healthy baby, an extended family, and a moral compass. It was one of those lazy, remote communities, surrounded by beautiful patches of lakes, where fishermen tossed their rods from the banks for recreational pleasure. They would throw their catch of the day back into the water or share them with their neighbors to keep up friendly relations. The *whiff* from a 'fish fry' for special celebrations made your mouth water. A family birth was one of those grand occasions.

The following week we returned to City Hall with as many documents as I could muster from America to verify my existence: My American Passport, US Driver's License, Voter Registration Card, Social Security Card, American bank account, and my new French bank account — everything except my Birth Certificate. I also carried the customized certificate to prove my identity and place of birth in American, embossed with the French Embassy Seal.

"Bonjour, may I help you?" the secretary asked.

"We would like to get married." François was beginning to sound like a broken record. He spoke to a different receptionist this time.

"Your documents need to be translated in French," she insisted.

"The Office of Vital Statistics said a translation is not required in European countries with the Hague Seal," I said.

"*Calme-toi,*" François nudged my arm to keep me quiet!

"It's required in France." she raised her voice not appreciating my comment.

In August, when the marriage ceremony was supposed to take place, Paris was deserted. I managed to contact a French lawyer on her way to court and asked if I had all the documents I needed and if she could do the translation.

"Have you given City Hall an Apostille?" she asked.

"I have given them a signed copy of a customized certificate with an American Embassy Seal."

"City Hall needs an authenticated Apostille seal proving your identity and place of birth in America issued by a public authority that can be recognized in foreign countries as members of the *Hague Convention Treaty.*"

"I have written to the State government requesting an Apostille but have not yet received it."

"Then you need to be patient and wait," she said, her voice

serious. "I repeat, without it, you're wasting your time and you'll never get married."

"I'm fed up! It's too darn complicated to get married in France. It's a piece of cake in America."

"I can assure you I am quite familiar with American laws. I travel there for business purposes. It's time to remove those rose colored glasses in France," she laughed.

"Are you French?" I asked.

"Yes, I'm French, and I love my beautiful country but the bureaucracy can be a bit of a nightmare, especially for foreigners."

The frustration of running around and waiting for approval from *Le Procureur de la République* (Public Prosecutor) took all the happiness out of getting married. We pondered the idea of tying the knot in Vegas where we could get married the same day without a birth certificate. A government ID photo is sufficient.

No one gave a hang about my birth certificate in America but I felt like a suspected criminal in France. My missing birth certificate opened up a can of worms and I spent weeks exchanging emails with the state government and contacting family members to get sufficient data to create a "Delayed Certificate of Birth." Some of the facts may have been misinterpreted but I wasn't about to divulge any suspicious information. Come hell or high water, I had to get this done.

Racing against time, I decided to do whatever was necessary to find a solution and even embellished a few things. One sigh of relief was that in France I didn't have to raise my right hand and take an Oath of Allegiance and swear on a stack of bibles.

So help me God.

Eventually, I received an "Apostille" from the US Bureau of Vital Statistics certifying that they had failed to locate a record of my birth and would create a "Delayed Certificate of Birth" on my behalf from the data I had provided. The Minister of Foreign Affairs in France created a "French Birth Certificate" using the same vital statistics. Several months later, I received a letter from the Courthouse that read:

I have the honor of informing you that your Declaration of Citizenship has been registered. Please bring a piece of identification with you when you pick up a copy of your French Citizenship.

The Clerk at the Courthouse said she would be sending my paperwork to the French Minister of Interior and asked for a utility bill with both of our signatures, plus two pieces of identification. I had already given enough papers to convict a criminal, but I returned the next day with the additional documents.

"You should receive an answer within ninety days," said the Clerk. "A word of caution Madame, before receiving your citizenship you will have an interview and you must answer the questions and not your husband."

François had already given me a fifty-page document about the rights and responsibilities of becoming a French citizen and asked me to be sure and read it. Bored stiff, I left it on the nightstand for months thinking I'd have plenty of time until the evening he came home with a crazy smile stretched across his face.

"What's up my Cheshire cat?" I asked.

"Have you read the French citizenship document?"

"No I haven't. I set it aside. It's very long, it's in French, and it's boring."

"You should have read it by now," he said raising an eyebrow. Then he handed me a notice from the French Republic Minister of Interior with the French motto: *Liberté, Egalité, and Fraternité,* which read: *On May 17 2006, at 2:00 p.m., you are summoned for your citizenship.* I had less than two weeks to prepare for my interview at *Le Commissariat de Police* and panicked.

"This is great news, Chérie! You should be very happy. Don't worry. I will think of something."

A couple of days later François had written fifty brief questions and answers about the French revolution, what it means to become a French citizen, and why I wanted to become one, etcetera.

"Are the questions and answers in English?"

"I hope you're kidding!" he said.

Actually, I wasn't. I spent every day cramming the information trying to memorize it and François quizzed me when he came home in the evenings from work.

The Brigadier Chef (Police Sergeant) at the police station was as tough as nails in the interview. A fiercely brave woman with the zeal to dispute also showed her sensitivities to other's feelings.

When she realized I was a nervous wreck, she softened up a bit. François sat next to me as quiet as a mouse. After warming up and calming down, I regurgitated so much information and thought to go for the brownie points. It seemed a pity not to throw it all out there after having had so much difficulty keeping it down. At the end of the interview, which lasted an hour, she stood up and shook my hand.

"I am going to send your application to the Office of the President for a final decision."

"How long will that take?" asked François.

"Up to a year," she said.

"How'd she do Sergeant?"

She smiled for the first time. "Perfect! You have nothing to worry about."

When I got home, I passed out for a few hours from the stress. After waking up, I bolted out of bed and sang at the top of my voice as I smoothed out my clothing and hair. "Celebration now, Come on!"

"Not so fast!" François shouted.

"Let's wait for your official citizenship then we can party."

After I received my French birth certificate, I received my French citizenship, my French passport, and French identification card. François promised me a French poodle after becoming a

French citizen, which I now was. I thought about having to wake up early in the mornings by the dog's time clock and stopped barking. The gift of being a French citizen was doggone good enough.

August was hotter than it had been for years in France. Elderly people were dying from the oppressive heat and lack of air conditioning. Paris was in the midst of a *vague de chaleur,* a severe heat wave. We were sitting in a café, the only one open for blocks, near a tiny fan circulating warm air, when François's mobile phone rang. He spoke for a few minutes, looked up, and smiled.

"Our documents have been approved. We can get married now."

Relief flooded my system and turned into unbridled excitement. "We're getting married!" I yelled.

Moments later, the waiter put two small glasses of champagne in front of us and said *"Félicitations!"*

Five out of the six people in the café stood up and clapped.

An elderly woman — the spitting image of Jessica Tandy in 'Driving Miss Daisy' with salt and pepper hair pinned behind her ears — remained seated. She lifted her head and smiled.

"When's the Civil Ceremony?" she asked.

"August 12th," I responded.

"My granddaughter is getting married the same day in England."

"Are you a writer?" I asked, glancing at page after page of tiny lettering. I found French penmanship indecipherable from writing on thin lined graph paper in school at an early age, I imagined. I have yet to find notebook pads with normal lines.

"Not professionally," she said. "I quit school at age fifteen.

Since that time, I have been reading and writing religiously trying to understand everything I can about the bible. In the future we should be better informed about God's existence."

"Are you Catholic?" I questioned, figuring since she mentioned God it was okay to ask.

"My father was a Swiss Protestant; my mother a French Catholic and my grandmother scorned me. One day she said you're like an uncivilized dog. You've never been baptized. From that day on, I have been curious about religion. I want to learn more, but we cannot possibly know all the truth about God. And what about you," she asked.

"I'm protestant," I said.

"Being catholic is no picnic," François chimed in. "My soon to be wife and I would like to get married in a catholic church but it's forbidden."

"It's punishment for getting divorced," she said, her lips twisting into a grin.

After receiving the unexpected news, we had just ten days to prepare for the ceremony. Our friends, François's family and most French people were on their summer vacation. We stayed behind waiting for a decision.

François was very concerned. "We'll have to try and find two witnesses."

"Can't we just ask a couple on the street and pay them something?"

"It's not that simple. We must have documented proof with signatures. I'll call my cousin. Hopefully, he is still around."

François pulled out his mobile, dialed, and shared the news.

"*Félicitations,*" Henri roared with such joy even I could hear the phone call. "We'd be delighted to do whatever is necessary to welcome Vernetia in the family. It's wonderful news and the timing is perfect. My daughter and I are not leaving for the countryside until the end of August. We'll be your witnesses."

Later that afternoon, the secretary at City Hall called François and asked if we wanted to meet the mayor before getting married. I found the custom appealing and we accepted. A few days afterwards, the Deputy Mayor, specialized in International Affairs, invited us to her office. A meticulously groomed white poodle with dark oval eyes, short wet nose, a teddy bear face, sporting a pink bow tie and matching toe nails, trotted behind and sat by her desk observing. My eyes were drawn to the elegantly dressed perfumed woman in a flowered dress, beaded necklace and dangling earrings. On her right hand, she wore an exotic costume ring.

"Welcome to France." she said with charisma. "Your marriage vows will be a testament to the solidarity between our two countries." She gave instructions and answered all of our questions. Before leaving the meeting, much longer than expected, we had forgotten all about the administrative hassles that led up to the grand occasion.

The day before our wedding, I woke up terrified from a nightmare and panicked.

"What if he becomes a control freak after we're married and I lose my independence? What if I faint during the ceremony?"

François assured me that my fears were irrational and ridiculous.

"So what are you wearing sweetheart?" he asked.

A lump formed in my throat. I let out a gasp. Goodness Gracious, I hadn't even thought about it.

Finally, after all the stress, the big day had arrived when I would become François's bride. Henri arrived early and waited for us at the City Hall Square. He came on his motorbike all decked out in a fancy grey suit, white shirt and red bowtie. The ninety-year-old motorbike enthusiast was in his glory waiting for the soon to be bride and groom. Anna, his daughter, came with Champagne, her black and white greyhound, who waited in the car. He was not allowed to attend the ceremony. He sat on his hind legs by the window in the back seat staring out regally with an aura of aristocracy, ears standing straight up and his red neck collar matching his master's bowtie.

The Mayor stood behind the podium in the exquisite marriage room constructed in Neo-Renaissance style in the nineteenth century. My knees were shaking, my palms were sweaty and my feet were unsteady in my French high heels.

"Vernetia Smith," she asked. "*Consentez-vous à prendre pour époux François, Philippe, Jean, Charles, Duval?*" (Vernetia Smith, do you take François, Philippe, Jean, Charles, Duval to be your husband?) I stood mute and she paused.

"She can't hear you." François whispered, squeezing my clammy hand.

"*OUI,*" I said in a high-pitched squeaky voice.

" *François, Philippe, Jean, Charles,* Duval *consentez-vous à prendre pour épouse Vernetia Smith?*" (François, Philippe, Jean, Charles, Duval, do you take Vernetia Smith to be your wife?)

"*OUI,*" he answered loudly and proudly with noticeable confidence.

"*Au nom de la loi, je déclare que* François, Philippe, Jean, Charles, Duval *et Vernetia Smith sont unis par le mariage.*" (In the name of the law, I pronounce that François, Philippe, Jean, Charles, Duval and

Vernetia Smith are united in marriage.) The mayor stepped down from the podium and congratulated us, *"Félicitations, Madame et Monsieur Duval."*

François and I shared a delicious kiss and then the five of us headed to a lovely restaurant to celebrate our marriage. Once seated, Champagne wagged his tail, licked my hand and put his head on my lap. Henri delighted us with a sweet story about World War II.

"At the end of the Normandy landing," he smiled, his light blue eyes lit up with remembrance, "the American soldiers hadn't slept in a bed for thirty days. My wife and I were thrilled to offer accommodations to two American boys. They bought us Nestle coffee and we couldn't sleep all night. We haven't given enough thanks to America for helping to save our lives," he lamented.

"What a beautiful memory." I said.

"Oh oui, oh oui," he replied. "Oh, how I'd love to see Joe and Bill again."

"Have you forgiven the Germans?" I asked.

"Mais non! Mais non," he said. When his eyes welled with tears, I changed the subject to other things.

After lunch, Henri drove the bride and groom, the short distance home, in a seat rigged to his motorbike, honking his horn. Streamers trailed behind in the summer sun. François held up a *JUST MARRIED* sign in one hand and clung to Champagne with the other. I waved to the small crowd on the street with a bouquet of red and white roses.

Back at the apartment, Anna and the caterer had prepared an intimate champagne celebration. After having lapped up more than his portion, Champagne passed out underneath the table snoring. When the weather cooled down, we left for Venice and cruised along the winding canals on a gondola. While being entertained by an accordion player singing *O Sole Mio* we sipped on a glass of Italian red wine in the beaming sunshine and talked about a church wedding in Boston.

Not long after getting married, François, was anxious to start a new life with his American wife and have as many children as possible. Our dream was to have a daughter with long fat braids and we'd call her Virginia. François was deeply saddened when I was unable to conceive children. Prior to my life with François, I hadn't given childbearing much thought. However, I knew — without question — François would be the best father in the world and having children together would have been one of the greatest joys of our lives. Unbeknownst to me, François had been doing a lot of clinical research about childbirth. He asked if I would consider artificial insemination with a donor offspring. "*Ma Chérie,*" he said with tears in his eyes. "I'd do anything or pay any price to have a child with you." After reading the complicated documents, I got cold feet and declined.

Just thinking about the gorgeous children we would have had with tons of hair, I wished a thousand times I had given it a chance with beautiful images of Virginia.

20

MINGLING AT THE GALA AND
THE MÉTRO

The annual meeting for lawyers was held at the Chamber of Commerce in Paris previously named Hotel Potocki. It was one of the most famous *Hôtels Particuliers* (Private Mansions) in the 19th century and was owned by a family of exiled Russian counts. I arrived at the evening gala and climbed the expansive winding marble staircase, admiring the extraordinary crystal chandeliers and a medley of exquisite paintings, and waited for François.

There were about five hundred guests at the reception held in the grandiose ballroom. Wearing a chic outfit made from fine silk, I paraded in my French high heels. Most of the invitees were already there dressed in business suits but it was surely an elegant venue to strut in one's fancy apparels. I had all day to doll up for the event and hadn't gotten so many gawks since I landed in Paris. After an hour or so, I was bored to death. No one moved an inch.

"Is this a party or a funeral?" I grabbed François's hand. "Let's mingle!"

"But it's not the French way," he said with hesitation.

"Nor is it the American way," I groaned. "This is not my idea of having fun. I'd rather roost in the exquisite lounge. Ready? Let's go!"

He sighed as I dragged him across the room.

"My name is Vernetia," I said extending my hand firmly into a small group of strangers.

A distinguished looking gentleman asked, "You're American?"

"Yes, I am." I tried to disguise my accent when I spoke in French but it wasn't happening.

"What firm are you with?" a classy man in a black suit asked.

I smiled. "I'm not."

"So what are you doing in Paris?"

"Nothing," I said with a nonchalant shrug.

"How nice," said a female lawyer, taking it all in, and gave a snort of laughter.

But she wouldn't get the best of me. I raised my chin a little higher. "Actually, I'm a budding writer."

Her eyebrows lifted as if she were suddenly impressed. "Really, can I read you?"

"No, I'm still in bloom."

François interrupted, blushed and embarrassed. "It's my wife's first book."

An older gentleman with an air of clout and gravitas turned to François. "I like Madame's openness and humor. What a breath of fresh air." Our intrusion seemed to delight the guests. As François made his rounds, I decided to mingle some more, making conversations and a couple of friends along the way, including Noémie, a woman from Martinique. She was excited about teaching her new American friend a thing or two about the island and I was eager to learn.

"Martinique was discovered in the Fifteenth Century by Christopher Columbus and the official language of the West Indies Island is French. King Louis XIV acquired the region in 1674 and Martinique became an overseas French Departments in 1946.

Napoléon Bonaparte's first wife, Josephine was born in Martinique and grew up on a plantation that kept slaves. Napoleon divorced Joséphine because she had not given him an heir. He re-married Archduchess Marie Louis of Austria who gave him a son."

Noémie's contagious smile and island personality was so engaging I listened to every word while she reminisced in charming English about her family gatherings on the Island. "My bloodline can be traced back to a mix of African, Chinese, European, Caribbean and Lebanese roots," she said proudly. "When we were children, we climbed trees and picked oranges, mangoes, apricots, coconuts and offered them to our guests. In the mornings, my mother bought baguettes, piled us into dad's mini-van and drove us to our rented home by the sea. Our door was always open to family and friends. The islanders have become more individualistic, more European, but I try to maintain that spirit of openness that I have always loved."

"By the way," she asked. "Will you and François be around on *Quartorze Juillet*? It's Bastille Day and my Birthday! I'm going to throw a big bash and I'd love to have you at my party."

"We'll be there," I said, nodding my head enthusiastically, definitely."

She gave me her address and then we parted ways. François sauntered over and tapped his watch. "It's getting late!"

While standing near the door before leaving, a man with a strong Eastern European accent tapped my shoulder, touched my hair, and gave me his business card. François had gone to the cloakroom to get our coats.

"Call me sometime Madame," he said with a lascivious look in his eyes sizing me up. "I like your neck!"

"Strange fantasy you have." I said. "My neck is like an ostrich. Anyway, I won't be calling you. I'm married." I held out my left hand, bringing attention to the ring. "Would you like to meet my husband?"

When we arrived at Noémie's party the following week, the patio was packed. We immediately felt the warmth and synergy among the guests. You could hear the island band on the lawn for blocks. She rushed to the kitchen, offered us drinks made with guava, mango, papaya, served with scrumptious *hors d'oeuvres* and a blend of Créole spices.

"Generally speaking," she stated as I licked my lips. "We cannot live without spicy food and music. I grew up in a family of musicians. My father was a violinist and performed at Island parties and weddings. He taught us how to listen to music, especially jazz. Once he met an American saxophonist on the seaside. Later that day, he was at our home grooving and playing jazz with my dad. We learned to play the piano when we were children. One brother plays the guitar and the other brother composes music for a Caribbean band."

After dancing for hours, we dined on a spicy home cooked meal at midnight. A huge coconut cake in the shape of the Island was the dessert with flutes of champagne. The guest huddled around the star of the night and sang Happy Birthday in French and Créole dialect. We continued dancing non-stop until dawn to the pulsating Zouk rhythm of a drummer, a guitarist, and a soloist rocked the house. We returned home early the next morning ready to drop.

Although my life in Paris had taken a euphoric turn like making new friends, there were also some grueling days. Nothing is exactly what you hoped it would be when you arrived in a new city, especially in a foreign country and a different language. Lured all over Paris with an abundance of energy, the Métro was vital for making new discoveries. Like clockwork, it arrived every three minutes.

One late afternoon I met a gregarious French woman at the Métro whom I asked for directions. During our conversation, she asked if I could give her daughter English lessons. She talked for a while in broken English and we exchanged telephone numbers. She was a lawyer like François and said it would be nice to meet him.

"*Maman, avez-vous déjà appelé cette dame pour les cours d'Anglais?*" Mother, have you called that woman yet for my English lessons? Fleur, ten years old, as cute as a rosebud, was bewitched by my accent when I spoke French. When I arrived at her home, she would open the door beaming. After taking my coat, she asked:

"*Vernetia, qu'est-ce que je peux vous servir?*" What can I serve you?"

"*Maman,* " she called out. "*Pouvez vous préparer des biscuits et une tasse de thé pour Vernetia et servez-les dans de la porcelaine, s'il vous plaît?*" Maman, can you prepare some cakes and tea for Vernetia and use the China, please? After the first lesson, Fleur insisted on pouring my tea, breaking the chocolate into perfect squares, and served it on a fancy tray.

"Fleur has very refined manners for a young girl." I remarked to her mother.

"Yes, and she thinks she's Marie Antoinette."

Well into our English classes, Fleur opened the door and I sensed there was something wrong. I was thinking perhaps she might quit her English lessons.

"Vernetia, I need to talk to you."

"Okay, what's up? " She put my coat beside her on the sofa. Usually she hangs it up on the coat rack.

Looking at me straight in the eye, she asked, "*Pouvez-vous être ma grande soeur?*" Can you be my big sister?"

"But you have a big sister."

"*Oui*, but I would like an American sister too."

"You'll have to talk to your mom about that Fleur." I was astounded and lost for words.

"I've spoken to her already."

"And what did she say?"

"*Elle m'a dit que c'est vous qui devez décider.*" She said you must decide.

"I'd love to have a little French sister." I squeezed her hand.

Fleur grinned with dimples in the cheeks, hung my coat properly on the coat rack, and went straight to the kitchen to prepare a fancy tray with tea, chocolates and cakes and returned to the table smiling for our lesson.

"Next week can we go to *Le Zoh*?"

"The zoo?" I said with a wide smile.

"*Non, Le Zoh* and I will give you the names of my favorite animals in French."

"It's okay for you?"

"Yes, in English and in French, okay?"

"*Oui, Oui,*" she said, "*Parfait!*"

Cutting across the woods of Vincennes in a mad rush going home, I ran straight into a group of children strung together with a rope. A blue eyed girl with blonde ringlets, wearing a fat red jacket, let go and stopped me in my tracks. "*Faites attention*, she shouted, *s'il vous plait.*" While I pleaded for forgiveness, the rest of the children looked on bewildered. When it became clear that the person she had scolded spoke with a strange French accent, she dropped her head down, "*Pas grave.*" Don't worry she said in a gentle voice and all was forgiven. Walking away, I heard laughter and soothing lullabies from a distance and wondered what François would think of my little French sister.

Many of the Métro stations take you well into the art world of Paris. While riding on Line I to *Le Métro Bastille* it made my hair stand on edge as I watched the train, go around the bend, crossing over the *Bassin de l'Arsenal*, once excavated to fill the moat of the *Bastille Castle*. I'd stare out the window at *Les Bateaux Mouches* (the cruise boats) and pinch myself because that is where it all began at *Le Métro Bastille,* a ten minutes walk to my *pied-à-terre* when I arrived in Paris.

Another admiration was the pronunciation of the Métro stations. I'd repeat the names over and over again under my breath while riding on the train. It took forever to pronounce the stations more or less correctly, but it was a pleasure to behold the cadence of the language: *La Bastille* (LA BAH STEE-YUH), *Charles de Gaulle* (SHAHRL duh – GOHL) and *le RER* (AIR EU AIR) suburban train." *Oh La La*! So much to learn! Was it even possible?

Much of my inspiration came from people watching. I could easily create a story while riding on the train, but I quickly learned that if you smile at Parisians you don't know they may think you're insane. In America, people are easily approachable. They will greet you with "Hello" or "Good Day" in a friendly way even if you don't know them. French people are not as trusting with strangers and tend to cling together with family and friends they have known all their lives. But there were exceptions.

I was sitting on the Métro reading a book when a woman got on the train cuddling her immaculately trimmed poodle wearing a rhinestone collar and a sparkling blue vest covering the *café au lait* fluffy manicured coat. Mesmerized, I discretely watched but it was difficult to see the dog's face behind the bangs. She starred me down with her watery eyes yapping. Next thing I knew she was resting her head on my lap. *"Cosette, Cosette!"* Her master smiled and quickly took her back.

Considering there are more than 4 million passengers that take the Métro every day, which does not include the riders on the RER — the suburban trains — it is surprisingly safe. Most of the eccentrics are beggars trying to make some easy cash. Romanians carry boom boxes blasting music, evoking images of a love story while singing *Ne me quitte pas* (Don't Leave Me), an Edith Piaf favorite. Contrarily, there are many organized pickpockets working in teams in the Metro, asking questions or bumping into a potential victim to distract them, especially during the peak of rush hour.

One afternoon, I was sitting comfortably on the Métro when a middle-aged man, perhaps once gainfully employed, paced back and forth down the aisle begging. Having carefully chosen his audience, he bellowed out in eloquent oratory his political assessment of the world in exchange for cash. Clanking coins filled his cup to the brim. He was different from the freeloader the previous week with one foot all bandaged up sliding down the aisle on his rump. "I had a car accident and I can't walk. Please help me," he pleaded. Saddened by his pathetic story, I gave the cripple five euros. When the doors opened at the next station, he jumped up and ran to the next car to do his dirty tricks. François said it was a ploy to get money. The larger question for me was what choice do they have, being poverty stricken, uneducated and unable to find jobs?

Another day, I stumbled on a boy about ten years old at the entrance of the Métro pan handling. *"J'ai faim,"* I'm hungry, he pleaded in ragged clothes. I went to a concession stand and bought him a sandwich. "*Mo-ney,*" he insisted. When I walked away, he yelled: "*Mesquine pauv' conne,*" you cheap stupid bastard!

Another Saturday afternoon, I paused inside *Métro Châtelet* and listened to a beautiful chorus of accordion players and vocalists harmonizing pulsating South American tunes. While exiting the turnstile, a teenager forced his way behind me:

"*Est-ce que je peux entrer avec vous, s'il vous plaît. Je n'ai pas de ticket?*" May I enter with you, please? I don't have a ticket.

Usually the fare dodgers jump the turnstiles. I didn't mind one person sponging but suddenly another and another squeezed in. Reluctantly, I let them trail behind and muttered, "You Jerks!" Annoyed, I rushed out of the station at *Métro Franklin D. Roosevelt* and missed my connection.

"Excusez-moi," I asked a woman. "Where is *Place d'Iéna?*"

"Madame, you are on the *Avenue des Champs-Elysées.* You need to go back into the station, change at Line 9 and take the direction for *Pont de Sèvres. Place d'Iéna* is the second stop."

"Will I need a new ticket?"

"Yes, of course, or you can cheat and come with me. I am going in that direction. Pay attention," she insisted. "If you are caught by the controllers, you will have to pay a hefty fine."

Having displayed a bit of generosity with the earlier passengers, I accepted her invitation. I glanced around and spotted *les contrôleurs* in uniforms writing tickets. I backed out immediately and waited in line to purchase my own.

On my way home reading a newspaper, a tramp reeking of alcohol stood in front of me holding out a tin pail. I ignored him but watched him from the corner of my eye. Suddenly he grabbed my shoulder shaking it.

"I have no money, I'm sick, I'm hungry," he stammered. François warned me that I should never open my bag on the train. I held my head down and clenched my purse under my arm. Vexed, he stood in front of me and whacked my face.

"*Espèce de cinglé,*" You crazy fool! I screamed, staring into his beet red face.

"*Fait chier,*" Piss off, you shit, he responded, laughing and unzipping his trousers. Shocked, I took a deep breath and fled to another car, his maniacal laughter following me.

I'd had some weird experiences in and around the Métro, but on the flip side, I'd met some exceptionally kind people who went out of their way to give directions or answer questions. If you think their kindness may have been an entrée to making a French connection, think again. Parisians are often non-trusting and reserved. On a couple of occasions, I pushed my luck and ask if we could stay in touch, and was told *bien sûr* of course, but that never happened.

It's easy to meet people in America even on the train. Once I was riding the "T" in Boston with my legs crossed wearing my favorite jeans. On one side of my jeans a twirling branch with pink cherry blossoms ran down to the bottom of my pant leg. The color of the jeans was an electric blue. The woman sitting beside me commented:

"I love your jeans. They are very stylish. May I ask where you bought them?"

"In Paris," I said.

"Oh my, I should have guessed. I love Paris," cheeks dimpled, she looked amused. Oddly enough, we got off the "T" at the same stop and walked up the street together. As fate would have it, she lives directly across the street from me on Beacon Hill and owns the entire building. We've stayed in touch and she recommended an agency to manage my apartment. When I am in Boston we meet at Café Vanille, a Paris café on Beacon Hill.

"Have you met any of the neighbors?" she asked.

"Not really," I said. "I'm not around very much."

"Beacon Hillers are pretty snobbish. Get yourself a dog. It's a good icebreaker." Would an encounter like that happen in the Paris Métro?" I am willing to bet *Never*!

"Why are you so fixated on meeting French people, *Ma Chérie?*" François asked.

"I prefer the richness and diversity of different cultures."

Thanks to our mingling, we have a group of friends from various countries including France that we hang out with and have tons of laughs.

21

BORDEAUX VINEYARDS AND TOURAINE CASTLES

"There is so much more to see in France than Paris," François said, anxious to show me other places. The first on his list was Bordeaux, the most celebrated wine region in the southwest of France and the evolution of its history. He and his family once lived in Arcachon and the close proximity to Bordeaux gave him an opportunity to visit frequently. This was my first time, and I barraged him with questions. On one of his visits to Bordeaux with his parents, François ordered a coke-cola with his meal.

"How old are you young man?" the waiter asked.

"I'm almost seventeen."

"Coke is like medicine," he said. "Salute a small glass of fine French wine."

I was about to salute Bordeaux wines for the first time straight from the vineyards with Francois' friends, and I could hardly wait!

One of the best times to visit Bordeaux wineries is in the fall and you can walk in the vineyards and tastes the ripe berries of Cabernet Sauvignon, Merlot and Petit Verdot wines. François and I arrived for a long weekend in the small village of Saint-Germain de la Rivière. With roots more than two hundred years old, Clément's home was perched on an incline among a sprinkling of odd shaped houses. "Welcome to Bordeaux," Clément said, happy to meet me for the first time and to see his old friend again. Then he took a moment to show us around his residence inherited from his grandparents. The latest renovations included a modern bathroom and a giant Jacuzzi. Very low ceilings, fat wooden beams, and massive stone fireplaces in every room were the only things remaining from the past. Sprawling vineyards were visible from the naked windows, including the bathroom. "Beautiful place," François said smiling.

After getting acquainted with Clément and meeting his wife from Gabon, Africa, we ambled along for hours in the vineyard plucking sweet grapes from the vines. A haven of tranquility, I played with their poodle and meowing cat for amusement and waved to an occasional neighbor rambling down the road. At 1 o'clock sharp, we lunched for more than three hours and drank an assortment of fine Bordeaux wines. The centerpiece on the table was an amazing platter of *pied de cheval* — Number 1 huge raw oysters shaped like a horse's hoof, and a large assortment of French cheeses. We ate a long hearty meal with the sliding glass doors opened wide, the brute force of rain flooded the ground, and balls of hail came falling down. Suddenly, the evening sun burst through the sky leaving a magnificent patchwork of rainbow colors. Clément's wife and Gabonese family spoke with a strong French accent, but I managed to understand some of the lively debate, especially when her cousin made extravagant hand gestures like President Chirac criticizing the Gabon government.

On a lighter note, Clément's brother, the family comedian, recounted stories that were hilarious. Once his friend lost his job, signed up for unemployment, and needed to look for work while receiving benefits. He told the reporting officer that he needed a vacation.

"Don't worry," the counselor advised. "Come back when you're good and ready." "That would never happen in America," I laughed.

The next day Clément drove us to the picturesque village of *Saint-Emilion* located on the Right Bank. He informed us that "*Saint-Émilion* is the most prestigious of all the Bordeaux wine making towns with narrow medieval cobblestone roads on the slope of a hill." We strolled in the charming village, took pictures of the Eglise Monolithe, a 19th century church sculpted from a giant rock, and paused in front of an underground chamber on the street once used for wine storage. I asked Clément what were his favorite wines.

"The ones made here," he said. "*Saint-Émilion* wines are pleasing on the palate. I love the seductive quality of the merlot wines, the aromatics and the balance."

We continued our journey driving west to the city of Bordeaux and visited *Musée des Beaux-Arts* and *la Cathédrale Saint-André* reconstructed in Gothic style from the 12th to the 16th centuries.

Before taking the TGV back to Paris, we drank wine at a rustic pub, and lunched at an old fashioned restaurant, profoundly gratified with our exciting long weekend where we indulged in Bordeaux wine tastings and met Clément's beautiful African family.

When we got home, I stared out of the window while editing my manuscript. It was during the school break and most families had already left for their fall vacation — even the habitual joggers were not around. That glorious Sunday morning cast a magic spell and a griping enchantment. The room was relatively sunny and a soft breeze from the outside carried a faint odor entering my nostrils. The scent of Bordeaux sweet grapes on the vines entered into my consciousness. Serendipitously, I picked up the phone and called *Château d'Agassac* to satisfy my yearning, thinking I might even write a short chapter about my vineyard experience.

I spoke to one of the winemaker's assistants and bombarded her with questions about the majestic *Château D'Agassac* thinking François and I might visit one day. I hadn't expected to get so much interesting information:

She began by telling me that *"Château D'Agassac* is a breath-taking castle located at the gates of Bordeaux on the Left Bank of the Garonne River. We are committed to respect the environment by practicing sustainable cultivation of grapes, focused on the future. Nowadays we are one of the most famous *Haut-Médoc* wine estates." She said, "Our sole purpose for cultivating wine is to maximize pleasure and our wide variety is suitable for conviviality and hedonistic moments. We have 100 acres where the flora and fauna (plant and animal life) are preserved daily with passion and respect for the environment. It is a jewel in the Médoc region. When we arrive on winter mornings, a thick fog overlooks the 13th century Château and the beautiful park. It becomes almost mystical!"

"Why do wines have such distinct differences in taste?" I asked.

"It is due to the difference in climate, wine growers, the wine-making process and also the aging or wine blending. By force of nature, the Left and Right Banks have different characteristics and the wines are obviously different in color and taste. The main difference between the Right and Left Bank is the soil. On the Left Bank of the Garonne and the Gironde estuary (i.e. the tidal mouth of a large river where the tide meets the stream), the soil is mainly composed of varying thickness of gravels, deposited by the Garonne. These filtered gravels have heat and an accumulation power promoting the grapes maturation. On the Right Bank, there is a wider range of soils of varying composition: clay, limestone, sand and some gravel that have the property to capture and retain rainwater, giving the vines a regular water supply."

I asked if the Left Bank produces better wine than the Right Bank, and what is the best season for color, smell and noise.

"One Bank is no better than the other," she responded. "This is very subjective. Spring is when the flowers on the vines distribute fine and delicate fragrances. It's the nature awakening season, the return to life. Red is the color that we await with impatience. It announces our harvest time with deep and bright red in the skin of the grapes and the quality of a great vintage. The noise is like a wine melody when it flows into the glass. It is neither white nor red. It is provocative and melodious when the wine is at its peak, and it is more acute if the nectar is still in its youth." I was completely fascinated when she said "The smell of fall fragrances is especially breathtaking; the perfume floats in the air and fore-shadows the beginning of a serene harvest, a scent that mixes both the human fragrances of cool and misty mornings with the warmer, delicious scents of the sun. If only a moment, the perfume delightfully drifts into the air."

Before our conversation came to a close, she talked about "*la fête de la Fleur,*" the renowned Flower Festival.

"Every spring," she explained, "The Flower Festival celebrates the small, sweet flower blossoms in clusters carrying the hope that the entrance of the plants in the final stretch will lead to a qualita-tive and quantitative harvest."

"Madame," she added, "I'd like to invite you and your husband to come and bask in the romance of our fairy-tale castle, experi-ence the different tastes of wine, and observe the stages of our winemaking process. "It's like making love!"

After our trip to Bordeaux, François was anxious to take me to Tours in the Southwest of Paris, the oldest city in the Loire Valley with almost a thousand castles. He called our friend Patrick whose family lives in the region. He would be in Tours on vacation for a month in July and invited us to visit. I eavesdropped on the conversation, clapping my hands.

"Of course, we'd be delighted," said François. "Will you have enough room?"

"*Mais, oui,*" he replied.

"When shall we come?"

"Come when you want and leave when you want!"

Honoré de Balzac was born in Tours and called it: "laughing, loving, fresh, flowered, perfumed better than all the other cities of the world." Two weeks after our invitation, we took the TGV at Montparnasse Station in Paris and an hour and a half later we spotted our handsome lanky friend towering over the crowd under the sky filled with sun.

I'd first met Patrick at his African Art boutique near the *Avenue des Champs-Elysées,* where he boasted about speed walking to work from his apartment in *Saint-Germain-des-Prés* in less than thirty minutes. Passionate about music and art, his voluminous classical collection and exquisite pieces of African art flaunted his Paris apartment.

"Did you remember to bring your swim suits?" he asked.

"Yes, of course," François said.

"And you, Vernetia?"

"Oh, I prefer swimming in the nude," I said and he laughed.

We got into his father's vintage Jaguar convertible and drove down a windy road laughing and joking until we reached his home. Patrick opened an iron gate with the remote revealing the family's villa perched among trees guarding their privacy. The only thing in sight was a scattering of rooftops below the climb. I detected an air of pre-eminence from Monsieur Raspail, Patrick's father, when he greeted us at the entrance.

"Welcome to Tours," he said, his voice low and deep. "Have you visited the region?"

"I have," François replied. "This is Vernetia's first time."

We followed Patrick and his Dad to the living room with oriental carpets, antique furniture, and a hand woven tapestry hung on the wall. The vestibule near the entrance with soft lights highlighted sculptures and artifacts from Congo, Benin, Cameroon and Zaire. We paused to study them. The family was passionate about travelling to Africa. Madame Raspail, tall, slim, elegant with an affectionate smile, invited us to the living room and returned to her wheelchair. A large bay window opened to a magnificent view of wooded trees surrounding a large swimming pool. After lunch, Patrick took us on a tour of the property.

In the 18th century, the medieval city changed into a cosmopolitan region loaded with cafés, boutiques and art galleries. During the Renaissance, the *Loire Valley* was nicknamed 'the playground for Kings,' 'the Garden of France'...'laced with rivers and rolling landscapes.'

Our excursion in Tours began early the next morning eye balling fairyland castles with discernment. François was anxious to visit his ancestors — *Henry II, Aliénor d'Aquitaine and Isabelle d'Angoulême* lying in state — so we drove to the Fontevraud Abbey in Anjou, once the largest abbey in France. François flooded us with information about his ancestors. Patrick sensed that I needed a break from the history buff and asked if I were ready to leave.

"Would you like to drive home, Vernetia?"

"I'd love to!"

He handed me the keys.

"Vernetia you don't have a French license and it's a dangerous idea." François argued.

"Don't worry, my darling, relax!" I sped away, bull headed, hugging the curves while a gentle breeze lifted my Afro curls. I glanced at the speedometer vacillating between forty and forty-five.

"Am I driving too fast?"

"It's okay," Patrick said. I came to a razor sharp curve in the road and slammed on my brakes when I saw a stream of motorcyclists approaching. The force sent the car reeling and we nearly got rear-ended.

"Why did you break?" Patrick raised his voice. "You weren't driving too fast."

François was furious. "As soon as you can, pull over and give Patrick the DAMN keys!"

I drove on and the back seat driver pouted all the way home. I discovered later that the speedometer registered in kilometers, which meant I was driving at a moderate speed.

We returned late that evening to a lavish dinner and took our assigned seats at the table. I was delighted when the conversation shifted from Tours and the hairbreadth escape on the winding road.

Monsieur Raspail opened a chest filled with booze and served aperitifs with refined flavors. Denoting confidence and a sense of grandiosity, he boasted with pride at the table. "I have a doctorate in history from the University of Chicago. I'll always cherish those days in America. Unfortunately, I have forgotten my English."

He and François were in their glory reminiscing in French about the good old days in Chicago. Meanwhile, Patrick escorted me to the guest room upstairs with a large Jacuzzi tub. In the mornings, we watched Patrick from our balcony diving like a dolphin in the oversized pool of soft-hued blues that changed colors with the sun. François and I swam with him in the evenings. Patrick said he was seriously contemplating selling his African boutique in Paris and buying a ranch in Paraguay and wanted us to visit him if he did. It seemed far-fetched to François.

"What a dreamer," he said.

"I believe in making dreams come true. Look at me."

"I am," he said and then he kissed my shoulder.

Along with discovering the countryside with François by my side, my French life was getting sweeter and sweeter by the day.

22

EVENING CLASSES & MUSEUM LECTURES

I became even more adamant about improving my French so back to school I went. Elementary schools were used for adult evening classes in several districts in Paris. When I arrived for my French lessons, I could hear the children playing in the courtyard, delighted by their chatter and laughter.

In the classroom, instructions were carefully written in white chalk on the blackboard. Paper, pencils and crayons were neatly organized under the desktops. Books were stacked on small shelves, reminiscent of my childhood days at school. I sat in the first row so that I could stretch my long legs out and not crush them under the tiny desks. Adults were forbidden to enter the building until the children left, even if the rain poured down on our heads like the coldest of showers.

Evening classes organized by City Hall were not very comfortable but were surely the best deal in town. I felt guilty taking a seat from someone more deserving, but my suspicion was that City Hall cared more about students imparting French knowledge and less about their status or income. Initially the classes were large but a third or more of the students dropped out fairly quickly thinking the classes were going to be easy because they were 'dirt cheap,' but that was hardly the case. The teachers were very strict and the homework carefully monitored.

I attended a French conversation group for adults at L'ARC, an International Christian organization for developing friendly relationships with interactive activities. The membership was inexpensive and it was located in Saint-Germain-des Près, one of the most exclusive neighborhoods in Paris. The first thing one sees when entering the room is a huge world map covering one side of the wall and a smaller version at the center of each table, surrounded by participants from around the globe. The conversations were mandatory in French. When accents from foreign countries were incomprehensible, the French instructors intervened and made the translation.

At another school with normal size seats, I sat across the room from a tall, attractive student with an Australian accent.

"What are you doing in Paris?" I asked while waiting for the class to begin.

"I'm a dancer."

"Oh," I said surprised, "Where?"

"The Moulin Rouge," she said proudly.

"I've never gone."

She crossed her legs at the ankles. "You should. It's a lot of fun."

"Do you think my husband would enjoy it?"

"What man wouldn't?" she said with a twitter. "By the way, the name's Loren."

François had surprised me as many times as I have hairs on my head, and I was long overdue reciprocating. Loren and I secretly arranged a rendezvous one night when she would be performing at the famed burlesque club. I asked François to accompany me to a restaurant in the 'naughty red light district' of Pigalle where Ivy climbed the façade of the building. The interior resembled a country house in the middle of the city with a charming fireplace.

Loren reserved a cozy corner for two behind a red curtain. It was so small we had to squeeze in sideways. *Le Basilic* was her favorite restaurant in the district. I trusted her advice and we headed there.

When we entered *Le Basilic*, François had a brief chat with the waiter in French about the dark wood interior reminiscent of a Middle Age Castle. He found the restaurant charming with creeping ivy surrounding the door at the entrance. It reminded me of ivy ascending a brick enclosure that separated my apartment on Beacon Hill from the neighbors. I found it delightful and reminiscent of a garden climbing the wall, a sight to behold when I brewed coffee in the mornings and listened to French melodies. François said he hadn't eaten at the cozy *Le Basilic* before which pleased me even more.

"*Vous êtes des amis de Loren?*" Are you Loren's friends the waiter asked, sensing we needed a little pampering.

"We're in French school together," I smiled.

"She's a lovely lady," he said, leaving us with menus. "I'll be back in a few minutes to take your order."

Meanwhile François asked, "Have you got something up your sleeve Vernetia? Do I deserve all of this?"

"No tricks sweetheart; you've earned the right to be fussed over sometime. You always make our outings about me, so I decided to invite you to a fancy restaurant to say '*Merci*' that's all."

For the entrée François ordered *Risotte à la truffle noire* (parmesan cheese with black truffles) and I chose raw tuna, olive oil, lemon, pine nuts and mixed herbs. For the main course, François ordered *noix de Saint*-Jacques *avec pommes de terre truffée* (florentine golden scallops, spinach and cream sauce with truffled mashed potatoes). I ordered a *demi-magret de canard, sauce poive vert* (half-duck breast with green peppercorn sauce). For dessert, he chose cheese cake with fruit sauce and I chose a rhubarb tart. François ordered a bottle of *Lussac Saint Emilion* red wine.

Towards the end of our scrumptious meal, Loren stopped by

and poked her head in behind the red curtain dressed in a loose white shirt, tight blue jeans and introduced herself to François. Except for the sexy costume (I imagined), Loren was already in a performance mode and "Wow" did she look provocative! Her face was exotic and seductive. I couldn't imagine she'd need any last minute touching up. Even François mentioned she was gorgeous, which is highly unusual for him to express a remote attraction to another woman when we're together. He's too much of a gentleman for that. She looked like a pin-up girl with sparkling eyeliner, long extended eyelashes, shimmering smoky-colored makeup, hot red lipstick with a sultry look, and a smile stretched across her face — Was I meeting a different person? Loren was ready for the stage.

"Bonjour François!" She greeted him with a wide smile, flashing her pearly whites. "Here are your tickets for the *Cabaret*. I will see you from the stage tonight at the Moulin Rouge."

He stood up startled and shook her hand. "We're going to see you dance?"

"Indeed. My colleagues know you're coming so please introduce yourselves and have fun!" I fibbed when I hadn't mentioned that our dinner was just the beginning of a long evening and night out, so it came as a bit of a shock. François joked, "I can only imagine what she's going to look like behind all those feathers!"

At the cabaret, we were ushered to our seats with a center view of the stage where a bottle of champagne in a bucket of ice waited for us, dazzled by the dance troupe wearing rhinestones and sequins under glittering lights. While they danced, their bare breasts could be seen behind gigantic multicolored *peek-a-boo* feathers. During the performance, Loren kicked her long legs towards the ceiling synchronizing with the other topless dancers during the night. In the Nineteenth Century, the 'Can-Can' was outlawed for several years because of indecent exposure.

Le Basilic was the last time I saw Loren. We kept in touch for a short time but she had moved on to whatever she was doing and so had I. The last I heard she met and married a Frenchman and moved back home to Perth, Australia.

As for the dreamer, I registered for an "advanced" French class beyond my comprehension.

The professor allowed me to stay because she wanted to have an American perspective. There were six students — a Brazilian, a German, a Syrian, a Lebanese, an Iranian, and the faint-hearted Ms. America! Everyone, except me, had been living in France for years and spoke French fluently. They were there to improve their writing skills and enjoy the lively debates. Since I wanted to improve my French, I thought, "What the hell. Perhaps I will learn faster in an advanced class!" I quickly realized it was absurd. I tried to participate but it would have been difficult at any level while Ms. America was the brunt of the attack.

The Brazilian student, politically spirited, banged her fist on the desk after I introduced myself. "Bush's invasion of Iraq was not necessary. It was greed, plain and simple. His goal was to secure petroleum and transport oil to higher-price markets," she said staring straight at me. The mere sight of an American made her cringe. Outraged, she jumped to her feet, thrashing her arms and snapping her fingers, as if she wanted to dance the Samba on top of my head. "It's a crime he bombed Iraq and killed so many innocent people," she shouted. "I'd like to ring his neck." I cowered in my seat scared silly.

The second week, our assignment was to research leaders who played a role in the French Revolution: Lafayette, Robespierre, Saint-Just, Babeuf, Barras, Danton, Mirabeau and Napoléon Bonaparte. I was vaguely familiar with Napoléon and Lafayette and could hardly pronounce the names of the rest. Out of my element, I wished I'd studied European History in college. American History didn't help. François tried to coach me but I became frustrated and quit.

A glutton for punishment, I decided it was time for an even greater challenge. Letting go of my imagination — Art History at the grandiose Louvre museum was my mission! The moment I entered, I was happier than having horse manure to fertilize the garden. I arrived early and took a seat on the side. Soon, the lobby was packed with attendees waiting for the conference to begin. I carried a book but was too anxious to read it. I was eager to engage in some form of communication, but the lobby was so quiet you could almost hear a pin fall. The silence was unsettling. I pinched myself thinking, "You're naïve, a dame fool, or a stubborn mule." I was about to attend my first lecture at the largest and most visited museum in the world and I only spoke a smidgen of French. The Musée du Louvre was formerly "a royal palace where kings and queens lived and died, a castle that had witnessed grandeur, bloodshed from wars and terror." It was my greatest wish to be there! Museum curators, academicians, and cultural heritage professors spearheaded the lectures. The critics included Oriental, Islamic, African, Chinese, Japanese, American and European Art. Although my French was terribly inadequate, the state of the art overhead projectors for the best known works of art in the world, helped with my lack of comprehension.

Each week I was the first to arrive and became more and more intimidated, realizing I was in an exceptionally talented crowd. One night I put my coat on the chair beside me hoping someone would at least say *Bonjour* or ask to sit down." This might invoke a short conversation?" The silence among the large crowd seemed unnatural.

Excusez-moi de vous déranger, Excuse me for disturbing you an elegant woman asked. "Is the seat next to you available?"

Bien-sûr, pas de problème, asseyez- vous, s'il vous plait. Of course! No problem. Please, sit down. She asked me a question about Renaissance art and I froze.

Je suis très fatiguée ce soir. I am very tired this evening, I said.

Nervous, nothing about art came to mind. She gave me a half smile and opened her book. The following week, I spoke to another woman who sat beside me.

"*Avez-vous l'heure, Madame,*" I asked. I hid my watch under my shirtsleeve, which was my little trick for initiating conversation.

Bien sûr, of course. She gave me the time in French — end of conversation!

The next week, both women surprisingly approached me and we spoke softly in the lobby about American painters. I explained that the Museum of Fine Arts in Boston has a large collection of French Impressionists. From that point on, we sat together inside the auditorium for the lectures and became a friendly group of four women and one man. They were passionate about art history and had attended lectures at the Louvre for years. After a few weeks my vocabulary was slightly on the rise.

One evening, the gentleman in our close-knit group invited the ladies for a drink after class. When the semester ended Aurore, the first woman I approached in the lobby, became a dear friend. She still teases me about the first night we met.

Je suis trés fatiguée, she said cracking up. "I found your comment about being tired a bit strange."

I asked why no one talked in the lobby.

"The French are reserved," she said, "especially at the Louvre."

"Is it reserved or snobbery?"

"At the museum, both probably," she said with a shrug. She eyed the woman who always dressed like an art painting. "I believe she thinks she's an aristocrat and would not socialize outside of her class."

Before the lectures ended, I spoke to an usher who worked at the Louvre museum school. "Stop by sometime," he said. "It will break up the monotony. I need to improve my English and you need to improve your French." He joked about the snobs in the auditorium. I enjoyed his wit, but it made me uncomfortable. I didn't want to sound like a loud-mouth American. When he handed out the programs at the lectures, his persona changed — Restrained, Cold as a Granite Rock.

One evening he stepped out from his booth for a short conversation.

"Are you coming to Toni Morrison's lecture?"

"When is it?" I asked.

"Next week."

"Can I get a ticket?"

"The tickets are sold out but I suggest that you go early the day of the performance. With some luck, there might be a cancellation."

"Toni Morrison? I doubt it," I said.

I arrived an hour earlier the day of her lecture, only to find a huge crowd waiting at the entrance. I asked a woman in French if she knew anyone who might have an extra ticket.

"I'm American," she responded. "I don't speak French."

"Where are you from?" I continued in English.

"California. We are members of the Toni Morrison Society from different parts of America."

"I'm from Boston," I replied. "But I live in France."

"Oh my goodness, you are SO lucky. And you don't have a ticket?"

"Nope, I didn't know about the event until today."

"How could you NOT know that Toni Morrison was going to be at the Louvre?" She spoke as if it was the only interesting event in Gai Paris.

"Lillian," she called out. "Ask our boss if she still has that extra ticket?"

"I'm willing to pay whatever she charges," I said.

"That won't be necessary ma'am," she replied, handing over one. "The price of the ticket is sufficient."

While we waited for the big event, members of the society were very inquisitive about my life in Paris and my marriage to a Frenchman. One of them blurted out, "That's it! God willing I'm coming to France to find my soul mate. Life is too damn short."

We were the first to enter the auditorium and I sat fifteen rows from the stage. Soon Ms. Morrison entered wearing her signature scarf and the audience gave her a very long applause. She began reading excerpts from her novel, *A Mercy*. The story was moving and the Frenchman translator, who sat beside her made it seem like a ballroom dance. The fans went bonkers!

The morning of the Toni Morrison event, I rushed to WH Smith, a British bookstore, on rue de Rivoli in Paris and bought "The Bluest Eye" to have it autographed. I read it in English and wanted to try reading it in French. I asked François to join me after work with a copy of my manuscript. "What-if," I imagined. "Everything in life is unpredictable or has surprising opportunities." After the lecture, I had a chance to shake Ms. Morrison's hand and then I returned to the book signing area and found François waiting in a long line. Soon Ms. Morrison came out of the auditorium, sat behind a desk, and began autographing. I asked her assistant if I could leave my manuscript.

"That will not be possible!" She seemed annoyed that I would even ask.

Standing at the desk holding a bright red folder, Ms. Morrison looked up.

"Is that a manuscript you want me to read, perhaps?"

"Yes," I said with a quivering smile.

"Give it to my assistant," she said with a wink. "I'm looking forward to it."

I left the book signing desk with an autographed copy of "The

Bluest Eye" and was ecstatic that Ms. Morrison was going to read my manuscript. Several months later, I received a call I had not expected.

"This is Toni Morrison's secretary in Paris. She asked me to call and let you know that she is extremely busy, but plans to read your manuscript."

My heart leapt.

I waited several months for an answer before sending a letter to Princeton University where Ms. Morrison taught Creative Writing.

The response read:

"I can no longer read manuscripts. Once I open that door, it closes mine."

"Damn!" I yelled disappointed.

Back to square one.

23

FOR BETTER, FOR WORSE — BUT
A COLONOSCOPY?

T he drama began while eating a spicy meal at a Malaysian restaurant in Paris twisting with pain. My symptoms included vomiting, diarrhea, and acute abdominal discomfort. François insisted that I consult a specialist so I called my doctor in Boston.

"You might need a colonoscopy and there are some excellent gastroenterologists in France." Now, really, how many new brides want to ponder this procedure in the early months of their marriage?

The temperature was a sweltering 37° Celsius, 95° Fahrenheit, when I arrived at Bégin Hospital in the afternoon for a consultation in the Gastroenterology Department. The good news — only four patients were ahead of me. The bad news — all four were seated by an open window fanning rapidly to enhance the breeze. "How strange," I thought.

After sitting for a few minutes, I quickly learned why when water rolled down my face like a dripping faucet and I joined the group of fanners. When a nurse walked by, I leaped towards her like a froghopper and asked, "The air-conditioning is not working today?"

"*Il n'y pas de climatisation,*" she growled. There is no air conditioning!

Meanwhile the specialist came into the waiting room calm and unfazed. I was completed agitated and gasping.

Air-conditioning was not as essential in the past in France as it is today with global warming. There are hardly any heating and cooling ducts in old French buildings used for heating and ventilation to deliver and remove air. French style windows are hinged on the side and open inward or outward depending on the design; American windows slide up or down so it is easy to put air conditioners in the windows or have central air throughout one's home. Air conditioning is omnipresent in most American cities and it is necessary to carry a light jacket or sweater on the trains, buses, restaurants, and stores at all times. François has an aversion to air conditioning, but the summers are getting increasingly warmer. "No two ways about it," he said. "I'm getting an air conditioner next summer."

"That's wishful thinking." I thought. "But how in hell will it fit in French windows?" Air conditioning is still rare in homes in France but has been installed in hospitals and some buildings as of the 21st century.

Back to my strange rendezvous at Hôpital Bégin —

"Good Lord," I said standing up, "Get me out of this inferno!"

"Madame Duval," the specialist called out. "I'm running late but you're my next patient." Miraculously, a half hour later there was a burst of thunder and lightning flashing in the hospital window, the sky ripped apart, the rain came down in buckets, and a soft breeze swept throughout the waiting room.

"I'd like to schedule a colonoscopy," the Specialist explained.

The minute I got home, I called François at the office with the news about my consultation. I began by evading the real topic.

"Did you know there is no air-conditioning at Hôpital Bégin?"

"Yes, that's right. I forgot to tell you."

"The specialist wants me to have a colonoscopy but I'd prefer having it when it gets cooler. What do you think?" Suddenly I felt better after breezing through that — but not at all ready for the surprising argument that followed.

"You always want to change things!" he shouted. "You postponed our vacation in Great Britain because it was too cold, our trip to Spain because it was too hot. You only have to stay one night," he yelled. "Absolutely not; had you paid attention (referring to an earlier botched rendezvous attempt), it would have been finished already."

François' stubbornness had begun to emerge — "Why shouldn't I express my reluctance to have a medical procedure during a heat wave without air conditioning? Who knows, it could be potentially dangerous." I hadn't heard of a hospital in America without air-conditioning and I told him so. "You're not in America, Vernetia," he shouted. I furrowed my brow, clenched my jaw and looked intensely into his eyes and shouted back. "The rendezvous that needed to be rescheduled was not entirely my fault. I didn't know I couldn't take aspirins before the procedure."

PAS D'ASPIRINE, C'EST OBLIGATOIRE. "It was written in bold letters, 'You must not take aspirins.' Furthermore, the French is close to English, so there is no way you would not have understood it.'"

"Written, in large black letters," I yelled! "If it were so damn important you should have told me. You're French. I'm not!"

"I am not a mind reader; neither did you ask!" He yelled back, clearly not appreciating my comment.

That evening, François came home apologizing with my favorite box of dark chocolates. "I don't want to spend a night without you, *Chérie;* I'm simply concerned and want your exam to be finished."

Finally, he was back to being the François I knew and loved.

Sometime later, I checked into the hospital for my daunting procedure. François had an important meeting at work, so I went alone. Having been dismissed for taking aspirins, I knew my way around and was rather calm. Bégin is a military hospital with a very good reputation. My first contact on the ward was a male nurse. He was like a colonel, cold as the North Pole, and tough as a burnt steak. He made me so nervous I forgot my French.

"Can you speak English?" I pleaded with the Iceberg.

"No," he answered affirmatively without making eye contact. He went through a long list of questions:

"Have you taken any aspirins?"

"No," I said.

He growled, studying my chart. "Are you SURE?"

"Absolutely," I said trying to convince him. *Did he think I was stupid?*

"*Bon!*" he replied. "Your nurse will bring your things. *Vous avez une chambre privée et un ventilateur avec une belle vue sur les bois de Vincennes.* You have a private room and a fan with a beautiful view of the Woods of Vincennes.

He left me to my own devices. Soon after, another nurse approached me.

"Don't worry," she said. "Your procedure only takes about thirty-five minutes. The worst part is the two liters of prep you have to drink after dinner and before midnight. It's not so bad with a squeeze of lemon."

I asked if I could be the first on the list.

"That's not my decision," she said. "You can ask the anesthesiologist when you see him. I'll see you in the operating room tomorrow morning with your Specialist." she smiled and shook my hand.

The Chief anesthesiologist from Africa with an air of confidence came into my room and sat at the foot of my bed. We spoke nearly ten minutes about my life in France. I believed his visit was partially to distract my attention after reviewing my records from an American clinic where I almost croaked from an allergic reaction to pain killers. He rescheduled my appointment a half hour earlier.

"How's the lemon drink Ms. America," the night colonel asked. *Allez faire du jogging pour le Tour de France.* Go. Go. Keep moving! Get that drink moving in your system! He was as cold as an ice cube when he checked me in and now he had mellowed with a great sense of humor.

"You don't need to worry," the Specialist assured me after the procedure was over, "but you should not eat spicy foods again." She sat beside me on the bed and sketched my stomach and my colon. "I would like you to stay another night."

The last day, the specialist walked me and François to the door, shook our hands and bid us farewell. On the way out, I saw the night colonel in the corridor. He smiled and waved goodbye. The procedure for the new bride went smoothly and I sent the surgeon a thank you note in French:

Merci sincèrement à vous et à votre personnel d'avoir rendu mon séjour à l'hôpital agréable. I thank you and your staff sincerely for making my stay at the hospital gratifying.

Et voilà! François and I survived our first 'unromantic' experience, at Hôpital Bégin where I convalesced for two surprisingly pleasant nights.

It was time to bring the romance back!

François kept his promise to take me to England after the procedure to meet his British friend that he has known since their teens. Before meeting George and Charlotte, we spent a couple of days in central London, a short walk to Kensington's Palace. The first night we saw the renowned musical comedy, *Notre Dame de Paris*. The scene where hunchback Quasimodo held Esmeralda's dying body in his arm, while waiting for his own death, was heart wrenching. When Quasimodo sang *Your Love Will Kill Me* and *Dance, My Esmeralda*, I could not stop myself from crying. "At the heart of politics, France has always had some 'fear of strangers, of what is different,' as portrayed in Victor Hugo's masterpiece, published in 1831, when immigrants, bound for deportation, found shelter in *Notre Dame de Paris* and were forcibly removed by the police after the church doors were taken down.'" The stage manager made an announcement in the middle of the performance:

"I need everyone to leave the theatre immediately. Please go to the nearest exit."

François grabbed my hand. "LET'S GO." he insisted. "The IRA (Irish Republican Army) may be up to their tricks again." Forty-five minutes later, we returned to our seats. At the end of the musical, François purchased two CDs, one in English and in French. The sound track resonated in my head for days.

The next morning George and Charlotte picked us up at the train station in Ashford, in route to Deal, driving on country roads and through rolling hills. It was so inspiring I envisioned writing a tale about it. Driving on the wrong side of the road I sat behind George and next to Charlotte. François sat in the front seat beside him.

"Strange seeing you drive on the passenger's side, George!" I uttered.

"We'd all be dead if I were driving on the opposite side," he said with a laugh.

That evening George and Charlotte prepared a show stopping charcoal-grilled barbeque with salmon strips, swordfish and English chips, diced lemon and cocktail sauce. A whiff of the spicy barbeque sauce from the grill followed my nose. Later we feasted our eyes on a traditional *Banoffee* (bananas and toffee) — an English pie made with cream on top of a pastry shell and later a delicious French dessert *Le Marie Antoinette*, made with two pink macaron shells filled with rose cream and sweet raspberries. We ate our hearts out until the wee hours of the morning on the deck, indulging in the pleasure of French wine and champagne and saluted the bygone years that François and George cherished.

An awesome surprise to celebrate the great reunion waited for us — a 5 bedroom Cottage at the beautiful Leeds Castle in Kent, England!

A relaxed environment, François and I got out of bed leisurely in the mornings starring out at the castle grounds and the river from our bedroom windows. Black swans with long elegant necks, geese and ducks swam around in the castle moat. While some of George's family and friends were early risers and preferred morning strolls with cool breezes, François and I took delight in the room of our preference before touring the castle. An angler, George flung his rod and line into the river at the break of dawn hunched over in a chair with a sweater covering his shoulders in the biting cold. We watched him from our bedroom window on the second floor, unable to see what he used as bait when he caught two large carps and tossed them back into the water.

Most days around noon George, François and I went on our leisure wanderings, strolling around the tranquil grounds and gardens. Charlotte prepared dinners every other night at the cottage with delicious French wines, platters of assorted British and French cheeses and desserts, as well as an early breakfast or buffet style lunch. My favourite dessert was the crusty cherry pie straight out of the oven with English custard pudding on top.

One night en route to the "Oak on the Green" restaurant, George drove his car with Charlotte, François and I, and their family and friends trailed behind. In the pitch-black, I recalled the name of Stephen King's novella *Full Dark, No Stars*, wondering what it was about as we entered a code to exit the Castle grounds in the absence of any light. I felt uneasy because we could only see the high beam headlights which guided us. Upon our return, we had become accustomed to the darkness as we walked from the car to the cottage admiring a myriad of stars blinking in the full dark over the treetops.

In the evenings we lounged in the living room sipping a cup of British tea or having a glass of wine and talked about everything, including the history of the famous castle, years of solid friendships, vacations, Megan and Harry's step back as senior royals, the US election and Brexit. We got used to our friends British accents and even learned some expressions, like ace brill (that's really great), creamed and crackered (worn out) and dosh (money). From the outside walls of our cottage, we couldn't hear anything, except the sweet melody of birds chirping and fluttering around in the early mornings.

After our parting lunch, George drove us to Ashford to return to France on the Eurostar. Our romance was firmly back on track.

Our Italian friends in Boston boasted about the Amalfi Coast.

"Vernetia you and François must go to the Isle of Capri and the Amalfi Coast in Southwest Italy. Every nook and cranny of the beautiful coastline is romantic with unforgettable vistas, charming towns and dreamy beaches, with dramatic cliffs and sparkling-blue seas."

We love central and northeastern Italy with its winding canals, beautiful bridges and architecture but we hadn't visited the Amalfi Coast. Antonio convinced me that we could do it in a week.

I've always wanted to do something extra special for François because he never says no to any of my wishes. To the contrary, he's quiet about it and before I know it, it's right there in front of me. He doesn't put a price tag on anything. If he thinks I will like it, he will buy it sooner or later. Money is never the driving force behind his actions.

François and I have traveled to beautiful places but most have been historic and cultural. Now I want to surprise my hopeless romantic with an idyllic vacation to keep the spark burning, and this is how I will do it:

Step 1: Have him clear his schedule.

Step 2: Decide how to reveal the secret.

Step 3: Convince him to pack his bag.

The vacation will require some very clever planning. While there is nothing François enjoys more than surprising me, he does not like being surprised. JO has a gift for convincing his dad to do unusual things so I'd have to get him involved. I will go to a travel agent and work out the details. We will stay at a classy hotel suite for a week and be catered to like a king and queen. May is the best month to visit the Amalfi Coast, with perfect temperatures, lush blooms, and few tourists. Hoping when all is done he will be shocked and estatic and I would say for the first time, *"Gotcha,"* with a big smile on his face — *n'est-ce pas?*

24

CHURCH WEDDING IN BOSTON

One crisp morning, I woke up early all pepped-up and searched the Internet for airline tickets to Boston. It was the perfect time to plan our spring vacation, and, perhaps a *real* wedding. While pondering I thought, *you'd better be damn sure you're ready to do this because François will never forgive you if you chicken out at the last minute.*

Out of the blue, the church wedding bells I'd always dreaded became vivid in my mind. With sudden invincible courage, I convinced myself that it was the right thing to do and I called Old West Church in Boston to schedule a date to get married. The ceremony would take place following the Sunday morning service.

Ever since our civil wedding in France, François pressured me to have a church wedding. It was not as important for me but he would never be satisfied until we marched down the aisle together. He wanted to reaffirm our love and commitment with God's blessings. Each time the conversation arose, I cringed. Planning a wedding across the Atlantic would be nerve wracking, I surmised. And my biggest fear was — *What if no one shows up after all the preparation?* François assured me if we were the only ones present at the church wedding it wouldn't matter.

We were both fond of Old West Church. It played a major role in American history and it was there that "No taxation without representation" was phrased. The magnificent organ was considered to be one of the finest of its genre. Prior to the Emancipation Proclamation, Old West Church was a safe house for people escaping slavery on the Underground Railway. Tourists came from afar on Sundays and the parishioners were always welcoming. The history of the church and the intimacy of the congregation were the things we admired most about attending.

I was a novice at this and needed François's guidance, but first I would have to tell him what was going to happen. He was having a great day at work and was in a wonderful mood so if the conversation didn't go well, I could always yell, "April fools!"

"Sweetheart," I said, approaching him gently. I poured a small glass of vodka, setting it in front of him. "I found some attractive airline tickets to Boston for our vacation."

"When's that?"

"I will leave May 15th. You'll come June 1ˢᵗ."

"We're not leaving together?" he said with a growl.

I shrugged. "I need some time to settle a few outstanding affairs."

At times I had mixed feelings about keeping the family's apartment in Boston with the headaches and expenses of managing it from a distance, but I couldn't imagine not having a base (my own space) when I had my fill with France. Additionally, François loves Boston and when he retired we could spend three months in the US whenever we wanted to. He was ambivalent about becoming a US citizen so that timeframe seemed to be sufficient for both of us. But this dilemma occurred when François was still working and I needed to go a couple of weeks in advance to make the marriage arrangements at the Methodist church that we both enjoyed while visiting Boston.

"By the way," I said, wondering just how he'd respond. "I called Old West Church and booked a date to get married."

"Is this an April fools' joke? If so, I don't think it's very funny," he retorted.

"Would I kid you about such an important matter? I'm very serious my darling."

"Really?" he said, blowing out a sigh of relief. "That's fabulous! What brought this on so suddenly?"

"Well, if you think it's too soon," I said, ribbing him, "we can put it off a few more years."

"Goodness No," this is the best news I've heard since our civil wedding! Let's have dinner out tonight sweetheart and celebrate this grand occasion!" Before darkness fell around us, we headed over to our favorite restaurant near home.

"Yes, Old West Church. Great choice, Vernetia," he said, leaning back in his chair excited. "I like the intimacy of the church and the people are always welcoming. There were never more than forty people each time we attended and they made a big fuss over us the minute we arrived."

"The Church is available on Sunday, June, 14th," I explained. "I'll need to meet with the minister beforehand and make some preliminary plans."

"No problem, do what you must my love bug! I'm shocked that we are finally getting married in my favorite American city. I can't believe it!"

"In many ways it's like planning our civil wedding in France," I said. "Once we set our date to get married, I thought about the good times ahead and became less frightened."

"I remember it all too well my little worry wart. I was never afraid to marry you, worried perhaps that you might say no, and neither am I afraid to marry you again. I'm thrilled. What a fabulous idea. When did you make these grandiose plans?"

"Today," I said.

The waiter interrupted. "You two look happy — May I get you a bottle of bubbly?" My eyes locked onto François. At the same time, we both said, *"Oui."*

When I arrived in Boston, I hit the pavement running. My first appointment was with the new minister of the church, whom we had not met during our previous visits. He was a charming African American man, statuesque and very slender. His large black eyes bulged when he joked with a contagious laughter and his dry humor was similar to my Frenchman. He kept me laughing during the meeting. We talked about some personal things and we had a lot in common. He was definitely not your typical pastor.

The rest of the week, I ran around exhausted. I popped in to the caterers, shopped for a wedding gift for François and a dress for the wedding. François wanted me to wear a long gown with a train. It took some time to convince him that I preferred a simple, elegant dress. I hadn't mentioned my chic white silk suit with splits in the jacket that I carried from France, but each time I tried it on it didn't look right for the wedding. By the end of the week, I found time between appointments to poke my head into Macy's and Lord and Taylor's. Hanging on a rack as if it were waiting for my arrival, I spotted a dress that caught my attention.

"Incredible," I said to the saleswoman. "That's it!"

The cream satin beauty covered with hand stitched lace was gorgeous, but I hadn't notice that the cut of the dress made me look emaciated until I tried it on at home in front of a large mirror. I fretted over it for hours and decided to wear my white sexy suit with splits in the three-quarter length jacket from Paris.

After a Sunday stroll, I took a short cut across the Boston Public Garden and headed home. From a distance, I heard a saxophone playing *My Heart Will Go On*. I was deeply moved and sat down on a bench in splendid weather and listened with interest while the saxophonist played with a jazzy groove. A small crowd gathered around her in the garden. The lyrics made me ache for François. At the end of the performance, I asked if she played gigs at weddings.

"Gigs, sorry, I don't understand," she said.

"Are you French?" I recognized her accent immediately.

"Yes, I'm in Boston since a few months."

"Would you play at my wedding?"

"I played never at a wedding," she replied.

Before leaving with my pleas, she reluctantly agreed. Life was on.

Meanwhile back in France, François was as happy as a lark making rapid plans. Some I was privy to and others I was left out completely. François is a pro at making surprises, so I knew things were in good hands. He designed the wedding invitations with our wedding bands, Old West Church and its history. In the interest of time, he notified the invitees via email and asked for an immediate response. He was so elated he hadn't realized that he was doing most of the planning on his side of the Atlantic. We invited thirty-five guests, plus members of the church.

Still not satisfied with both outfits hanging in my closet, I made time to continue looking. François knows I have a conservative streak and reminded me that it was a once in a lifetime decision.

"Buy what you love regardless of the cost," he convinced me. "You should be the most beautiful bride in Boston."

Had he not insisted, I may have avoided Sax Fifth Avenue. I saw lots of beautiful gowns and evening dresses but I hadn't noticed any in white. The saleswoman brought out a classy, cream-colored beauty that had just arrived in their new summer collection. I fell in love with it immediately. François may have preferred that I wear a long wedding gown, but I believed wholeheartedly that he would love my beautiful dress.

"It's swimming on me!" I said forcefully to the saleswoman.

"I know, but how glamorous! When's the wedding?"

"Next week," I said.

"Oh my goodness, that's cutting it close. But don't worry. I can order it from our headquarters in New York and you will have it in two days."

"How do you know it will fit?"

"It's my business to know," she said with conviction. "This is a size four and I'm certain a size two will fit you perfectly."

"Size two, are you kidding?"

"These are our designer dresses and they run on the larger size. Anyway, we can make the alterations here at the store if necessary."

I wrote a fat check and prayed that the she was right. Two days later, just as Sax promised, UPS rang the doorbell around 10:30 a.m. I was happy and nervous opening the over-sized box. I threw off my jeans and sweater and carefully pulled the dress on. Facing the mirror, my jaw dropped.

"Oh my God, it's a perfect fit!" I screamed.

While I modeled my gorgeous dress, it reminded me of my ballet lessons, *Le Lac des Cygnes*. The Swan Lake by Tchaïkovski — 'Under the spell of a sorcerer, Odette spends her days as a swan swimming on a lake of tears and her nights in beautiful human form. Prince Siegfried and a lovely swan name Odette quickly fall in love.' Tchaïkovski's music provoked memories of my young life in my ballerina classes. I'd suddenly turned into a black swan in my wedding dress.

Even though the larger size of my dress in the store seemed much longer, I believed François would not care about the length. I called the saleswoman to thank her.

"It's a shorter version of Michelle Obama's dress that she wore for the Inauguration." With a smile lighting my face, I hung the dress up and gingerly placed it in my closet.

François was on Cloud Nine when he arrived in Boston, getting more excited each day while we finalized our wedding plans. The traditional marriage vows with promises to love, support and comfort one another through sparkling fresh eyes was exactly what the hopeless romantic wanted. François was in the den watching TV when I pulled on my dress awestruck, lost in admiration.

"Hey! Come take a look at my gorgeous wedding dress," I shouted.

"No! I'm not supposed to see my bride before she walks down the aisle."

"I, François, take thee, Vernetia, as my wedded wife, to have and to hold from this day forward, for better, for worse, for richer, for poorer, in sickness and in health, to love and to cherish, till death do us part" remained indelible in his heart. He said he hadn't felt we were wholeheartedly husband and wife in our daily lives because we hadn't renewed our wedding vows in the church. I was saddened to learn that he carried this burden for such a long time.

One evening, before the neighbors came home, the saxophonist arrived at the apartment carrying a large case with her instrument for the rehearsal. François and I wanted to sing a duo at the wedding with the melody of Armstrong and *Go down Moses* interpreted by Claude Nougaro, jazz composer and soloist, born in Toulouse, France, but we had no time to practice. I imagined François's deep baritone voice ringing out in the church. Still, listening to her play Bach on her saxophone in the pulpit was heart-warming.

François craved a romantic, fairy-tale wedding — an old-fashioned high-stepping horse-drawn carriage with the heads and necks of the horses bobbing up and down, making the clip-clop sound of hooves trotting on the cobblestone streets in Boston. One afternoon in the financial district, we saw a line of magnificent horses and carriages waiting on the side. I figured if the future bride could bribe the coachman with an attractive tip, he might carry us the short distance from the church to our apartment.

"We'd like to hire this beautiful horse-drawn carriage for our wedding on Beacon Hill," I said, petting the horse between his eyes and his neck.

"I'm sorry. Carriages are forbidden on the Hill."

Days before the wedding, we received an urgent message from the Minister of Music and Arts at Old West Church who asked if we could come to the church immediately.

"I'm sorry to inform you that Pastor King cannot officiate at your wedding. He was rushed to the hospital." The news and the timing were devastating and I was dying to know what happened.

"How is he?" I asked but she offered no explanation.

While François continued to ask other questions, I whispered, "Maybe he will have recovered by Sunday."

"You're dreaming!" he muttered.

"Don't worry," she said. "We'll meet with another pastor that I have in mind. I am confident that you'll like him and I'll be assisting with the ceremony."

After getting the news, we had the blues all day running around town. Up to that point, everything was almost flawless. Although we had no other choice, we trusted the Minister of Music and Arts' recommendation. She was very professional, Russian, and her accent added an interesting dimension. We had a delightful conversation about a great vacation we'd taken in St. Petersburg, Russia for White Nights. When we met the minister who would preside over the wedding, he was very charming. He spoke some French and enjoyed conversing with us. Despite the unfortunate circumstances with Pastor King, we felt confident that the new minister was going to be simply perfect.

The morning of the wedding, I heard the early bird puttering around in the kitchen. *What on earth is he doing?* I had already arranged for the caterers to take care of everything. When I greeted him, he had already prepared two large platters of appetizers with an exquisite presentation.

"Wow," I asked. "What's that?"

"*Foie gras* from France made with fattened livers of geese."

"But we don't eat meat."

"It's a special treat for our American friends."

"No kidding! What a nice French touch."

"And *caviar*," he said, smiling.

"Fantastic. How'd you get it through freaking customs?"

"I kept my mouth shut for the grand occasion."

"You weren't scared they would discover it?"

"Frantic! Fortunately they didn't."

"That's not all," he continued.

"You're joking!"

"Take a look in those boxes."

I opened them and found beautiful French Favors for each of our guests, plus other things he had smuggled on the plane including a large bottle of French champagne. I had also brought back a special bottle of pink champagne on the plane for François's wedding gift, and we had a couple of bottles on reserve from previous vacations, so we had plenty of bubbles.

"*Oh, La La,*" I yelled, "Holy Moses!" And then I paused in panic. "Oh No, we forgot the darn flowers!"

"We didn't, you did," he said with sarcasm. He kissed my nose. "They're going to be delivered when the caterers arrive. I also ordered flowers for the church."

"Sweetheart you're amazing! What can I say except "thank you so much" my professional wedding planner. "You're the best! I never thought about all these things."

"One last detail," he smiled. "I'll put an announcement in the Beacon Hill Times."

"Brilliant idea," I said. "Go right ahead."

The day had finally arrived for the big event. The ceremony would follow the Sunday service where the members of the church were anxiously waiting. It was a chilly morning with a sprinkling of rain, so I was able to hide my wedding dress underneath my raincoat. Guests came from New York, Connecticut, Maine, the South Shore and East Boston. A friend from Pennsylvania had already checked in at the Boston Marriott Hotel. Before her arrival, she mailed two bottles of California Zinfandel wine to a neighbor to hold for the reception. On the eve of the ceremony, we hung out with three friends from New York. They treated us to cocktails at the Taj Mahal Hotel, facing the Boston Garden, and later that evening we dined at Legal Seafood in Back Bay. I was relieved knowing that some of our guests were already in town.

Thelma was hospitalized shortly before the wedding and could not attend the ceremony. François and I visited her with gifts: a bottle of Yves Saint Laurent *PARIS* perfume — the scent of a rose in full bloom — and two beautiful silk scarves — a Hermes scarf with apple blossoms and another Hermes love garden scarf with butterflies in burnt orange trim. She wore hats to church on Sundays with wide brims dipped on one side and silk scarves draped around the neck. Did she think she was part of the British royalty where hats were an essential part of an outfit? When she wore large dark sunglasses with her ensemble, she looked like a star from Hollywood. I went to her room first and when François entered moments later, I yelled SURPRISE and she beamed with joy.

Thelma and Charlie were like our guardians. They treated us as if they were our parents. I often thought about what our lives might have been without their tough love and guidance. We may have been homeless, penniless, sexually abused or even suicidal — highly unlikely but no one knows except God. While they were very strict and illogical at times, they exercised constraint rather than have us wind up in situations that called for drastic measures. Maturity takes time and complications can take a toll on everyone's lives. For their eternal love and guidance, I am truly grateful that they made so many sacrifices raising us to be polite, respectful, kind, and smart young ladies in the absence of our parents.

At the hospital Thelma introduced François to her doctor, thrilled to have him meet her brother-in-law from France. She apologized profusely for not being able to attend the wedding. We played it down as if it were just another day. I knew she was going to be okay when she started with her zany jokes. "Vernetia you'd better hold onto François's arm while you're in Boston unless you want to return to Paris alone. There're lots of women out there looking for a good man." Then she held my face. "Pretty woman, please get your hair cut and styled for the wedding (as if I wouldn't). I don't want you to lose this beautiful man." François just blushed. I laughed and said "Thelma for God's sake, we're already married and don't worry my dear, François seldom goes anywhere without me."

"Okay, just saying." She walked us to the door and kissed us goodbye. "Next time you come home please bring some more of those beautiful scarves in French colors, and thank you from the bottom of my heart." When I told her François was a lawyer, she asked if he had met her daughter Karen, a graduate of law at Columbia University and that she practiced law with her dad.

My brother Charlie offered to take us to lunch while we were in Cambridge doing some last minute shopping. I told him François did not eat meat so he chose a restaurant with plenty of daily seafood and fish. François gave it a 'thumbs up' just looking at the array of attractive dishes. We wanted to treat Charlie for lunch but he insisted on picking up the tab. We were pressed for time but postponed our next appointment at the caterers. It was impossible to leave him after having such a lovely afternoon together.

I asked Charlie if he was going to give the bride away thinking he would surely say yes. "Hell no," he said with a laugh. "I'm your brother, not your father."

François looked on mystified. Actually, I liked what he said, realizing that we were now equals and I was no longer under his wings.

"No problem," I said with a laugh. "François and I will walk ourselves down the aisle."

When I got home, I listened to Charlie's upbeat message on the answering machine.

"Beautiful man — I approve! I'll see you guys at the wedding."

Happily, our wedding day had finally arrived. Charlie sat on the first row with his wife. Thelma's daughter Karen sat next to him wearing her mom's wide brim hat slightly cocked to one side with a Hermes scarf. Our brother Carl and his wife sat beside her. François's sons, JO and Xavier, were traveling around in Europe with friends and Renée's doctor advised her against taking the long haul across the Atlantic. She was with us in spirit and we knew she'd have something special planned when we returned to France.

I was ecstatic but a flash of sadness appeared with images of Virginia knowing she would be with us if only life had taken a different direction. Words could not express the absence of my loved ones. I wished Virginia had been there to share my big day and to meet the love of my life. Derek my loving nephew who died from Cycle Cell anemia would have blown us a big kiss, his round eyes narrowing, and the sides of his mouth crinkling, radiating with happiness. I knew they were all looking down upon us, as well as my parents. "Those we love don't go away; they walk beside us every day."

When we entered the church we sat in the last row across the aisle from each other. I glanced over at François and he was glowing while I fretted about who was coming. When each of our guests arrived, I smiled and my heart stopped racing. Camille was dressed like a fashion plate straight from Paris holding the arm of her French husband. Isabelle and Pierre from Marseille, the largest city in France on the Mediterranean coast, sat next to them. When the Wedding March began, I took off my raincoat and locked arms with François. He looked straight into my eyes and stared down at my wedding dress with a wide smile. As happy as two 'clams in mud at high tide,' we strolled down the aisle while the organist played "Here Comes the Bride." The guests turned around gazing and smiling; cameras were clicking and flashing.

After our marriage vows warm embraces were overwhelming. François wiped my tears away with is his finger.

When the ceremony ended we strolled with our guests, the short distance to the apartment, laughing en route to an intimate reception and had completely forgotten about the horse-drawn carriage. We had arranged for the saxophonist to greet the guests when they arrived. For entertainment, we hired a Chinese violinist from the New England Conservatory of Music. She had recently won a prize at an international violinist competition in Vienna. She would play pieces from Vivaldi, Wagner, and Bach. Her performance would be a surprise so we asked her not to arrive before the champagne salute.

After setting up the stand, she glanced over her music sheets. You couldn't hear a pin fall. The guests were entranced when she began playing Moon Light Serenade. There were claps of joy at the end of each rendition. She bowed graciously and smiled. The intensity of the music and François' stare across the room caused me to weep. He moved in closer and held my hand while being serenaded with romantic pieces. She placed the bow and instrument back in the case and said goodbye to the guest.

During the reception, François placed a beautiful emerald diamond ring on my right hand that he brought back from France for my wedding gift. I gave him a gold tiepin. I wanted to give him a Rolex watch, nothing fake, but found that it was outrageously expensive. After our guests left, we danced until dawn.

Newlyweds now for the second time we would leave Logan Airport the following evening to return to Paris. Before our departure, I spoke discretely to an agent.

"Do you have any First Class seats available?"

"Do you want to change your seats?"

"We'd like to if possible," I said with deferential respect.

"So what's your question?"

"If there happens to be two empty seats in business class, would you mind giving them to us?" We just got married and we're returning home to Paris and nothing could top that!"

"I'm sorry. It's not possible."

I didn't say anything more, but I knew it was remotely possible because once on Air France, a French agent offered us business class seats on a fairly empty flight and we hadn't asked. We would be squeezed in the center aisle with no wiggle room for more than six hours. I kept an eye on the crowd hoping the passengers sitting next to us would not spill over into our seats. Minutes before the departure and after everyone was strapped in, a flight attendant tapped me on the shoulder and asked us to come with her. Revved up when she changed our seats to business class, we tried to keep calm, snuggling up in our convertible seats feeling like a King and Queen.

"I'll always love you, my beautiful bride." François whispered in my ear.

"And I'll always love you, my handsome groom." Well into the flight, the captain made an announcement.

"Ladies and gentlemen we have newlyweds on the plane. Congratulations from the crew!" The flight attendant filled our champagne glasses and the passengers in business class, "Cheered!" We were saluted with big smiles stretched across our faces. On the way out the captain tipped his cap and shook our hands.

"Merci beaucoup, *Capitaine*," we said smiling from ear to ear elated by the extraordinary kindness of Air France.

"You know what I want now?" I asked François when we stepped off the plane.

"Besides me Ms. France?" he asked.

"A flight in a hot air balloon drifting with a breeze and say our vows with a flute of champagne en plein air (outside!)"

"*Oh La La*...you're dreaming again!

Hand in hand, we walked, ready to dive into the sweet life.

When we returned to France, Renée had organized a family Champagne brunch at the celebrated Paul Bocuse restaurant, an upscale dining establishment, next to Lyon with 3 stars maximum in the Michelin guide. She took delight in introducing her son and daughter-in-law to Paul, one of the most famous chefs in the world. We dined most of the afternoon on some of Paul's signature dishes like his "Black truffles soup with a majestic crown of puff pastry" and his famous "filet of red mullet encrusted with pota-toes." There were so many extraordinary dishes including a large variety of French cheeses and otherworldly desserts. I loved the Lemon Tart – *oeufs à la neige grand-mère* – "egg whites piled up like a mountain of snow with sugar, honey, pistachios and almonds," YUM!"

For our wedding gift Renée gave us an art déco eight-piece tea setting displaying a sleek symmetrical design in exuberant shapes with rich bold colors in green, orange, blue, yellow and purple. The set includes cups, saucers, dessert plates and a long rectangular dish for savory snacks, a round plate for a pie or a cake, and a fancy cutting knife with the same pattern. The delicate cups are slanted at the bottom in a V shape; the handles of the cups have the shape of an earlobe; multi-African faced masks in blue and gold colors on the outside. The cups are white inside. When served with red tea, the "look" is unforgettable. The collection is entitled "*So French*" written at the bottom of the plates. It's a mixture of African culture and porcelain china produced in the region of Limoges, France. Our marriage celebration in America and in France was a full circle moment like the beauty of stars orbiting in a galaxy.

EPILOGUE

My life in France has been extraordinary even with the rocky parts. I'll always be grateful that the road I traveled gave me a heightened sense of awareness with a pair of fresh eyes in the most mesmerizing city in the world. Stories create culture, and France is no exception. Its rich history makes it the perfect setting for anyone daring enough to bridge seas, languages and cultures in search of adventure, love and happiness.

Happiness is Mom's sweet kisses and love that shined through as a child. The happy tone in her voice sounded like harmonious chiming bells. "Congratulations Sweetheart," she would have said, "You did it! Now go out there and discover a world of adventures." Dad would have winked with a big grin on his face and squeezed me so tight I could hardly breathe. "My little trail-blazer," his eyes glowing, "I'm so proud of you baby."

Happiness is when I gazed up at the stars filled with excitement and disbelief and thought, "Gee whiz! How'd you do it Vernetia?"

Happiness is when François asked me to marry him and we'd spend the rest of our lives together always and forever. He showers me with red roses symbolizing eternal love and blue roses symbolizing mystery or achieving the impossible.

Happiness is the state of joy that I felt walking down the aisle holding François arm, even with a flicker of sadness missing Virginia but I knew she was with us in spirit on our special day.

In hindsight, I've earned my new life in a country with magnificent castles, renaissance architecture, art masterpieces, cobblestone alleys and passageways, quaint villages, rolling hills, stunning landscapes and a stroller's paradise. The lure of cruising on the Seine at sunset through the heart of Paris still makes my heart flutter. Each time I get a rush of adrenaline, I am confident that I made the right decision to follow my Paris dream. Occasionally things get under my skin like the grey melancholy skies and the nerve-racking French bureaucracy. When I become cynical, I tell myself, "If you don't like the weather, wait a second. If you don't like the French bureaucracy go back to America and you'll find that red tape inefficiency is ubiquitous!"

I will always cherish the first gift François gave me before he left for Cannes on his Christmas vacation. I declined his invitation not knowing if I would ever see him again. His gift was a small book, entitled Alexandre Dumas, *les Aventures d'un Romancier*. Despite Dumas' aristocratic background and personal success as a celebrated French author, he had to deal with discrimination related to his mixed-race ancestry. In 1843, he wrote a short novel *Georges* that addressed some of the issues of race and the effects of colonialism. "When in a salon a man insulted him about his mixed heritage. He gave this response: "My father was a mulatto, my grandfather was a Negro, and my great-grandfather a monkey. You see, Sir, my family starts where yours ends."

I've felt Virginia's presence and the teachings of my parents on my journey. I've made new friends and have learned many lessons, none of which I take for granted. One thing that comes to mind is the difference between friendship in America and friendship in France. It took time but I finally got it — understanding the mechanics of it all. While entertaining around the dinner table seemed awkward at times, I learned to hold back rather than express inconsequential ramblings to avoid being an outcast. While it is easy to make friendships that lack depth, real friendship is not easy to come by and it takes time.

Marianne, a dear Parisian friend that I have known for a long time, greets me at the door once a week with a broad smile dressed elegantly. "Bonjour Vernetia, entre, s'il te plait." She gives me a kiss on both cheeks and then we head straight to the entertainment room where delicious homemade pastries are waiting for my arrival. I call her my professor because there is nothing she enjoys more than helping me improve my French. We spend hours together talking about everything under the sun having a ton of laughs, while she critiques my strong French accent. The "R" is the hardest letter to pronounce in the throat with a guttural or nasal sound and vowel distinctions. With her persistence, I've progressed but not to my full satisfaction. Yet it is indeed a pleasure to be in her presence.

I've learned to keep a respectable distance with new and old acquaintances. When I want to be a bigmouth American and have a thousand laughs, I hang out with a small group of multicultural friends. The French friends that I have made are extremely kind and I can confide in them completely. The subtleties of human behavior make me realize how fortunate I am to have found love with an extraordinary Frenchman that helps me navigate and appreciate the cultural differences.

Still, there were some hilarious moments that I'll always cherish:

One sunny afternoon while casually promenading under the trees at *Le Jardin des Plantes,* a Seagull, I imagined, glided over my head and a clump of dung landed on the side of my face and splattered down the front of my new French jacket. The outdoor toilet was not fully equipped so I ran for help in the park's café located under sprawling branches. The manager rushed to the kitchen and handed me a jug of water and a large dishcloth. He read my facial expression, clenching my jaw and biting down on my bottom lip.

"Droppings all the time," he said, "Sometimes in the soup!" We laughed aloud and waved good bye. Moral of his story: *Shit happens!*

Even in the dentist office I was amused. One afternoon I was folding with cramps while I waited. "Would you like a cup of warm mint tea?" his assistant asked. It was the first time I'd ever been offered a cup of tea in a dentist's office. She served it on a small tray with a morsel of sugar.

"When you get home," she counseled. "Go to the pharmacy and buy a Caoutchouc."

"What's that?" I asked.

"I can't tell you in English. It's a bouillotte," she said unable to find the right word.

"Humm...A caoutchouc, bouillotte...C'est chaud," I pondered.

"You're fragile like me. You need warmth," she said and drew a wide rectangular bottle with a round head and flat bottom.

"C'est fait avec le matériau du pneu de la voiture," she explained. It's made from the material of a wheel on a car.

"*Oh La La,* what the heck is it?"

"Is it leather?"

"*Mais non.*"

"Is it rubber?"

"*Mais oui!*"

"Do you put hot water inside la bouillotte?"

"*Oui, Bien sûr,*" Yes of course.

"Oh my goodness," I laughed aloud. "It's a hot water bottle!"

When the dentist called me into to his office, I stretched out on the reclining chair listening to new wave music, surrounded by the latest technology in dentistry, while he drilled in my mouth.

"Would you like a shot of novocaine in your stomach to numb the pain?" he asked with a straight face.

What's the purpose of our short time on earth if we don't explore our grandiose dreams and make exciting plans while we can? My stumbling blocks and setbacks made me even stronger while I ventured out on my journey and I am elated that I pursued my dream that swept me off my feet and landed me into the arms of an irresistible Frenchman.

Sometimes I'm asked if I miss my life in America.

Comparing France to America is like comparing apples to oranges. While comparisons and contrasts are topics of interest, they are often not the makings of reality. Things that are different from one country to another are not always good or bad. There is no perfect territory on the planet. Embracing France wholeheartedly doesn't mean I dislike America. On the contrary, it means I'm enjoying my new life in France and appreciate America differently, realizing the longer one lives in a foreign country the easier it becomes home. François and France have replenished the inexplicable void in my life and my discontentment has vanished. To say that I'm overjoyed is not an exaggeration and to imagine my destiny would unfold this way is nothing less than miraculous.

"Pineapples in Paris: My Sweet French Life" recounts how I snuffed out the darkness and found happiness, laughter and romance in the *City of Light* — a mesmerizing story of my extraordinary adventures in Paris in the pursuit of a new beginning and my refusal to cave into adversities, paired with my willingness and resilience to take chances. Along the way, I found the love of my life, and have achieved an inner peace. I've cut through the blue, white, and red tape of living in France, took a big leap and I've never looked back. What a ride and a *'joie de vivre!'*

My life with François is solid as a rock and our love is sublime. "I've come a long way baby," and I'm truly blessed. I am both American and French and like famed Edith Piaf sang, *Non, je ne regrette rien* — No, I don't regret anything!

☺

Ma Petite Française,

Bravo pour ton français hier soir !

C'est incroyable le vocabulaire

que tu as.

Bonne journée. TGiW.

Bisous.

☺

Bonne journée ma
Papillote d'Amour,

cet après-midi il fera 17° !

gros bisous et à ce soir !

François

Me

My Vennekiva
I love so much

Bonne journée ma
Chérie

☺

Bonne journée.

Encore du vent. Probablement
de la pluie bientôt.

Obama a refusé d'être vice-président.

À ce soir. Aujourd'hui il y
a des primaires dans le mississipi.

Gros bisous !

Bonne journée ma Chérie.

Beau temps, c'est vendredi
et plein de baisers

A tout à l'heure, j'espère !

François

Thank you for accompanying
me last night to the party.
It may rain(or snow?)
today...
Have a nice day
Kisses from

François

Babynette,

Your hair is beautiful.
It's too bad to have to
go to the office and
leave you here.
Kisses. See you tonight.

← béret

← baguette
de pain

Très bonne journée
ma petite franco-américaine !

Il va faire encore beau.
gros bisous. Et repose-toi ou
travaille sur ton livre.
A ce soir.
François

Dear Pouyette,

Ko-nite I'm on vacation!

See you on the Champs-Elysées.

Bonne journée.

Kisses

Français

René and Renée

François and Vernetia

Made in United States
Orlando, FL
20 July 2024

49322188R00178